# EXUBERANCE

Cover design: Lídia Puccetti | lidiapuccetti.com
Image credit (woman): Lídia Puccetti / Midjourney
Image credit (ladybug): Pixabay

ISBN 978-0-6458661-0-0 (paperback)
ISBN 978-0-6458661-1-7 (eBook)

Printed in Australia. Typeset in Lucida Bright and Lucida Sans 10.5 pt.

The events and characters in *Exuberance* are a work of fiction. However, the insights into the medical condition at its core are based on thorough research and lived experience. The author acknowledges her experience is unique and cannot be generalised.

Most of the quotes used throughout this book are in the public domain.

The quote by J. Krishnamurti that appears on page 52 is from *The Book of Life*, August 1, HarperSanFrancisco, 1995, copyright © Krishnamurti Foundation of America. Permission to quote from this work has been given on the understanding that such permission does not indicate endorsement of the views expressed in this novel. For more information about J. Krishnamurti (1895-1986) please see: www.jkrishnamurti.org.

A catalogue record for this book is available from the National Library of Australia

NATIONAL LIBRARY OF AUSTRALIA

BV CONCEPTS

# EXUBERANCE

## BEL VIDAL

# About the author

Bel Vidal is the pen name of a Bolivian-born Australian writer who since 1988 has called Sydney home.

Her works of fiction, non-fiction and poetry have been widely published both in English and Spanish, under her pen name, her real name and other pseudonyms. Soon after arriving in Sydney, she was the recipient of an Australian Council of the Arts grant to publish a bilingual collection of poems and short stories, *Arcoiris de Sueños / Rainbow of Dreams*.

An earlier draft of *Exuberance* was short-listed for the Varuna-Harper Collins award for manuscript development, and was awarded the five-day Varuna Awards Residential Masterclass.

Bel works in communications and media, using her writing skills towards advocating for positive social change. She is also a book lover, film buff, bush walking enthusiast, keen photographer/designer, adventurous traveller, avid storyteller, occasional rock and roll dancer and blogger.

Find out more at **belvidal.com**.

# PREAMBLE:
# AVOIDING ELENA

*What is life? A madness.*
*What is life? An illusion, a shadow, a fiction…*
*for all life is a dream, and dreams are only dreams.*

- Pedro Calderón de la Barca, *Life is a Dream*

Dave's mobile rings, startling him and piercing the silence of the office. He looks at the time on his computer screen, it's almost 9.00 pm. Even the cleaners have been and gone, and he's still here. He flips his phone open and immediately recognises the number – he knows that landline by heart, even though he hasn't called it in years.

'Mario?' He asks, hesitantly. The last time they spoke, it hadn't ended well.

'Hello, Dave,' a woman's voice replies, surprising him even more. 'It is not Mario. It is Elena.' She had always been very particular about the enunciation of her name: 'It is not Ellen, or Helen, it is Elena, with the emphasis on the second "e"'.

She speaks slowly, as if savouring the words, and has managed to hang onto the same Spanish accent she had when Dave first met her, in the late 1980s. Has it really been ten years?

She had a very limited English vocabulary at the time, and it used to amuse him when she used words like emphasis, or subterfuge. 'Oh Dave, always using subterfuges to get your way,' she would say to him, quite often.

'Elena! Talk about a blast from the past!' Dave exclaims. 'How are you? How is Mario?'

'Fine, Dave, we are both fine. Listen, I called your mobile because I am not sure if you are still in the same place at Balmain.'

Dave notices that she still doesn't use contractions, always saying 'I am' instead of 'I'm', 'we are' instead of 'we're'.

'Sure am, but I'm still at the office. I'll call you back from my desk phone so it doesn't cost you a fortune,' he says, hanging up. When he punches her number, his hand is trembling.

'It has been a long time, Dave. We miss you!'

The three of them used to spend a lot of time together,

when they were all living at Balmain. Before Mario and Elena bought a place in the Southern suburbs about an hour's drive away from him.

'Work, Elena ... It's killing me!'

'Are you still at the accounting firm in the city?'

'Still here. Bloody 9.00 pm and still here! And you?'

'Same job, different shop. But there is so much to talk about! I wanted to see you – I have an invitation for you. I am a having a party for my 30th birthday, it will be the event of the year! Listen, I am in the city on Friday – what about we meet for a coffee at Piccadilly's and I can give it to you?'

He says yes. He could never say no to Elena.

∂

Dave and Mario go back a long time, to high school, where they had been inseparable. After graduating, their lives followed quite different paths.

Dave grew his hair long, turned to meditation, experimented with sex and drugs, dropped out of uni to work for the public service, quit work to backpack in the U.K., and finally finished his accounting degree only to discover that he abhorred his chosen profession. Mario managed to remain unchanged, as if somehow living outside the real world. He didn't date, drink or smoke; he read Scientific American, borrowed books on science, astronomy and eastern philosophy from his local library, worked at a computer repair shop during the day, and went to technical college at night.

Sometimes they wouldn't see each other for months, but whenever Dave was having a crisis, financial, existential or any other kind, the doorbell would ring, and it would be good old Mario, there at his door when he was needed the most. Dave didn't know how Mario did it, but he always knew when to drop in.

Dave always tried to get Mario to come with him on double dates, to meet girls. He never did. Mario never dated anyone until his cousin introduced him to Elena, not long after his twenty-third birthday. Mario's mother was from Spain, and Elena was thrilled that he could speak Spanish fluently. Within a year, they were married and had moved to the other side of town.

Dave opens the Johnny Walker kept in the bar fridge for office parties, lights up a cigarette, and reclining on his leather chair, his feet up on the desk, remembers the first time he and Elena met, the day Mario introduced them. Dave had soon discovered that he could talk to her, with her broken English, about more things than he could talk about with most of the girls he knew.

She had come to Dave's place to fetch Mario, who was helping him fit a sound system in his car. Dave had offered her a soft drink upstairs, and they had spent the following hour talking about forced emigration, languages, poetry and the Russian composers, while he played her the four versions he had of Tchaikovsky's 1812.

Only when they realised that it was dark outside did they remember that Mario was still in the basement, struggling with the car stereo on his own. Laughing, they raced each other down four flights of stairs, and she won. He'd never seen anyone with so much energy.

'Well done, mate,' he had whispered to Mario, giving him a pat on the back. 'You've got yourself a phenomenal gal.'

❧

A few months after Mario's wedding, Dave became seriously involved with a teenager, Sonja. Their relationship was very difficult, not unlike others he had had before and has had since. She was eighteen years old (Dave was twenty-four), and really screwed up for a person so young. Like Dave, she was seeing a therapist. She was trying to come to terms with stuff like having been sexually abused by her uncle when she was eleven and other similar issues. So she had great difficulties with trust and many a time would cry after making love or wake up screaming in the middle of the night.

Dave had his own troubles to deal with at the time, having recently discovered that the man he had always thought was his dad wasn't his dad at all, that his real father was still alive and living in some county in Ireland. That was probably why he couldn't handle Sonja's panic attacks very well. He reacted by getting even more agitated than she did, and they wound each other up for hours on end.

One night Sonja and Dave drove all the way to Mario and Elena's place during one of their crises, to ask Mario for counsel. It was after midnight and all the lights were off but they rang the bell anyway. Just when they were about to give up, Mario opened the door in his pyjamas and let them in. He sat there for a while, listening patiently to their troubles before responding.

'You need to let go of the past, let your mind become an empty vessel,' he was saying. At the time he was reading a lot of Krishnamurti, the South Indian philosopher whom the western theosophical societies hailed as the twentieth century's messiah.

Before Mario could finish, Elena came out of their bedroom,

half-asleep and blurted, 'Do you people know what time it is? David, have you forgotten that Mario has to get up at six in the morning?'

They quickly said their goodbyes. Sonja whispered in Dave's ear as they were leaving, 'What's the matter with her? Hasn't she ever seen anyone in trouble before?'

'This isn't the first time she's treated me like rubbish,' Dave answered. 'But it sure is the last.'

Elena's attitude towards Dave had visibly changed after her marriage – he suspected she resented him for spending so much time with her husband. Soon she had developed enough skill in English to be caustic, calling Dave user-friendly every time he brought something over for Mario to repair (his computer, his car, his stereo, his relationships), and accusing him of resorting to subterfuges when he began to offer payment.

Ultimately, however, it hadn't been Elena who damaged his friendship with Mario.

Pouring himself another glass of scotch, Dave remembers Mario and Elena with mixed feelings, unsure whether he's looking forward to this meeting on Friday or not.

There she is, waiting for him at Piccadilly's, sipping from a glass of white wine. She's more voluptuous than the last time he saw her, and her black hair is shorter. He can't say she is beautiful, but there is something out of the ordinary about her. Maybe the intense look in her big hazel eyes, or the way she dresses, wearing colourful clothes and exotic jewellery that make her stand out from the rest. Of course, there are those impressive breasts of hers, which he tries not to look at. But it's more than her looks; she emanates a kind of energy, even just sitting there, absorbed in reading the menu, unaware of his gaze. What's the word?

*Exuberance.* That's right; she's still as exuberant as she was the first time they spoke, the day she came to his apartment to fetch Mario, wearing a straw hat, sandals and gypsy clothes.

They order more wine, and talk about the women Dave has been seeing lately; she asks him about a couple of girls he hasn't seen in years, including Sonja. They talk about Mario; they have always talked about Mario. All of a sudden, Dave touches her cheek, as if to make sure that she's real.

'I wish some of the girls I dated were more like you ...'

Elena blushes and looks away. He knows he should stop, but doesn't. 'Elena, there's something I have to tell you – '

'No,' she interrupts. 'You do not have to. I know.'

'What do you mean?'

'I know you are attracted to me. I always knew.'

'Since when?'

'Mario told me, the day you and I met, when he was fixing your car and I came to fetch him. He has always had a way of knowing these things.'

Elena pauses for a moment, and this time it is she who brushes Dave's cheek with the tips of her fingers.

'You know, back in those days, I liked you too. Physically, I mean,' she says.

It's Dave's turn to blush.

Seeing that he is not going to say anything, she goes on.

'And in other ways. That is why I became a little ... snappy. Self-preservation, I guess. I would never do anything to hurt Mario. Besides, if you and I ever got involved, we would have a very intense, passionate affair. Out of this world. But it would not last very long. We are too much alike.'

'Elena,' is all he can say. She's summed up the story of his love life in one sentence. It would not last very long.

'No Dave, I like you, but we would not last long,' she says, and leans forward, her eyes closed.

'You're right, maybe we wouldn't ...' he says. He closes his eyes as he kisses her, wishing, for a fraction of a second, that Mario didn't exist.

When Dave opens his eyes he's still at the office, and it's past midnight. The bottle of scotch on the desk is nearly empty, and the room is spinning around him. As he runs to the toilet, nauseated by the alcohol and his own thoughts, he decides not to go to Piccadilly's on Friday. It will be better that way.

# PART 1:
# A BORROWED LIFE

*None of us want to be
in calm waters all our lives.*

- Jane Austen, *Persuasion*

# PART I.
# A BORROWED LIFE

*Many of us want to be*
*to calm where all our lives*

Jane Austen, Persuasion

# ~ Angel in the gutter ~

It's January, 1999. Dr Elizabeth Suenho's practice, shared with two other consultant psychiatrists, is in an old brick cottage on a quiet street lined with Jacaranda trees. Less than four kilometres away, the final touches are being applied to the new Sydney Olympic Stadium, preparing it for its inaugural game scheduled to take place in March.

From outside, the practice looks just like a family home. Inside, bedrooms have been converted into doctor's consulting rooms, the living area into a waiting room, the dining room into a reception, and the large eat-in kitchen into a common room.

At this time of day, the early afternoon sun fills Dr Suenho's office. Angelica Fletcher, the last patient today, sits on the edge of her chair, next to the window, her red hair made more incandescent by the sunlight. This is her first time here, and she seems to be engrossed by the surroundings, as if unaware of Dr Suenho looking at her inquisitively from behind gold-rimmed glasses, a ruled pad on her lap and a pen in her hand.

Angelica notices a desk calendar, with today's date, Saturday January 16, and a quote by Oscar Wilde underneath it: "We are all in the gutter, but some of us are looking at the stars". A bookshelf holding titles such as *Beating the Blues*,

*The Road Less Travelled, Touched With Fire, Everyone Can Win*, and *My Mother, Myself*. There's a pin-up board stuck to the grey wall, with cartoons, health information posters and a photo of a young woman holding a curly-haired baby. On top of a metal filing cabinet is a potted Poinsettia, its red petals like flames of fire defying the neutral shades that dominate the room. And of course, there's the middle-aged lady with silver hair gathered in a bun above her head, sitting opposite, patiently waiting for Angelica to speak.

'I don't really want to be here,' Angelica finally says. 'It was my mother's idea. For months, she has been begging me to look for help, but I don't think anybody can help me. She can't, my husband can't, and I doubt, with all due respect, that you can.'

'Nobody can help you if you don't want to help yourself,' Dr Suenho says. She's soft spoken, but assertive. 'I can recommend medication, give you exercises and tools, but you have to be willing to do the hard work, Mrs Fletcher.'

'Please call me Angie.'

'Of course, Angie. Tell me why your mother thinks you need help.'

Angie scrutinises Dr Suenho, trying to determine why she feels she can trust her. She has a gentle, grandmotherly air about her, and several qualifications listed on her business card: Consultant Psychiatrist, MB BS MPH FRANZCP – whatever all those abbreviations mean. But above all, Angie realises, it's the fact that she has been recommended by Sinéad. Angie trusts Sinéad with her life, even though they've only known each other for eight months.

Dr Suenho takes the opportunity to examine her new patient. In her early thirties, tall and robust, with hazel eyes framed by long ginger eyelashes, a round freckled face and porcelain skin, she would look just like one of the rubicund angels in renaissance paintings, if it wasn't for her hair. The ends of her red mane are dyed a dark burgundy, too severe for her angelic features. Something else catches Dr Suenho's attention: the complete absence of a spark in Angie's eyes. Depressed, she scribbles in her notepad. One can always tell by the eyes.

Angie draws a big breath and holds onto the sides of her chair with both hands, as if bracing for a rollercoaster ride, then launches into the monologue she rehearsed all night in her head, as she lay in bed staring at the ceiling, unable to sleep.

'Picture this, Dr Suenho: You have just turned thirty, and everything is going seemingly well in your life. You have been married for nine years, your apartment is nearly paid off, and you are planning to start a family soon, without the burden of a mortgage. You are working full-time managing a one-hour photo lab, and you have recently started a part-time Arts degree at university. Although your husband is a tradesman – an offset printer – and would never go to college himself, he is very supportive of your desire to obtain a tertiary education.

'Out of curiosity, you decide to take a creative writing class as one of your elective subjects. For your first assignment, you need to write a short story. For weeks you have been wracking your brain trying to think of an idea, and poof! It comes to you in a dream: a meeting between a man and the woman he has been secretly in love with for ten years, his best friend's wife, Elena. You wake up the next morning with her name reverberating inside your head, and her husky voice, clearly saying, with a Spanish accent: *It is not Helen, or Ellen, it is Elena.*'

At this point, Dr Suenho stops taking notes and pushes the red button on the small tape recorder sitting on top of the desk. She leans forward to give Angie her undivided attention.

'You are so excited about the short story you have written,' Angie continues, her eyes fixed on a point in the distance, 'that you show it to your mother, and her only comment is that it is *too personal*. How can it be personal, if you couldn't be any more different from Elena? She's exuberant, she's exotic, she's outgoing, she's mercurial and passionate. She is in fact, your opposite, not to mention that she's Spanish, and you've never met anyone from Spain in your life.

'After reading the story countless times, it dawns on you: Elena may be nothing like you, but Dave is too much like someone you know, although you haven't seen him in several years – your husband's former best friend, Tiger. You haven't even changed the suburb where he lives in your short story – no wonder your mother picked it up straight away. Even she knows that Tiger's very nickname derives from the fact that as a child, he was a mascot for the Balmain Tigers Rugby team.

It takes three sleepless nights, filled with obsessive thoughts about Tiger, for you to gather up the courage to call him.'

৵

## 10 months earlier – March, 1998

Angie sits at a table in a Spanish restaurant in Liverpool Street, loud flamenco music playing in the background. Her mood isn't flamenco at all. She's tired, she's nervous because she's seeing Tiger for the first time in four years, and she's disturbed by the fact that she has lied to her husband, telling him she was going to the library after work. She has never lied to Jimmy before.

A tall man in his early thirties wearing a navy blue suit, with his light blond hair in a crew cut, approaches her from behind and covers her eyes with both hands.

'I can smell your Catalyst aftershave, Tiger,' she says, laughing nervously.

'Gee, you have a good memory!' Tiger says, kissing her gently on the cheek before sitting down.

'I remember it because it's so penetrating,' Angie says, immediately regretting her choice of words.

'Well, you smell like a rose, and you look like one!' says Tiger, winking.

Same old flirt, Angie thinks, blushing. She's conscious that she's anything but rose-like at the moment. Before heading to the restaurant, she spent twenty minutes in front of the mirror in the restroom at work, trying to find a trace of the suave and sophisticated Elena of her story, to no avail. The reflection was that of a round face as pale as death, with black rings under the eyes, the ginger hair flat and badly in need of a trim. She regretted not having worn makeup, even though she seldom did. Fumbling through her bag, she found an old tube of mascara, which she promptly applied.

'It was such a surprise to hear from you today!' Tiger says, opening the menu. 'At first, I thought something might have happened, something bad, and was glad when you said both you and Jimmy were okay. Listen, do you mind if we order soon? I'm starving.'

'Sure.'

While Tiger devours the paella they have ordered to share, Angie struggles to drink a glass of wine. She rarely drinks alcohol, but she remembers how cool Elena looked sipping her wine while waiting for Dave at Piccadilly's.

'Tell me, Tiger, why did you stop calling us?' she suddenly blurts out. Tiger looks at her startled, his jaw hanging open, and a few grains of saffron-tinted rice fall from his mouth to the table.

'I've been so busy, Angie,' he explains, sweeping the rice on to the floor with his hand. 'You know how it is – you both work long hours too. The weeks fly, the years fly. How long has it been? Two years?'

'Four. But no, why did you really stop calling? You and Jimmy had been friends for years before I met him; you don't throw away a thirteen-year friendship because work is too busy.'

Tiger is usually a good liar, but confronted with Angie's reproachful look, he finds himself at a loss.

'All right. If you want to know, I'll tell you,' he says, pushing his half-eaten paella aside. 'It's to do with Liz. Remember when she overdosed? I rang Jimmy as soon as I found out; I needed to talk to somebody. Jimmy listened for a while and then all of a sudden, started to talk to me about his work and some problems that he'd been having with his supervisor. Here I am, telling him that Liz, the girl that I've been seeing for ten months, just died of a fuckin' heroin overdose and he starts bullshitting about work! How self-centred can the guy be?'

'That's not what Jimmy said ...' Angie is nearly in tears. 'He said to me he couldn't discuss something like that over the phone, he wanted to see you in person, but you didn't show up.'

'Angie, it wasn't only that time. He'd been aloof with me for months. That was the straw that broke the camel's back.'

'Yes, but he always felt uncomfortable about Liz, knowing she was on drugs. You know how he feels about those things. And maybe he started talking to you about work to distract you.'

'Angie, hang on,' Tiger says, lifting one arm as if to shelter himself from an attack. To his disbelief, Angie is weeping. 'I want to know what this is all about. Honestly, I approached Jimmy several times, I wanted to talk things over, but he seemed to be avoiding me. So I moved on, I have other friends, other circles now. Life goes on.'

'Did you ever stop to think that I needed you? Did you ever realise you were also my friend?' she says. 'Did you know that apart from Jimmy, I never found another friend like you?'

Next thing she's muttering about how she hates her job, how lonely and isolated she is, how she can't make friends at uni because she's always tired and in a hurry, and how Jimmy is always working late and they hardly spend time together. She completely fails to emulate the cool and sophisticated Elena – blowing her nose, smearing mascara all over her face and crying like a baby.

It had been so much better in the short story.

Tiger brings his chair closer and of course he asks her why now, why has all this come up all of a sudden. Having anticipated this question, Angie has prepared the answer: "It's all because of a short story." But instead, she has an attack of the hiccups – this often happens to her when she's anxious. She decides that the best thing to do would be to send Tiger the story in the mail and let him read it for himself.

'Sorry to cut the evening short,' she says between hiccups, 'but I think I'd better leave now.' She gets up from the table, red-faced, and heads towards the door. This whole thing has been a bad, bad idea.

'Wait, Angie. I'll drive you home!' Tiger says, leaving a couple of twenty dollar bills on the table and hurrying after her. He knows that Angie and Jimmy have never had a car.

During the half hour drive he repeatedly tells her that he'd love to be her friend; that he'll call her and they can meet sometimes. They can go out for lunch; he can introduce her to his friends. Looking out the window she nods, thinking yeah, sure. As if that's going to happen now.

When they arrive at Angie's place, Tiger turns off the engine and tells her that he's genuinely worried because she sounds depressed.

'And I mean depressed, you understand? Needing anti-depressants depressed. I should know, because I've been on them for ten years. Angie, you know you can call me whenever you need to talk. Don't let things get this bad. You can even go see my shrink, he's very good,' he says. He writes her work number in his pocket diary and promises to call her the next day with his psychiatrist's details. Yeah, sure, she thinks, and kisses him goodbye.

Jimmy is waiting when she walks in the door. It is 10.00 pm, and he is in his nightclothes, sitting on the sofa with his arms folded and his forehead furrowed. It strikes Angie that Tiger doesn't seem to have aged a day since she last saw him, whereas Jimmy looks a lot older than his thirty-three years, maybe because his golden brown hair is receding and he's put on a few kilos.

'Angie, you shouldn't have stayed out this late knowing that neither of us got any sleep last night,' he says, reproachfully. The night before, her tossing and turning had disturbed him so much that he had gotten up to watch documentaries until dawn.

'I ran into Tiger at the train station,' Angie says, avoiding

Jimmy's gaze. Once you've told your husband your first lie, it becomes easier the next time. 'I went for a coffee with him, because I wanted to ask him why he stopped seeing us,' she explains. And then, hesitantly: 'He says it was because you'd become too self-centred and aloof.'

Jimmy's bottom lip twitches slightly. He turns around and heads towards the bedroom.

'I don't give a rat's arse what Tiger thinks,' he barks half-way down the hall. 'All I want is to get a decent night's sleep.'

After this sorry episode, Angie doesn't call Tiger again, and thank God, he doesn't call her either. But she can't believe the way she cried at the restaurant, the unhappiness that poured out of her. She can't believe what Tiger told her about Jimmy's self-centredness. She can't believe that Jimmy is not interested in knowing anything else about her meeting with Tiger, acting as if it never happened.

Gradually, Angie's disbelief turns into discontent. Discontent screams like graffiti across the walls of her home; she sees it in her own face, reflected back at her in the mirror, in her computer screen at work, and every time she looks at her husband in the eye.

One night she dreams she's ice-skating, sliding gracefully on the surface of an immense, deserted frozen lake. Suddenly, the ice begins to crack beneath her feet and she falls through. In a panic, Angie looks around for help, and spots Jimmy sitting on the shore, completely absorbed in building a house out of Lego blocks. Struggling in the freezing water she calls him, but no sound comes out of her mouth. Eventually, he looks up and waves, smiling – then returns to his task.

When Angie wakes up she is sitting in the shower recess, still in her nightie, the running water hitting her scalp and shoulders like cold needles. And she sobs like she did at the Spanish tavern, until she is choking on her own tears and the freezing water, while her husband sleeps blissfully in the next room.

The perfect life she thought she had crumbles around her in a matter of weeks, and she doesn't even know what the catalyst for this early midlife crisis is. Is it the damned short story? Is it Elena, so irrepressible, so full of everything Angie has always wanted to be and isn't? Is it Tiger? Does it matter?

She cries at the slightest provocation, she can't sleep, she has lost her appetite and her concentration; she can barely drag herself out of bed in the mornings. Jimmy attributes Angie's mood swings and low energy to the fact that she is trying to do too much, working the long hours she works and studying on top of that.

'Too many late nights', he says. 'Too many weekends spent at the computer, doing assignments. You don't even have time to visit my family anymore, and they are tired of hearing the same excuse: uni assignments. Maybe you should consider dropping a subject.'

Angie's mother, however, recognises signs she knows all too well, although she has never before seen them in her daughter.

It's early May, and turning cold in Sydney. Norah, Angie's mother, asks Angie to come with her on the five-hour drive to the Sapphire Coast, to visit Grandma Pearl for Mother's Day.

'We'll stay overnight and come back on Sunday,' Norah says.

'But Jimmy's parents are expecting us on Sunday,' Angie says, gazing at Jimmy. She isn't looking forward to spending Mother's Day with Jimmy's parents. If Jimmy's family gatherings are a trial in normal circumstances, she suspects they would be excruciating in her current state of mind.

'You go with Norah, Angie,' Jimmy says, to Angie's relief. 'I'll catch the train to Gosford on Saturday and come back the next day, like you.' He doesn't tell her that Norah has already asked him about this, that everything has been arranged.

Norah and Angie leave early on the Saturday, the morning breeze ruffling their hair. Norah has packed tuna and mayo sandwiches, Angie's favourite, to have on the way. She's brought a thermos with coffee, and Tim Tams for morning tea. But Angie is not interested in food or in her mother's attempts at light conversation. She winds up her window and stares out in silence through the glass fogged by her breath.

Norah feels daunted, not knowing where to start to say what she wants to say. Then she clicks her tongue, as she does when she has an idea. She stops at the side of the road and fumbles inside the case of tapes that she keeps under the seat, until she finds the one she's looking for. Seconds later, the silence is broken by a soprano's voice singing an aria from Mozart's *Marriage of Figaro*.

*Giunse alfin il momento, che godro senz'affanno.*

The response is immediate.

*'Deh veini, non tardar!'* Angie exclaims. 'That was Aunt Jo's favourite aria. Remember?'

'Of course I remember. And it was yours, too. You used to ask her to sing it for you every Sunday.'

'Yeah,' Angie says, and falls silent again, thinking of Jo standing in the middle of the living room, moving her hands theatrically and singing in her heavenly mezzo-soprano voice, Norah accompanying her at the piano.

The Moore twins grew up performing together at family gatherings, at weddings, at school recitals. They were physically identical but Josephine, the one with the gift, always overshadowed Norah, who was happy to hide behind the piano while all the eyes and the expectations were fixed on her sister.

Jo was destined for great things, they all thought. And they all waited, and waited, for the great things to happen.

By the time the twins had turned thirty, Norah had been married for several years and owned a house in the suburbs. She was a creditable piano teacher, and had a placid seven-year old daughter. Jo, on the other hand, lived the carefree life of a bohemian, never lasting in a job or a relationship more than a year, and having done nothing with her gift apart from singing at parties and at her niece's request during her weekly visits to Norah. Sunday roast at Norah's seemed to be the only constant thing in Jo's chaotic life, and the only decent meal she ate in the week.

The family's hopes for Jo had long given way first to disappointment and then to indifference; so they were shocked when they found out that Jo had applied for a grant to study opera in Milan for a year, and that the grant had been approved.

'When I saw my thirtieth birthday looming around the corner, I thought it was about time I did something worthwhile with my life,' she told her family over lunch when they gathered to celebrate the twins' thirtieth birthday.

At the beginning of autumn, 1975, Jo climbed onto a plane Italy-bound. She was wearing a short lemon coloured dress, bright like her future, and was brimming with vitality and optimism.

'Remember what happened to me, when your Aunt Jo died?' Norah asks Angie, turning the music down.

Angie looks at Norah with one eyebrow raised. This is something that is never mentioned between them, under some sort of code of silence that Angie, Norah, and her grandma Pearl have adhered to for over twenty years. The same code stops them from ever uttering Angie's father's name.

Of course she remembers; although she wishes she didn't.

**August, 1976**

Angie is seven years old. Her father brings her home from school, as he always does when he's around. They open the front door and walk into mayhem. Norah is screaming in the bedroom. Grandma Pearl's soothing but firm voice rises above the wailing, telling Norah to calm down.

'How can I calm down? How can you be so calm?' Norah cries.

'Someone has to keep their composure,' Pearl answers. 'Besides, there's still hope yet.'

Angie's father takes her to her room, and turns her little black and white TV on.

'Stay here,' he says, leaving Angie with the Looney Toons.

But she doesn't stay in her room. She's thirsty and wants a glass of milk. The space between her room and the kitchen is filled by whispers. Muffled voices in her parent's bedroom, Josephine's name bouncing from the walls, Norah saying 'I want to come,' her father saying 'you're obviously not in shape.'

A telegram on the kitchen counter, addressed to her grandmother.

Emergency STOP Come urgently STOP Josephine in I.C.U. STOP Call Nina Giovanni for particulars.

Pearl leaves that night, and comes back two weeks later with Josephine's coffin. Pneumonia, they tell Angie. Pneumonia, they tell their relatives and friends at the funeral and at the wake. Norah inconsolable, Pearl sorrowful but composed, Angie's father keeping to himself, as if in shock.

After the funeral, they send Angie away to the Sapphire Coast, to stay with Norah's relatives for a few weeks. One night, as she's about to fall asleep, she hears a tap on the window. It's her father, gesturing for her to come outside. She goes out by the back door, wearing pink pyjamas with Sylvester and Tweety printed on them. The grass is damp and she's barefoot. Her father lifts her up and sits her on top of the brick fence.

'Hey ladybird, I have to go away for a while,' he says, kissing her on the nose. Angie is used to her father going away; he's a wine merchant, always travelling. He is away more often than he is at home, but when he's around he has all the time in the world for her. Angie is the apple of his eye, and she adores him. He's promised that when she's older, he'll take her with him, but not yet. 'I'm leaving first thing in the morning. I just wanted to say bye. Your grandma will pick you up tomorrow – she wants to stay in our house while I'm away, because your mum is not doing very well.'

He holds her for what seems a long time, then, ruffling her hair, he carries her back to the house and sends her inside with a gentle push. Angie is about to climb into bed when she hears him again, tapping on the glass, this time signalling for her to open the window.

'One more thing, little bug,' he whispers. 'Promise me you'll be good to your mother.'

'Okay, Daddy,' she says.

'Don't just say okay. You have to say 'I promise'. A promise is a serious thing.'

'I promise, Daddy,' she says, solemnly. And then she frowns – it seems to her that her father's eyes are getting watery, but she can't be sure in the poor light – she can't even tell the colour of his baseball cap. 'You okay, Daddy?' She asks.

'I'm fine, baby. See you soon.' He says, and turns around, walking to his car without looking back.

When Angie arrives home the next day she finds her mother in bed, with the curtains drawn. Angie offers to let some light in but Norah shakes her head. That day, and the next day, and the next week, and the next month, Norah remains in bed, enveloped by darkness. Sometimes she gets up, and wanders around the house like a soul in penance, looking ghostly in her white nightgown.

Grandma Pearl takes Angie to school, picks her up, cooks, and cleans. She bathes Norah with warm water every afternoon and combs her ginger hair, as if she were a child again. Grandma Pearl smiles and tells Angie that everything will be okay, but Angie notices the tear marks on her grandma's cheeks. Angie shows Norah her drawings, her homework, she recites the timetables for her, but Norah just looks through her, as if Angie were invisible.

A man starts visiting Norah regularly, a spiral notepad sticking out of his pocket. Words float in the air after the man leaves, words that Angie can't quite understand.

Nervous breakdown, shock, deeply disturbed, severe depression, abandonment, grief.

The words weigh on Angie like the darkness, like her father's absence. It has been months, and he hasn't returned.

One day there is another commotion at home. When the neighbour brings Angie home from school, an ambulance is leaving, Pearl is crying, Norah's room is empty, and it remains empty for weeks.

Unlike Aunt Jo, unlike Angie's father, Norah does come back after a while. Slowly she gets better, the colour returns to her cheeks and the spark to her eyes. Sometimes she even smiles. She starts to teach piano again, and after a few months she can look after Angie without the help of Pearl, who goes back to the Sapphire Coast.

Once in a while though, Norah catches Angie looking at her from the corner of her eye, as if the child can discern that a piece of her mother's soul has gone missing, never to be found.

≈

**May, 1998 – Norah's car**

'I remember,' Angie says to Norah, in a low voice. 'Your ... your nervous breakdown.'

She loathes those two words – she knows that these

words drove her father away. Not everyone is as strong as Grandma Pearl. Some people freak out at the first sign of trouble. Some people just parrot 'in sickness and health,' without understanding the significance of this vow. That's what relatives had said when her father didn't come back.

'Yes, my breakdown, my episode of severe depression. What strikes me most is that I was exactly the age you are now when it happened. Seeing the way you have been lately, so miserable, so apathetic, it's like seeing history repeat itself, like a curse...' Norah's voice breaks up and she pauses to clear her throat. 'The curse that took my sister away, nearly took me, and has now come to take you.'

She stops by the side of the road, and turns the engine off. Angie doesn't know what to say – Norah has never believed in curses.

'Angie, I don't know exactly what's afflicting you, but I know that there's help available. There's medication. I refused to take it for months on end, and I would have done something drastic like Jo, had it not been for your grandmother.'

'What do you mean, "do something drastic like Jo"?' Angie asks. 'Die of pneumonia? Or go overseas?'

Norah begins to cry. She fishes a pink handkerchief out of her handbag and buries her face in it, her whole body shaking.

'Mum? What's the matter, Mum?' Angie asks, panic in her voice. Since Jo's death, since the breakdown, Angie has seldom seen Norah cry, or laugh heartily, for that matter. As if she were afraid of both despair and happiness.

'Jo didn't die of pneumonia, Angie,' Norah manages to say. 'She took an overdose of sleeping pills. When your grandmother arrived at the hospital in Milan, Jo was in a comma, and never came out of it. She died a few days later in Grandma Pearl's arms.'

Angie feels light-headed. In her confusion, it occurs to Angie that Norah must be speaking about someone else's aunt, about a character in a movie she saw, or a book she read. They often go to the movies together, and exchange books, and talk about the characters and their tragedies. Norah prefers dramas to comedies.

'It was not only her death, but the way she died, all by herself, in a foreign country, surrounded by strangers, that affected me so deeply,' Norah says. 'She was my twin half, even though our lives grew to be so different. She wrote to me every week from Milan. And she didn't ask me for help.'

The car has become as long as a train carriage. Norah is at the front of the carriage and Angie is sitting all the way down at the back. She is hardly able to make out her mother's words – they seem to come from a great distance. The car is an endless desert, an ocean, a universe, and Norah speaks from light years away.

'Why?' Angie finally cries, loud enough to reach her mother across the rift in her mind, causing Norah to jump in her seat. Angie tries to speak quietly, she tries to remain calm. 'Why wasn't I told the truth?'

'Oh, Angie!' Norah says, extending her arms towards her daughter. But Angie waves Norah's hand away.

'You lied to me. You lied to everybody. You and Grandma Pearl. I would have never thought that Grandma – '

'We had to, Angie!' Norah exclaims. 'Jo's last wish was that we wouldn't tell anyone what she had done. Do you understand the significance of a last wish?'

Angie knows about last wishes. She remembers the last promise she made to her father, before he vanished. *Be good to your mother*, he had made her promise. Of course, her father isn't dead – he wrote many years ago from some obscure country in South America, to ask Norah for a divorce. He wanted to remarry. Still, Angie had promised.

She makes herself inhale and exhale slowly, her teeth digging deep into her lip, waiting for her mother to speak, to get it over and done with.

'I'm breaking my promise to Jo now,' Norah continues seeing that Angie has calmed down. 'I think it's important that you know that this curse, this illness, runs in the family. Jo killed herself, and I wanted to do the same, unable to cope with her death and your father's leaving all at once. After what happened to Jo, your grandmother hid all the pills, and I wasn't bold enough to slash my wrists. So I simply stopped eating, but my mother wouldn't have it. She wasn't about to lose another daughter. When she couldn't force food down my throat anymore, she sent me to hospital to have me fed intravenously. She didn't want you to see me like that.

'But I don't want to talk about that whole episode anymore. It's just too horrible. All I want, Angie, is for you to address this before it's too late. I want you to make an appointment with Dr Hamilton first thing on Monday – if necessary I'll take you there myself .... And I want him to give you a prescription for antidepressants.'

The afternoon has suddenly grown dark; black clouds fill the horizon ahead of them. A chill penetrates their bones; Angie switches off the air conditioning. *The Marriage of Figaro* has finished, and Norah doesn't bother to change the tape. She starts the engine and they drive in silence for a long time.

'I'll go to see Dr Hamilton,' Angie says at last. 'But I can't go see Grandma Pearl, not now. Drop me off at the next train station, I want to go home.'

Norah nods, and takes the next exit, thinking about how dismally she has handled this situation. It could have been worse, though.

She could have told Angie everything.

෧

Alone at home, every time Angie dozes off, she dreams the same dream: she sees the back of a woman standing inside a padded room, wearing a white restraining suit. Her red hair is cut short and uneven, as if it has been roughly trimmed with a knife, and her hands are tied behind her back. Angie suspects it's her Aunt Jo, but then again, it could be Norah – they were identical after all. When the woman turns around, it's neither of them.

It's her, Angelica, with a deranged look in her eyes.

When Jimmy comes home on Sunday evening he's surprised to find the house in darkness; he had expected Angie to be back before dusk. When he turns on the bedroom light, he jumps when he sees his wife's body jerk beneath the blankets, her hand emerging from under the duvet to protect her eyes.

'Shit, Ange! You scared the living lights out of me! How come you're in bed already?'

'I'm tired, Jimmy. Please let me sleep,' she pleads.

She doesn't tell him that she's been in bed the entire day. She has been staring at the illuminated red numbers of the clock radio, watching the minutes and the hours pass ever so slowly, thinking morose thoughts.

*What strikes me most is that I was exactly the age you are now when it happened*, Norah had said, and for some reason, this phrase keeps spinning around inside Angie's mind.

She can see history repeating itself, following its inevitable course, recurring right in front of her eyes, and under her skin, right now.

The curse befell the twins when they were thirty years old, and it has punctually returned to besiege Angie at exactly the same age. The curse not only took Jo's life and Norah's spirit, but it also drove Norah's husband away. Angie is convinced that her own husband, Jimmy, standing now at the doorway, blissfully unaware of what's going through her mind, will end up deserting her too, as soon as he realises what he's in for.

'Maybe you're coming down with something,' Jimmy says, turning the light off. Whistling, he goes to the kitchen to heat up the leftovers his mother gave him for dinner.

It is not until the next day, when Angie remains in bed, curled up in a foetal position, well past the time she should be getting ready for work, that Jimmy starts to truly worry.

'Ange, what's the matter?' he asks when he's ready to leave.

'You were right, Jimmy, I might be coming down with something,' she mumbles.

'Are you going to call in sick?' he asks, incredulous. Angie does not take a sick day because she might be coming down with something. She has been known to go to work burning with fever, or with a throat so swollen she can hardly talk.

But Angie doesn't answer. She covers her face with the pillow.

Jimmy calls Norah, who lives ten minutes away.

'I can't leave her like this,' Jimmy tells Norah when she arrives. 'She won't tell me what's wrong.'

When Norah walks into Angie's dim bedroom, she realises she has never understood the meaning of the expression 'what goes around, comes around' until this moment.

# ~ Elena's Awakening ~

That Monday, after Angie breaks into tears at her doctor's consulting room, where her mother has practically dragged her, Dr Hamilton agrees with Norah's diagnosis of depression. After all, he was the one who had supervised Norah's treatment over two decades ago. After Angie gives him a spiel similar to the one she gave Tiger, about hating her job and everything else in her life, Dr Hamilton hands her a prescription for antidepressants.

'But medication alone is not the answer, Angie,' he adds. 'You need to address the problems that might be causing your symptoms. If you dislike your job so much, you should consider changing it.'

Reluctantly Angie starts taking the medication, and just as she expected, the weeks go by and nothing improves. By the time June arrives, her outlook is as gloomy as before – not better, not worse.

So she moves on to Plan B, and gathers the courage to tell Jimmy that she would like to quit her job and study full time. She knows it won't be easy to convince him – she tried once before when she first enrolled at university, and Jimmy said no. He reminded her that they couldn't afford to pay a mortgage, the bills and the university fees on one wage. 'You can't have your cake and eat it too,' he told her back then.

One early winter night after dinner, Angie confesses to Jimmy that she loathes her work so much that not even with Prozac can she continue to face going to that 'horrible place' day after day.

'I've been missing so many classes because of work that I'm afraid I'll fail both subjects,' she says, looking at the remains of her dinner. 'Maybe that's why I'm feeling so anxious and depressed.'

At first, Jimmy looks at her in disbelief. The 'horrible place' is a photo lab in a shopping arcade at the heart of the city. Granted, it is a busy spot, but Angie has been working in similar places for nearly a decade, and has never used words like *loathing* and *horrible* in reference to them – in fact, she rarely uses such strong words in reference to anything.

'Is it really that unbearable, Ange?' He asks, a knot forming in his stomach as he realises she's dead serious.

'It's so unbearable, Jimmy, that the idea of having to work there for another fortnight after giving my two weeks' notice, makes me so sick I want to throw up.'

With raised eyebrows, Jimmy watches his wife clear the table and produce a spreadsheet that she has created on their home computer to demonstrate to him that, if they made some adjustments to the household budget, they could survive on one wage for a while.

'I think I'm burnt out, and just need a few months off to recharge my batteries,' she says. 'And if I can study full-time for a while, I'll finish my degree sooner, and I'll be able to get a better paid job.'

'Didn't I say, when they offered you the manager's position earlier this year, that you should say no if you didn't want the extra responsibility?' Jimmy replies, knowing that

I told you so isn't what Angie needs to hear at this precise moment, but unable to help himself. It is obvious to him that it had been that so-called promotion, which came with increased hours and responsibilities but hardly any extra money, which had pushed Angie over the edge.

Seeing her now, looking at him with puppy eyes while she waits for his verdict, he realises how much weight Angie has lost in the last few months. She has always been on the voluptuous side, but now, for the first time since Jimmy has known her, she looks almost gaunt.

'Well, there's no point in me forcing you to go to work, if I'm going to have to take you there in a wheelchair,' he concedes in the end.

Angie can't believe it has been so easy to convince Jimmy – she had anticipated an argument. Instead, Jimmy retreats to the bedroom without waiting for dessert, looking like Atlas, burdened by the weight of the world on his shoulders.

The very night after Angie gives her two-week's notice at work, she wakes up with a start around midnight, feeling a sense of anticipation in her chest, as if she were on the brink of discovering something transcendental. She gets up and instinctively heads towards the spare room, a spring in her step, completely alert though she has only just woken.

From the cheval mirror, illuminated by the moonlight, a woman with olive skin, dark eyes and high cheek bones is looking at her, smiling from ear to ear, exposing two rows of perfect white teeth. She's wearing a black velvet dress, handcrafted earrings dangle from her ears and her long dark hair cascades down to her waist.

Angie reaches out towards the mirror. Her fingertips

meet Elena's on the surface of the looking glass – Elena's fingernails are long and painted red.

'Hello, Angelica – I have been waiting for you,' Elena says, in her lovely Spanish accent.

With her heart thumping, Angie waits for Elena to go on – her voice has abandoned her.

'Do you remember, Angelica, what Jimmy said to you on your first date?'

'He – he said a lot of things,' Angie stutters. 'I – I don't remember them all.'

'He said: "Angelica, you are so busy trying to be, that you do not stop to see what you already are."'

'Yes, he did say something like that.' Angie remembers now. 'Because I was carrying on about being almost twenty-one years old, and not knowing what to do with my life. It's been nine years and things haven't changed much.'

'That is precisely my point, Angelica. You have become stuck at that stage, and you cannot see what you already are.'

'And perhaps you can tell me what I already am?' Angie asks Elena, who rolls her eyes.

'Think about it, Angelica. Ever since you wrote me into that story, you have been miserable, because you believe that I am the personification of everything you always wanted to be and that you are not. But what you do not see is that you already have all the attributes you have given me. Where do you think they came from? Stop looking outside: dig deep inside, Angelica. Look into the mirror. There are magical things in there.'

Then she's gone and the reflection in the mirror is Angie's, wearing rather unattractive winter flannelette pyjamas. But there's a spark in her eyes that wasn't there before.

'Angelica … ' Elena's voice lingers.

'Yes?' Angie answers, hungry for more revelations.

'It is time to wake up, now.'

But Angie doesn't. Every morning when she opens her eyes she expects to wake from this dream and revert to the miserable, disgruntled Angie she had become, but the weeks go by, and she doesn't.

# ~ Sinéad ~

On her way to the book club, Sinéad Kennedy stops at the travel agent's to get a quote for her airfare back home. She is seriously contemplating asking her mum and dad to send the money, as much as she doesn't want to disappoint them.

The brochure she'd been given at Tyrone University's international office had promised her that by broadening her horizons, by experiencing a different academic system in another country, she would "expand her mind, find independence and develop a whole new way of looking at life". So she had signed up to study a three-year International Relations degree in Australia.

But the experiment hasn't turned out quite as she hoped, maybe because she embarked on it for the wrong reasons. Forget expanding your mind. She ran away to the other side of the world to mend a broken heart, and it hasn't worked.

When she arrived in Sydney earlier this year she was twenty years old and had never before been outside her home town, let alone her country, and had no idea how lost she would feel away from her turf, even though she thought that growing up in the middle of political upheaval had prepared her for this and greater challenges.

Back home, along with the IRSP, the INLA, the IRA, the demonstrations, the riots and the bombs, the constant disruptions to her studies, there are also her parents, her sister, her childhood friends, the local church, the local pub, and she misses them. She misses Lillian, too.

What troubles Sinéad most is that she seems to have lost her ability to laugh at misfortune, her trademark sense of humour that her friends had celebrated back home. She isn't sure if it is her accent or what, but Aussies never seem to get her jokes.

Dr Suenho, the university counsellor whom Sinéad has been seeing for a while, believes that Sinéad is suffering from a reactive depression, the type that afflicts displaced people when they find themselves removed from their familiar surroundings and support networks.

'But I've always been very social. I thought making friends here, you know, networking, would be the least of my problems!' Sinéad said in one of their sessions.

'You'd be surprised, Sinéad, at what happens to people when they change environment. Introverts suddenly come out of their shells, and extroverts clam up.'

Dr Suenho recommended antidepressants to help Sinéad cope while adapting to life in Australia. Sinéad was reluctant to take drugs, so Dr Suenho came up with many other helpful suggestions, such as joining some of the interest groups at the university. She gave her a brochure called 'How to Get the Best out of Campus Life'.

Determined to try everything possible before giving up, Sinéad has decided to join the gospel choir, the book club, and the belly dancing classes. This will be her first time at the book club. She has also put her name down for casual work stuffing envelopes at a mail house, but in the last two weeks she's only got three days' worth of work.

The book being discussed at the book club's June meeting is Milan Kundera's *The Unbearable Lightness of Being*. When Sinéad arrives at the meeting, the others, who already know each other, are chatting in little groups and don't seem to notice her. She sits in a corner feeling out of place, vulnerable and invisible, just like Therese, a main character in the book they are about to discuss. Therese had felt like that most of her life, but the feeling is new for Sinéad, and she can't stand it.

Shortly after the meeting starts, a tall redhead erupts into the room, like a volcano clad in red velvet, and sits in the empty chair next to Sinéad.

'Hi,' the redhead says, producing the book out of a calico bag. 'I'm Angie. It's my first time here.'

Sinéad introduces herself. 'My first time too!'

'Shy ... Shy ... say again?'

'Shan-aid,' Sinéad pronounces slowly, smiling. 'Like the singer, Sinéad O'Connor.'

'Never heard of her. But it's a beautiful name! Does it have a meaning?'

'It's Irish for Janet. It means God is gracious.'

After the meeting Angie asks Sinéad if she wants to go for a coffee. There is so much more she wanted to discuss about the book, and there hadn't been enough time. Besides, the guy who was chairing the meeting kept interrupting her – so that others would have the chance to speak.

Two hours later, they are still at the university coffee shop. It is semester break, and the shop is practically deserted; the Italian brothers who run the place are delighted to have some business. By sundown, the two women move from Milan Kundera and his troubled Czechoslovakia to Sinéad's equally troubled Northern Ireland, and by the time they finish their third round of cappuccino and muffins, Angie takes it upon herself to be Sinéad's personal tour guide in Sydney.

'I've been working since I was nineteen, and have never had the chance to enjoy the things my own city has to offer,' Angie says. 'So many things to do, so many places to go … it's like I've been living in another country: full-time work country. So, what do you say, Sinéad? Do you want to discover Sydney with me?'

'Love to, but I happen to be broke,' Sinéad says, sighing.

'You'll be surprised at how many things are cheap or free: parks, galleries, museums, markets, second-hand shops. I've been looking them up on the internet, 'cause I don't have that much cash either, now that I'm not working.' Angie says, and starts giggling.

'What?' Sinéad asks. 'Want to share the joke, or is it private?'

'It just occurred to me, that when we work we have plenty of money but no time to spend it. When we don't work, we have plenty of time but no money. Crazy, hey!'

'One of life's greatest paradoxes,' Sinéad says, laughing while emptying the contents of her purse on the table. She separates out what she needs for her bus fare and counts what's left. 'Listen, sister, I have enough money and enough time for one more coffee, and then I must make tracks. Actually, I better make it a cup of green tea, or I'll be up all night.'

In the ensuing weeks they roam the streets of Sydney together, exploring the NSW Art Gallery, Hyde Park Barracks, second-hand shops in Newtown, Centennial Park, and the beaches, walks and harbour views that Angie had mentioned the first time they met. They go everywhere on foot, on the train or on the bus.

Between book club meetings they read and discuss the works of Virginia Woolf, Germaine Greer and Jeanette Winterson, Sinéad's favourite writers, and Angie reads aloud to her friend the poetry of Oscar Wilde, Emily Dickinson and Judith Wright.

Sinéad invites Angie to join her belly dancing classes, her gospel choir, all the groups she's been attending in her efforts to meet people. With plenty of time on her hands, Angie is only too happy to agree.

One afternoon Angie arrives to pick Sinéad up driving an old Toyota Corona. She explains that Norah, who is delighted to see Angie smiling again, has decided to upgrade her car and has surprisingly given Angie the old one.

'So I got a car, just like that!' Angie says, snapping her fingers.

Later, on their way to the belly dancing class, after they have been honked for changing lanes without giving enough warning, she explains that she obtained her license at eighteen, but because she never owned a car, she's a little out of practice.

'You should've seen me when I went to the shops last Sunday, driving for the first time in twelve years. I was petrified, and so was Jimmy. He says he won't let me drive him around, ever again.'

'Understandably,' Sinéad agrees, thinking it is about time that she got her own licence. The test couldn't be that hard, if Angie passed.

'Oh, it's more than my driving,' Angie explains. 'Jimmy's convinced that he died in a car crash in a previous life, and he'll do whatever is possible to avoid that happening again. He doesn't even have a driver's license.'

'Are you serious?'

'Absolutely.'

'Well, having you driving him around is certainly not going to help him overcome his phobia.'

'I'm getting the hang of it though,' Angie says, as she turns a corner so violently the left wheel climbs over the footpath. 'Oops! I take that back.'

'Holy Mother of Christ!' Sinéad exclaims, holding onto the sides of her seat.

'Sorry! Sometimes I think I should stick a P-plate at the back. But I didn't want to miss our turn.'

'Forget the P! You need an "M", for menace!' Sinéad says, and they both burst out laughing. 'By the way, that wasn't our turn,' she points out. 'See the sign? "No through road".'

Angie has no sense of direction, so with Sinéad not knowing the streets of Sydney, they get lost twice before arriving and again on the way back. For the rest of the winter, the sight of two women giggling whilst wandering lost through streets that often don't even appear in the old directory that came with the car, becomes a regular occurrence.


In early Spring, Dr Suenho tells Sinéad that she will be leaving the university counselling service to concentrate on her private practice, located near Homebush. Sinéad is welcome to make the trip there but she will have to pay for the consultations.

'That works out well, because I came today to tell you

that I have decided I no longer require your services,' Sinéad tells her with a smile in her face.

'I'm never sorry to lose patients because they've recovered,' Dr Suenho says, also smiling while she scribbles her final remarks on Sinéad's file.

That evening, Angie and Sinéad go to the choir's post-concert party, in Newtown. About eighteen of the thirty choir members are there, and most of them, including Sinéad, have exchanged their formal wear for jeans and t-shirts. Angie, inexperienced in these things, hasn't thought of bringing a change of clothes, and is rather hot in her long-sleeved silk blouse and black skirt, but this doesn't stop her from having a great time.

The terrace, which belongs to the choir's conductor, smells of incense, alcohol, tobacco and other substances that Angie, to Sinéad's amusement, doesn't recognise.

'You need to get out more, sister!' Sinéad says, exhaling cigarette smoke, careful to blow it away from her friend. They are sitting outside, on the veranda.

Angie is thinking that she has never felt better in her life, though sometimes she catches Jimmy looking at her out of the corner of his eye, as if looking at a stranger. The crease between his eyebrows is growing deeper and his hair thinner.

'You've gone quiet all of a sudden,' Sinéad says, bringing Angie back from her reverie. 'A penny for your thoughts.'

'Oh, it suddenly occurred to me that I'm living a borrowed life,' Angie says, clutching a glass of orange juice. She tries not to drink at all when she has to drive – she is enough of a hazard on the roads as it is. 'I'm going to wake up any day now, unhappy, depressed, overweight, trapped in a dead-end job, with no friends, unable to sing, drive or enjoy anything. The thought terrifies me.'

'Angie, maybe this is your real life, and the other one was the borrowed one.'

'Yeah, that's an interesting take. I wonder who borrowed my life during that time – who lived all the adventures I was meant to live in my twenties ...'

'Surely, your twenties weren't so bad? Frankly, I can't picture you unhappy, overweight and friendless. You are the friendliest and cheeriest person I've met since I've been here.'

Angie tends to forget that Sinéad hasn't been a part of her life for long; it feels as if she has known her since childhood; even though they've grown up with ten years and three oceans between them.

'You need to get out more, girl,' Angie says, laughing. 'But you're right about my twenties. They might've been uneventful, but most of that time I was quite content with my life. A secure job, a modest apartment and a decent husband were enough to make me happy, you know?'

'Uneventful! Sister, in my world, getting married, buying property and becoming a manager qualify as very meaningful events in life! Anyway, you are happy now, that's all that counts,' Sinéad says, taking the last puff of her cigarette and pulling Angie by the hand to join the other choristers inside. They have started a drunken but still exultant rendition of *Amazing Grace*.

# ~ Jimmy ~

One night Jimmy arrives home to find a note on the table saying that Angie has gone to a choir party with Sinéad and won't be back till after eleven. All the curtains are open and the lights are blazing in practically every room. Angie quit work at the beginning of June, saying that she needed a couple of months to recharge her batteries. It is mid-September now, she is still unemployed, her batteries are so charged that she is literally bouncing of the walls, and she is driving him to distraction.

Jimmy sighs repeatedly as he walks around the place switching off the lamps, the television, the stereo. A couple of weeks ago, Angie left the car parked outside Sinéad's place with the lights on, and drained the battery. She had to call road service to jump-start the car, or so she said, when she got back home after midnight.

In a way, Jimmy's relieved that Angie's not cooking anymore, because she would probably leave the gas stove burning, and he doesn't look forward to coming home one night to find the whole apartment building reduced to ashes.

Angie is full of unpleasant surprises these days. A few nights ago, she came home with her beautiful ginger hair dyed burgundy.

'I wanted a jet-black tint, but Sinéad said that it would be too dramatic against my pale skin, so we settled for burgundy. She applied the colour herself. '

When Jimmy met Sinéad at a recent university function, he nearly choked on his drink. He had expected a woman around Angie's age, not a teenager with spiky hair and a tattoo on her ankle.

'She's not a teenager!' Angie exclaimed later, when they got home. 'She'll be twenty-one next year.'

Teenager or not, Sinéad's opinion was obviously more important to Angie than anyone else's, so he hadn't even commented on her new hair colour. Not that she had asked for his feedback.

In her haste to leave, Angie has left a trail of chaos. The bed is unmade, with clothes scattered all over it, and Jimmy doesn't know whether they are clean or not. There's a pile of dirty dishes in the sink. There's a mug, a quarter full of cold coffee, sitting on the computer desk. There are several crumpled pieces of paper on the floor of the study. He picks one up and smoothes it out: the beginning of an essay on *Mrs Dalloway*.

> This is undoubtedly a largely autobiographical work. After reading Virginia Woolf's diary entries at different stages of her life, one can see traces of the author's suicidal despair in Maximus, the poet, morbidly obsessed with death. But there is also evidence of Woolf's exhilaration and love for life in Clarissa Dalloway, rejoicing at the sight of a perfect summer's day.

Angie seems to have started the essay four or five times and never gone past the first couple of paragraphs.

Jimmy notices that fish are swimming across the monitor

screen: the computer has also been left on. When he jiggles the mouse to clear the screen saver, he discovers that Angie has left the word processing program running, and the document she has been working on is still open. It's not the first time she has left her uni assignments unfinished and unsaved. Jimmy's about to close it, when the words "human desire" catch his eye. He reads a few paragraphs and finds himself blushing.

This is no *Mrs Dalloway*.

Dave remembered the night very well; it had been a full moon.

They met outside the movie theatre in Paddington, and he was astonished at the change that had come over Elena. She was looking radiant, as usual, but she wasn't dressed in her customary gypsy style; instead she wore a long black velvet dress which accentuated her curves. She wore her long hair pulled back with combs, and a handcrafted silver necklace with matching earrings.

Dave knew nothing about the movie they were going to see, but he was familiar with Almodóvar's work, and his fetish for exploring the most obscure aspects of human desire. As soon as the film started, he knew it was going to be in classic Almodóvar style.

Feeling awkward, he shifted in his seat and just then Elena leaned towards him, as if she wanted to say something but decided not to. Their faces were almost touching, and he couldn't resist the impulse of kissing her on the mouth. Surprisingly, she returned the kiss eagerly at first, but then pulled away.

Could this be something that Angie has downloaded from the internet? Jimmy wonders, with raised eyebrows and a dry throat. It isn't even the stuff that she likes to read – she's never been interested in 'bodice rippers'.

Jimmy checks – the document is one of three word files inside a folder called *Elena*. He clicks to open them, one after the other. They seem to be short stories, or chapters of a story. Angie has even dated the other two.

The first one is called *Avoiding Elena*, and was written in March. It's about David, who receives a phone call from his friend's wife, Elena. David hasn't heard from Mario (his friend) or Elena in years, and now Elena wants to meet with him. After he hangs up, Dave falls asleep in his office and dreams about the encounter, realising as he wakes that he had always been attracted to Elena, even though she had often treated him "like rubbish". Abashed by this discovery, and for his old friend's sake, he decides not to attend the rendezvous.

The second story, called *Six Seconds* and dated in July, seems to be a reversal of the previous scenario. In this version, the meeting does take place, but it is Elena who confesses to Dave that after writing a short story about him, she had realised that she had been attracted to him for a long time. She's terribly distraught by this realisation because she would never do anything to hurt her husband, who is such a decent human being, and has always been so good to her. But she can't deny it any longer and wonders if Dave has ever felt the same way.

'...what was I going to say?' thought Dave. 'That she had always been out of bounds because she was Mario's girl, so I never thought of her in that way?'

Not wanting to hurt her feelings, Dave began to say that yes, he used to think a lot about her, and dream about her, in the past, but––

Before he could finish, Elena leaned forward and kissed him.

Instinctively, he looked away, and the kiss landed on his left cheek. She kept her lips pressed against his skin for what seemed a long time. He didn't know what to do. Turn around, stay still? In a desperate effort to stop thinking about the awkwardness of his situation, he started to count. One, two, three, four, five, six. Six seconds. Those six seconds felt like ... forever. After that, Elena looked away and said:

'It is late. Take me home.' She hardly spoke again, while Dave's mind raced, thinking of what would have happened if he'd turned back towards her, just a little, if he'd let his lips meet hers.

The third story, the one Jimmy discovered open on the computer screen, is still untitled and had only been created that very morning - 15th of September. It's a sequel to the previous story. After Elena's six-second kiss, Dave becomes obsessed with her, thinking of "what could have been". He wants to see her again, but she refuses. She finally agrees to go to the movies, where they kiss. Elena storms out of the theatre, followed by Dave, and--

That's as far as it goes. Untitled and unfinished.

By the time Jimmy has read the three files, it's well after eleven and there's no sign of Angie. His head is thumping; he would've been shocked to find out that Angie read this sort of trash, but to discover that she has actually written it... is unconceivable. And yet, he wants to know more, he wants to know if Elena will betray her husband, if Dave will resist temptation and remain loyal to his old friend.

Jimmy notices that certain things change in every variation: the kiss, for example. The first one is imaginary, the second is ambiguous, and the third is explicit. In every story, Elena is more exuberant and provocative, and Dave is weaker.

What remains constant is the "decent" husband's obliviousness to what's going on around him; his capacity to live somehow outside the real world, immersed in the teachings of Jiddu Krishnamurti.

Ten years ago, when Jimmy met Angie, Jimmy's bookshelf had indeed been filled with books by and about Krishnamurti. During the turmoil of his teenage years, marked by worsening problems between his parents, the philosopher's teachings had given him a sense of peace and stability.

*It [truth] is there as sudden as sunlight, as pure as the night; but to receive it, the heart must be full and the mind empty.* This had been one of Jimmy's favourite meditations and he had shared it with Angie. It must've made an impression on her, as she had paraphrased it in one of her stories. Jimmy recognised it in the scene in which Mario counselled Dave.

In fact, Jimmy remembers, he spoke non stop about Krishnamurti all throughout their first date, and Angie had been dazzled.

They were sitting on a bench overlooking the Sydney Harbour Bridge, both keeping to their own side of the seat. It was a Sunday afternoon in autumn, and there was a mist in the air that made the Bridge look slightly out of focus, as though it were in an impressionist painting. They started talking about work – Jimmy had just finished his printing apprenticeship with Fairfax, and Angie had been working at the photo lab for a few months. She wanted to do psychology at university, but her TER hadn't been high enough.

'I don't mind the Quick-Pic shop,' she told Jimmy. 'But I'm only there temporarily, you know, until I figure out what I want to do in life, what I want to become.'

'See Angie,' Jimmy said, looking into the skyline, his face transfixed. 'Krishnamurti says that daily life is a process of becoming. I am this, and I want to become that. It's a continuous, painful struggle. Instead of wanting to do something else, to be someone else, maybe you should stop to see what you already are, right here, right now: a bright, sensible, wonderful girl. Be content with that, and the rest will fall into place in due course.'

Angie had lowered her eyes, blushing, and when she looked up again, there was something different in her gaze. As they walked back to the ferry, she had slipped her hand inside his, and gripping it, Jimmy had thought, Lucky I didn't tell her that living in the present is easier said than done.

But unlike the Mario of Angie's stories, Jimmy moved on from his philosophical phase. He donated all those books to the library shortly after he got married. His bookshelf is now laden with texts on real estate investment and financial planning, though he can't say he has finished any of them.

Tempted as he is to trash it, Jimmy saves Angie's "untitled" piece before switching the computer off. Ignoring the complaints of his empty stomach, he takes two headache pills and goes to bed. He pushes the pile of clothes over to Angie's side of the bed, and falls asleep as soon as his head hits the pillow. Ever since he was a child, he's always been able to switch off his brain at night, just like a computer, and leave his tribulations to the waking world.

He dreams of Elena and Dave kissing on the back seat of Dave's car, while Mario scans the shelves of his local library, looking for a book he read when he was young, a book that had all the answers, whose title and author he can't remember.

Jimmy wakes up at dawn with no recollection of his dream – he never remembers his dreams. Angie is sleeping soundly beside him. He has no idea what time she came home. He gets up and kneels on the floor beside his wife, and contemplates her for a while. She's breathing regularly and peacefully, her familiar profile buried in the pillow and her unfamiliar dark hair spread over her cheek and shoulders. Her eyes are moving fast behind her eyelids, and whatever she's dreaming is making her smile.

By the time the alarm goes off, Jimmy has decided that Mario's philosophy is not so flawed, after all: ignorance is bliss.

Still, every few weeks, he turns the computer on when Angie's not home – to check if she's made any progress with the story. He wants to know if Elena and Dave have done the deed. Each time, to his relief, the saga remains unfinished.

~

'Do you like it?' Angie holds her top above her belly, waiting for Jimmy to say something. It's a Friday night in early October. It's hot and humid, and Jimmy arrives home from work, tired after a rotten week, quite unprepared for what's waiting for him. On Angie's stomach, just underneath her belly button, is a tattoo of a ladybird, about two square centimetres in size. Bright red with black spots.

He tries to recognise Angie in the woman who stands in front of him, but this woman with dyed burgundy hair, long earrings, overstated makeup, Indian clothes, a loud voice and a ladybird tattooed on her belly is not his wife. His wife doesn't like to wear makeup; his wife is soft spoken and meek, and she didn't even have her ears pierced until a couple of months ago.

'Angie, you know how I feel about those things,' he says, firmly, when his voice comes back. 'I thought you would ask me before doing something permanent like a tattoo.' The pierced ears, he had thought, would heal in time. Her natural light ginger hair would grow back. Maybe it was all part of some sort of existential crisis that women face when they turn thirty.

But a tattoo!

'Most men think tattoos are attractive, you know? Some husbands even ask their wives to get one.'

'Was it her idea?' Jimmy asks.

'Whose?'

'The Irish girl. The one with the unpronounceable name.'

'Sinéad, Jimmy. Shan-aid.'

'Yes, her. She has one on her ankle, some sort of squiggle.'

'It's not a squiggle. It's a symbol for ... oh, never mind,' Angie sweeps the air with her hand. 'Of course it wasn't her idea. I'm thirty years old, Jimmy. I can make my own decisions about my own body!'

'You realise you won't be able to donate blood...' He knows it sounds idiotic, but it's the only thing that comes to his mind. Angie, the old Angie, had been donating blood once a year ever since they met, following his example.

'Oh, Jimmy. The things you worry about,' Angie says, rolling her eyes. 'You didn't even ask me if it hurt.' But before he can ask, she leaves for her belly dancing class, telling him not to stay up.

Next thing Jimmy is kneeling on the floor, staring at a hole that he's just made in the wall after kicking it with his steel-capped boot. Plaster all over the carpet, broken pieces of plywood. The paper-thin walls they have been working so hard to pay for, for nearly nine years. Worst of all, flashbacks

of his own father kicking the furniture, slapping his mother
... the man he swore never to become.

Later that night, after rearranging the furniture to cover
the evidence of his frustration, Jimmy walks the few blocks
to Norah's place and knocks on her door.

'Norah!' he exclaims when she opens the door, the breeze
of her ceiling fan blowing above her. He's never shed a tear
since he was a child, but his voice is trembling.

'Come in, Jimmy. What's wrong?' She's wearing her apron,
and has just finished setting the table. For weeks now, she's
been cooking dinner for Jimmy as well, because Angie is
rarely home when he arrives from work. Cooking seems to
be the second last of Angie's priorities, the last being finding
a job.

'Please, Norah, help me! I want my old Angie back!' He is
standing in the middle of the lounge, his arms hanging by
his sides like defective wings, a look of hopelessness in his
light blue eyes, traces of paint and plaster on his right boot.

Norah covers her mouth, and the tears she's been crying
in secret for the last few months roll down her cheeks in front
of her son-in-law. Jimmy is like her own son, the son she never
had; the son who is always in control, the one who always
helps others and has never before asked anybody for help.

'Me too, Jimmy!' she cries. 'Believe me, I want her back too!'

Be careful what you wish for, the saying goes. Jimmy wished,
as adamantly as he used to pray when he was younger, that
the alien who had taken possession of his wife's body would
go away. And she did, not long after the night they fought
about the tattoo. But what was left behind was not his wife.

It was her body, although tattooed, pierced, and tanned, but her spirit wasn't inside.

What strikes Jimmy most are his wife's big hazel eyes, devoid of fire, searching his face every night when he gets back from work, as if hoping that he will bring home what she has lost. And he would, if he only knew what to look for. What does a person's spirit look like?

He has always been Mr Fix-it, fixing everybody's broken down cars, computers, washing machines; and he can do nothing to fix the heartbreaking expression in his wife's eyes. Useless, good for nothing. His mother had been right after all, when she called him those names as a child. It hadn't mattered how hard he had tried to prove her wrong.

... And here he is, in the backyard of a psychiatrist's practice, sitting on a wooden bench underneath one of many jacaranda trees, waiting for his wife to finish her first appointment with Dr Suenho. He has brought a newspaper to read, but it remains folded on the bench, covered now with purple petals. He wonders if it might have been a good idea to go inside with Angie, even though he doesn't believe in psychotherapy.

Tiger, once his best friend, resorted to both therapy and medication for as long as Jimmy has known him. He used to swallow antidepressants, sleeping pills and tranquilisers like tic-tacs, but showed zero sign of progress. In fact, when Jimmy last saw Tiger, three or four years ago, he was even more disturbed than he had been the first day they met, back in seventh grade.

Unlike Tiger, Jimmy has always faced life's troubles without the help of shrinks (as Tiger called them) and drugs. To see Angie become one of those people who need drugs to cope with day-to-day existence has been a slap in the face, when all he's ever done in the nine years they've been together, is to provide her with everything she has ever wanted.

Jimmy looks at his watch: 1.15 pm. Angie should've been finished fifteen minutes ago. He scratches his head, wanting to know what's taking so long, wondering whether Angie is telling the doctor about him, complaining about his faults, revealing intimate details about their marriage ... things a stranger needn't know.

Or is she going through the "What my dad did to my mum" routine that shrinks invariably go through with their patients? He's never been to see one but he used to listen to Tiger talk about his therapy sessions often enough to be an expert.

Jimmy tries to picture himself in a psychiatrist's room. This is not easy for him – imagination is Angie's territory, not his. She's the one who remembers her dreams vividly, who exaggerates everything. Why, she even writes stories.

But he still tries; he even squeezes his eyelids shut, but cannot visualise himself talking to a therapist any more than he can see himself flying on the back of a winged dragon or reading a romance novel.

Then poof! It happens, like a videotape playing in his mind: Jimmy Fletcher, tall and slightly overweight, lying on his back on a beige leather couch, his arms crossed over his chest and his feet dangling from the edge. The room is half-lit, and he cannot see the doctor, but he knows it's a man.

'My dad used to hit my mum,' Jimmy tells the man, in a monotone, as if in hypnotic trance. 'My mum tried to hide it but my brother and I knew. My mum's way to cope was to drink herself into a stupor every day, when dad was at work. When she was plastered, she'd turn against my brother and me, telling us that we were useless mongrels like our dad. She would throw things at us: vases, plates, pots. But we were quick, Peter and I. It's hard to hit a moving target when you're drunk.

'I hated my dad for doing this to my mum, and Peter hated my mum for the things she said to us. To this day, he blames her for the fact that he didn't amount to anything, just like she said. A year younger than me, he's divorced, renting a studio, and having to work two factory jobs to be able to pay maintenance for his three kids. He even seems to hate me, because I have a good job, a good marriage - well, up until last year - and some common sense about financial and family planning. If he only knew that, despite everything I've achieved, mum's voice is as much inside my head as it is in his...

"But mum's better now, she's been sober for thirteen years, and dad has mellowed with age. Mum has become a Christian, and dad even goes to church with her. I don't hate dad anymore, I don't hate either of them; they are changed people. But there's something that bugs me sometimes, something that only occurred to me after leaving home: *did mum drink because dad hit her, or did he hit her because she was a drunk?'*

Jimmy presses the pause button on his mental video. There's something very wrong with this scene. Would he be confiding all these painful, intimate things, things he hasn't even told his own wife, to a stranger he's never seen before in his life?

Fat chance, even under hypnosis.

# ~ Symphony in D ~

In Dr Suenho's consulting room, Angie is about to reach the end of her story.

'Those five months last year…were like a dream. Armed with Elena's confidence, I was practically walking on clouds. And then, sometime in November, just after I finished the semester at uni, I took a false step into a rabbit hole and found myself free-falling all the way to hell, where Elena doesn't bother coming to visit me.

"My faithful visitors are Jimmy, my mother and Sinéad, but I don't want to see them. Actually, I don't want them to see me – not like this. I pushed them away, isolated myself, dropped out of the book club, the choir and the belly dancing classes, and became a zombie.'

Angie shifts in her seat and for the first time since she started her monologue, looks at Dr Suenho directly in the eye.

'This is where I am now, Dr Suenho. In the last nine months I've gone the full circle: hell, heaven and back to hell again. But this hell is worse than the first one. Without Elena, I'm like a puppet without strings, a balloon without air, a zombie. Can you help me find her again? Can you help me bring her back into my life? Can you?'

'You speak about Elena just like methadone users talk

about the highs they experienced while on heroin,' Dr Suenho says, pushing her glasses back with her index finger – they tend to slide down her slim, pointy nose.

'No, no!' Angie cries, shaking her hands. 'I have never tried heroin, or any mind-altering drug, but I know that they induce an artificial state of mind. What I experienced was NOT an artificial high. It was like … like coming home, like finding something I had lost long, long ago – my soul, myself, I don't know.'

Angie shuts her eyes tightly, searching her mind for an adequate metaphor. 'Think of a blind person who has been given the gift of sight, but only for a short time. After having known the difference, sightlessness would be twice as wretched. Do you understand?' Angie begins to sob.

Dr Suenho hands Angie a box of tissues, and switches the tape recorder off. She gives her patient a minute to compose herself, while she scribbles down a few key points: History of severe depression in the family (mother). Suicide (mother's sister). Lost father (desertion) – age seven. No apparent family history of manic depression. She underlines the words 'manic depression'.

'From what you've told me, Angie, I can confirm your family practitioner's diagnosis. What you went through early last year and are experiencing now is a clinical depression,' Dr Suenho says when she speaks at last, matter-of-factly. And then her tone becomes cautious. 'The period in between … I can't be sure yet, but it seems to have been a bout of hypomania triggered by the antidepressants. It doesn't happen very often, but it can happen when the patient has a predisposition, and it could've been a one-off episode.'

'Hypomania?' Angie repeats, bewildered, the tears suddenly dry in her eyes.

She's heard of kleptomania and megalomania, but not of hypomania. She thinks about the etymology of those words: they all come from Greek roots. Klepto means thief; mega, great. And mania ... stands for a mental disorder, which makes kleptomaniacs steal compulsively, and megalomaniacs have delusions of grandeur. Hypo, as in hypoglycaemia, or hypothermia, means low, or less.

*A lesser madness?*

Angie has always been fascinated by the meanings of words and names. She has a dictionary of etymology at home, and several thesauruses. She subscribes to the online 'word of the day', and crossword puzzles are one of her favourite pastimes - or at least they were - she hasn't been able to complete one in months.

Shortly after writing *Avoiding Elena*, she'd looked up the meaning of Elena, the name that had so inexplicably come to her in a dream: it was of Greek origin, and it meant *radiance of the sun.* Helen, daughter of the Queen of Sparta and the god Zeus, had reputedly been the most beautiful woman of the ancient world, and according to myth, her kidnapping had been the cause of the ten-year Trojan War.

'You could have a predisposition to suffer from manic depression. I don't need to explain what depression feels like, as you are in the middle of one. Mania, on the other hand, is a state of euphoria that comes in various degrees.' Dr Suenho is in the middle of an explanation when Angie is able to focus back on her words. She elucidates that acute mania can involve psychotic episodes and requires hospitalisation. Hypomania is mania in its mildest form, and it fits the description Angie has given her: one feels confident, exuberant, on top of the world.

'It's a great feeling, but alas, it's short-lived; it either develops into a full-blown mania, or, as in your case, reverts into depression. Do you follow me, Angie?'

Angie nods with a blank look. She's grappling with Dr Suenho's suggestion that what she thought had been a miraculous recovery from her earlier depression, an awakening that had led her to the path of self-discovery and assertion, had actually been a mild episode of madness.

Angie thinks of her mother, of the things that they could never openly discuss: depression, death, desertion, divorce (for some reason, they all started with the letter 'd'). Unspoken, these words hovered between them like a lingering smell, particularly when Angie was a teenager.

Back then, the taboo subjects found their way to the surface through other channels, mainly through Angie's poetry.

At this precise moment Angie remembers the first stanza of a poem she wrote at fourteen:

My nameless friend
Entraps me with his bittersweet spider web
Slowly taking possession of my body
Slowly taking possession of my brain
In a lover's game
Whilst I am nailed to the mattress, staring at the ceiling
Hearing the symphony of the silence
Orchestrated in my head.

When Norah stumbled across Angie's poetry scrapbook while cleaning her room, and read Angie's collection of poems, entitled "Symphony in D", she was so alarmed that she took Angie to see the school counsellor the next day, for a psychological assessment. Angie was given the 'all clear' by the counsellor, but the embarrassing episode had the effect that she suspected Norah had hoped for: her poetic inspiration fizzled. Much as she tried, she could not stick to trivial topics.

While Angie struggles to remember the second stanza of the poem, Dr Suenho flips through the files in her cabinet. She hands Angie a one-page printout, *Signs and Symptoms of Mania.*

'I want you to take this home and read it. When you come back next time, you can tell me how many of these symptoms sound familiar and we'll discuss them.'

Too many, Angie thinks, after glancing at the list: heightened senses, increased energy, restlessness, racing thoughts, rapid talking; excessive high or euphoric feelings; extreme irritability and distractibility; decreased need for sleep; sustained periods of behaviour that is different from usual; increased sexual drive; provocative, intrusive, or aggressive behaviour...

Angie remembers the second stanza of her foreboding teenage poem and succumbs to an attack of teary hiccups:

Somewhere amidst the echo
Of my never ending thoughts
I find the words
To welcome my oldest friend.
Insanity
Has finally found me again.

Dr Suenho gives Angie a glass of water and a sympathetic pat on the back. It is never easy to throw a patient mercilessly into the eye of a storm knowing there's no way to rescue them in a one-hour session. Some of her patients recover within months. Others have been coming to the cottage for years. In Angie's case, the signs point towards a diagnosis of Bipolar Type II, the mildest form of the condition.

'Angie, we've run out of time for today but I'd like to see you on a weekly basis. We need to work on one thing at the time, and it's important that we address your current state of depression before we deal with anything else. In the meantime, I'll increase your dose of antidepressants until you show some signs of improvement.' Dr Suenho takes a book from the bookshelf and hands it to Angie. 'I'd like you to read this book. It's a step-by-step program on overcoming depression,' she says.

Turning to the last page, Angie wonders how she is going to get through 169 pages when she has barely been able to finish a four-hundred-word newspaper article lately. Meanwhile, Dr Suenho writes a prescription.

Angie slips the prescription between the leaves of the book, together with the one-page list of symptoms, and gives Dr Suenho one last heartbreaking look as she heads to the door.

Outside, Jimmy leaps to his feet, leaving the newspaper behind on the bench.

'How'd you go?' He has jacaranda flowers caught in his hair.

Angie shrugs her shoulders. Dr Suenho hadn't been con-clusive, she'd said that it could've been a one-off episode, and Angie isn't about to tell Jimmy or anybody about the doctor's suspicions until she knows for sure. Besides, despite the 'signs and symptoms of mania' listed in that leaflet, which seem to make her a perfect textbook case, a part of her remains convinced that something that felt so right couldn't possibly have been an illness. *No, no, no!*

'Well, Ange? Do you think she can help you?' Jimmy insists.

'It's too soon to say, Jimmy,' Angie answers in a mono-tone. 'She gave me a book on depression. She upped my medication. She wants me to come once a week for a while.'

Jimmy wants to say something like 'Of course she does. At one hundred bucks a session who wouldn't?' but he bites his tongue. Norah has told him that you get seventy per cent back from Medicare. Norah has offered to pay for the gap in the fees if necessary, knowing that Jimmy is struggling with the mortgage and the bills on his own.

They walk in silence, each lost in their own thoughts. They caught the train this morning, because Angie no longer has the confidence to drive. As they make their way to the train station, they see a large park, crisscrossed by walking paths and bike tracks. In the middle there is a fountain, at the point where all the paths meet.

'I don't remember this park,' Jimmy comments. 'But then again, it's been ages since I've been over this side of town.'

'Can we sit there for a while?' Angie says, pointing towards a bench near the fountain. 'I'm wasted; that session was exhausting.'

She just wants to sit quietly, but Jimmy wants to talk.

'It will take years for them to reach full height,' he tells her, referring to the young trees in the park. Jimmy has always been interested in trees. He points to a bush here, a shrub there, and starts talking about how trees and plants improve a city's environment.

But Angie is hardly listening. She's intently watching bicycle riders pedalling around them. Young couples with their children puffing behind, middle-aged parents with their teenagers racing ahead. She can't help but wonder if she will be able to ride a bike with her kids in the park one day; to have the family that they had been planning to start soon.

Jimmy's voice flows in the air around her, merging with the racket that the birds are making among the leaves. Angie's attention shifts to the fountain. There is a large column of foamy water in the centre, surrounded by similar but smaller jets. They resemble women dressed in white tunics performing a manic veil dance. It makes her think of a reluctant bride facing a life of lovelessness, surrounded by her bridesmaids. All of them want to escape, their veils and lace dresses swirling uncontrollably around them as they try to free themselves; but their feet are fixed to the ground, to their starting place.

Angie too wants to run, to free herself, but she cannot. Worse still, she senses that Jimmy too, feels trapped – trapped in a marriage to a wife with the words *damaged goods* stamped on her forehead. If he doesn't feel this way now, it won't be long before he does.

Just then, Jimmy says something about marriage.

'What did you say?' she asks, because the word marriage has not been mentioned between them in a long, long time.

'Foliage,' he says. It wasn't marriage, after all. 'They could've been more imaginative about it when they designed this park.'

Variations on Angie's old poem, recited in Elena's distinctive Spanish accent, revolve inside Angie's head throughout that night, intertwined with Jimmy's gentle snuffles and the hoots of the owl that has been camping on the pine tree outside their bedroom window for the last few days.

When Angie started writing gloomy poetry at sixteen, the school counsellor, only a few years older than her, had deemed her a typical teenager - if a little on the morose side.

But this was understandable, considering that she came from a broken home and that she had seen her mother go through a severe episode of depression. It was a phase, the counsellor had said, and it would pass.

Many of Angie's 'morose' poems had come to her in dreams, not unlike the story about Elena. She would wake up in the morning with the words fluttering inside her head like butterflies trying to escape from a cage. She used to free them as soon as she got up, while the words were fresh in her mind. She would spread her scrapbook open on the bed, kneel on the floor, and scribble without editing what came out, as if someone were dictating.

Did this young counsellor, probably on her first placement, miss something? Something that Norah was able to discern, knowing what she knew about Jo? Has this madness, which Dr Suenho has so quickly identified, been incubating inside Angie for much longer than she dares even to imagine?

'I see that the – what do you call her – *shrink* has washed your brain, Angelica,' her long lost friend Elena says, sitting at the other end of the bed. Angie can barely make out her silhouette against the shadows, but she can clearly hear the disappointment in her voice.

'You mean brainwashed me,' Angie can't help correcting. She looks at Jimmy – he's facing the other way and sleeping as he always does, curled up like a baby. Angie lowers her voice, just in case. 'Dr Suenho wasn't trying to brainwash me. She was just giving me information. Stating facts.'

'Facts. Information,' Elena repeats, running her fingers through her long hair. 'Of course. Who can argue with the facts?'

She can, of course. It only takes her a few seconds to prepare her case.

'Tell me something Angelica: remember last Spring, when you performed with the gospel choir at Saint Andrew's church, when you sang Gershwin's *Summertime*? How did that feel?'

'It felt ... amazing!' Angie says, overcome by a pang of longing. It had in fact been so moving that she had cried with happiness during the concert. She hadn't realised she could sing until she had auditioned for the choir, urged by Sinéad; there was a performance coming up and two girls had dropped out. At the audition, the volume and pitch of her own voice had pleasantly surprised Angie. Norah had never encouraged her to sing, not after what had happened to her gifted sister.

'And afterwards?' Elena asks, and then answers her own question. 'You drove home after the post-concert party, past midnight, still singing *Summertime* at the top of your voice,' Elena sings a couple of lines from the song to illustrate, in a rich contralto voice. 'The car windows were wound down and the night air, moist after the rain, filled your lungs. You felt as if your chest was about to explode, as if your whole body was going to burst with excitement. You were overtaken by the radiance, brighter than usual, emanating from the street-lights, the lamps inside house windows and the flickering stars in the clearing sky. You had not been drinking, but you were intoxicated: with life, with this magical feeling of having stepped into another reality, higher than the ordinary.'

'It felt as if I wasn't driving at all, but gliding smoothly through the traffic and the night ...' Angie says, her eyes glazing. 'I've always wanted to fly. As a child, I often dreamt of flying; I wasn't a dove or an eagle though – I was a ladybird.'

'You experienced all those things, Angelica. You did not imagine them. They are facts. If you listen to this doctor, you will be denying some of the most fulfilling times in your life. You will be denying me.'

'Denying you? You deserted me!'

'Shhh ... You will wake him,' Elena points at Jimmy. Her index finger is unusually long and slim, like a spider's leg. 'I did not desert you. I thought you were ready to fly on your own, but you were not.'

'Don't believe a word she says!' Jimmy interrupts, still facing the other way. He often talks in his sleep, and he can carry out entire conversations with Angie, of which he will have no recollection in the morning.

'Hush, Jimmy. This is my dream. You shouldn't be able to hear her, anyway.' Angie says.

'Of course I shouldn't. I only pay heed to the voice of reason.' Jimmy answers in his sleep.

Angie turns back to Elena, but she's gone, and the first rays of light are seeping through the blinds.

Fully awake, sitting up in bed, Angie remembers the time Elena was referring to, the very night she'd felt that she'd reached the pinnacle of her new existence. It had been the night of the post-concert party at Newtown, when she spoke with Sinéad about living a borrowed life.

She was thirty, young, attractive, excelling in her studies, doing the things she loved to do with a new bunch of wonderful friends. A brand new life, full of opportunities and with none of the traumas and shadows of her childhood, was unfolding ahead of her.

It would've been only a few weeks after that memorable night that she tripped and came tumbling down the hill of her life, bringing her borrowed time to a tragic end. The trouble with reaching the pinnacle of one's existence is that it's all downhill from there.

Angie watches her husband, sleeping serenely under the bedspread that Norah made for them for their fifth wedding anniversary, to match the pastel green of their curtains. Her eyes hop from Jimmy to their colonial-style timber wardrobe, packed with clothes, many of which she bought last year and which are too loud or too tight for her usual taste.

Her eyes rest for a while on the wedding portrait on her dressing table, then on her old musical jewellery box (a memento from her father), and the teddy bear that Jimmy gave her last Valentine's day, when their lives were still blissfully uneventful. These are just some of the things that had been enough to make her happy less than a year ago.

And she cries in silence, asking why, oh why.

# ~ Norah ~

Norah has just finished setting the table for three when the phone rings. She's expecting Angie and Jimmy for dinner. All afternoon, while cleaning the house and preparing the meal, she has been praying. Praying for Angie to get better, for this doctor to be good, for Jimmy to be strong and patient.

Months ago, Dr Hamilton gave Angie a referral to a psychologist, but Angie shook her head and shrugged her shoulders every time Norah asked her if she'd made an appointment. Later Angie confessed that she had lost the referral and couldn't be bothered getting another one.

To Norah's surprise, the next time that Angie had gone to see Dr Hamilton to get a prescription for antidepressants, she had come home with a referral for a different doctor, a psychiatrist that Dr Hamilton didn't even know, whom Sinéad had recommended. Norah wasn't sure how much to trust Sinéad's advice – could a twenty-year-old girl, who had only been part of Angie's life for a few months, know more about what was best for Angie than her own mother, her husband and her family doctor?

Still, Norah had been glad that Angie had finally decided to see someone, anyone; and she is eager to hear a full report on the first session over dinner. But as soon as the phone rings, she has the feeling that she won't be hearing it tonight.

'I'm afraid we won't be coming for dinner,' Jimmy says at the other end.

'Why? What's happened?' Norah asks, concerned even though she's not surprised.

'Nothing bad. It's just that Ange was extremely tired after the session, and as soon as we got home she went straight to bed. She's fast asleep and I don't want to wake her up. I'd come on my own, but frankly, I'm not that hungry. I'm sorry.'

'Why don't you two come tomorrow for lunch? Chicken Marsala is even better the next day,' Norah says, trying to hide her disappointment.

'We'll see how she is in the morning. Good night, Norah,' he says and hangs up.

Norah puts down the receiver and goes to the kitchen to turn off the oven. She takes a can of chicken and vegetable soup out of the cupboard, then leaves it on the counter, not feeling very hungry herself. Clicking her tongue, she decides to make a cup of tea instead, and takes it to the veranda.

The cicadas are singing their usual summer night serenade, and occasionally a car drives past or a dog barks. It's a balmy night on a quiet street, much like any of the quiet evenings Norah had before Angie went haywire last year and Jimmy started to visit on an almost daily basis.

In the past, Jimmy and Angie had come for lunch every second Sunday, and Norah would visit them on the Thursdays in between. The other nights, she ate by herself. Still, she cooked every night, a meal for one. Cooking was her passion, second only to classical music.

When she bought this place, almost twenty years ago, there had been two deciding factors: the sunny study in which she would conduct her piano lessons, and the recently renovated kitchen with ample bench tops and solid timber cupboards. She had sold the house where she had lived with her husband as soon as she recovered from the breakdown. She migrated south, like the birds, to the other side of town. She never looked back, and never broke down again. This took considerable effort, and the careful construction of rules to live by. Not getting involved in another romantic relationship was rule number one. Taking calculated risks, living a quiet, healthy lifestyle, were among the others. She had been doing very well until Angie fell ill last year, and inadvertently brought so many painful memories back to life.

Not everything that happened last year had been bad though. Having Jimmy as a dinner guest so often had brought a welcome change to Norah's daily routine. It had also been a motivation to try new recipes. She became more adventurous, experimenting with the Indian, Vietnamese, and Moroccan dishes from her *World Tour* recipe book.

Now that Angie is housebound, Jimmy doesn't come any more. It is Norah who goes to their place every other day, to help Angie cook and clean, but quite often she finds the meals she has prepared for them untouched in the fridge the next day.

Drinking tea on her porch, watching the clouds gather in the moonless sky, Norah remembers the year gone by, and realises that she will have to clear up some unfinished business, if she wants Angie to get better.

She remembers last Mother's Day. After she told Angie about Jo's suicide, and Angie went home too upset to visit her grandmother, Norah asked Pearl for advice. They agreed that now that the can of worms had been opened, it was best to tell Angie everything.

'Once she gets over the shock, she'll want to know why Jo did what she did,' Pearl said. 'So you better prepare yourself.'

'But … where do I begin?' Norah asked.

'Let Jo explain it. Show Angie her letter. One thing will lead to the next,' Pearl said, and disappeared into her room. Norah heard drawers opening and closing. Pearl came back with an envelope and handed it to Norah. It smelled of potpourri.

When Norah returned home the next day, she drove straight to Angie's place, envelope in hand. From outside she saw that all the lights were off and the curtains were drawn, even though it was only 7.00 pm. She assumed that Angie and Jimmy had gone out.

On Monday she received Jimmy's phone call, saying that Angie wouldn't get out of bed. Norah convinced herself that by trying too hard to stop something terrible from happening, she had actually made it happen.

'Like a self-fulfilling prophecy?' Pearl said, when Norah rang her in tears, after she had taken Angie to see Dr Hamilton for the first time. 'Nonsense, child. It would've happened anyway; it was already happening when you tried to stop it. It has more to do with genetics that it has to do with you saying anything. It must be something that runs in the family. Maybe on your father's side – God bless his soul.'

'Well, I guess the letter will have to wait until Angie gets better,' Norah said, wiping her tears.

And the letter was filed away in her filing cabinet.

But Angie didn't just get better. Like a phoenix, she rose from her ashes a completely new person, almost a stranger. This new Angie was too busy having a good time to worry about her dead aunt. Why, she didn't even have time for her mother and husband, who were alive. And now... she's in the dumps again.

Angie won't be reading that letter any time soon, Norah thinks. In fact, she should never read it. I should have never told her anything, kept my mouth shut, let sleeping dogs lie.

At this thought, Norah puts her mug of cold tea down, goes back inside the house, and walks purposefully towards her filing cabinet. With shaky fingers she flips through the files. The envelope, addressed to Pearl, is where Norah left it last May, under "J" for Jo.

Jo's letter is handwritten in a wobbly script – her beautiful longhand barely recognisable. She had used the same onion skin paper and blue fountain pen she used to write her weekly letters to Norah.

> My dearest Mother,
>
> I am sorrier than you can ever imagine for what I'm putting you through, but I can't go on living, with the shame and the deceit that I've been carrying with me for so long. And now, the loss of the one thing I wanted more than I ever wanted anything in life.
>
> There was never an opera scholarship. I came to Milan to have my baby. Nina, the Italian friend I made during my European trip five years ago, offered me a place to stay while I figured out what to do next.
>
> Two weeks ago I fell down the stairs and by the time Nina got me to hospital my baby was already gone. The worst thing was that I had to go through with the labour, I had to 'give birth' to my dead child. I held it in my arms. It was a girl.
>
> And who was the father? I can hear you ask ... That, I can't tell you, because he is a married man, and I never told him I was pregnant. We had been trying to end our

on-and-off affair for years, almost since we started it. But it was like a long-entrenched addiction, impossible to break. What made matters worse was that I knew his wife and it killed me to hurt her, even though she had no idea of what was going on. They say that what you don't know can't hurt you, but I knew – and it hurt.

I thought this was my opportunity to cut this off once and for all, to start a new life away from him, just me and my child. But it was not meant to be.

I know this is a selfish act, but I have always been a selfish person. I know the pain I feel is no greater than the pain I will cause you, but I cannot bear it any longer. I only ask one thing – not ask, beg - don't tell anyone but Norah the truth about how I ended my life. I won't have to deal with the endless questions, the stigma and the rumours, but you will, and I don't want to put you through that on top of everything else. Tell the family it was a car accident or cancer ... I know you'll think of something.

Please forgive me. The lies, the secrets ... they were necessary.

Jo

Pearl had only told Norah, as Jo had instructed. And Norah told her husband, because trust had been one of the pillars of their marriage and there was no way she would lie to him about something so important.

Norah reads Jo's final words one last time. Then, with clouded eyes, she holds the letter over the gas-stove burner with a pair of metal tongs.

'You lied and deceived us for so long, and then asked us to lie and deceive on your behalf,' Norah says, bitterly. 'You lost your baby daughter, Pearl lost you, I lost my husband, but I'm not about to lose Angie, not on your account.'

# ~ Symphony under the stars ~

Reluctantly, Angie gets up to answer the phone. It's Wednesday or perhaps Thursday, and it's raining outside.

Regardless of the weather, all the weekdays are pretty much the same for Angie: when the alarm goes off at 6.00 am, she stays in bed until Jimmy is ready for work, then makes the effort to walk to the front door and kiss him goodbye. As soon as the door shuts behind him, loneliness attacks her like a deadly virus, and she often runs to the bathroom and retches over the toilet bowl, kneeling on the floor. Exhausted, she goes back to bed, and spends most of her morning staring at the ceiling, tormented by hopelessness and guilt.

She can't concentrate on reading, and she finds TV more depressing than her thoughts. The book that Dr Suenho gave her is gathering dust on her bedside table.

When she's not staring at the walls, she spends hours staring at the mirror, appalled by the vision of the plump, pale Angie, with hollow eyes and unkempt hair.

Months ago, the same mirror reflected a handsome, confident woman, exuding sensuality. She had bright colours on her eyelids, rosy cheeks, red lipstick, dark burgundy curls and dangling earrings. That is how she imagined Elena would look – except that Elena's hair was jet-black, and she had a natural Mediterranean tan which Angie couldn't achieve in a million years.

Her tattoo and the fading burgundy tint are the only testimony that those five months last year weren't a dream. Of course, there's also her very real credit card debt, which Jimmy has managed to reduce from a few thousand to a few hundred dollars. Up until last year, the credit card had been something they only used in emergencies - in other words, hardly ever.

In the afternoons, Angie forces herself to do the laundry or the shopping, but she can't find the strength to vacuum carpets and scrub floors. Norah drops by every other day and helps Angie with the cleaning and the cooking as her own mother had once done for her. Like Pearl, Norah never sheds a tear in front of her daughter.

Sometimes Angie manages to cook a meal unsupervised, but she occasionally hurts her fingers with the chopping knife. It seems that her dexterity has been swallowed up by the same black hole as her intelligence and vitality. Jimmy often comes home late and tired, and he goes straight to bed without eating.

Most days Angie is thankful that it's the university summer break, because she's so brain dead that she can't string two sentences together, much less write an essay.

Today, though, she wakes up thinking that perhaps university would give her some motivation, an excuse to get out, to face the world and other people, as inadequate as she might feel. That's why she decides to answer the phone instead of letting the machine get it.

'It's Sinéad. Remember me?'

'Hi Shine,' Angie says. 'I'm sorry I didn't return your call last night. I meant to, but then Mum came over and she didn't leave until after ten.'

'Never mind, I got you now. Hey, what are you up to this Saturday?'

'I'm supposed to go and see Dr Suenho,' Angie tells Sinéad, laconically. She could go and see Dr Suenho during the week, but Jimmy wants to escort her as he did last week, perhaps to make sure that she's keeping her appointments.

'Say hi for me, will you? What time is your appointment?'

'Noon. Why?'

'I heard about this 'Symphony under the stars' concert this Saturday. Apparently it happens every year in the Domain, and it's free. Have you ever gone?'

'No, and I don't think I'm up to it ...'

'C'mon, you'll enjoy it. There were one hundred thousand people there last year. It'll do you good to get out, have a picnic, listen to some music, and see other human beings apart from Jimmy and your mum.' Sinéad pauses, reconsidering. 'Of course, they can come too, if they want.'

'I can't enjoy anything at the moment, Shine. It'll be a waste of time,' Angie says, unable to think of an excuse, hating herself for letting Sinéad down once again. Her friend has been asking her out at least once a week for the last month or so and the answer has always been 'no'.

'Surely, you can't be miserable all day, every day. There must be something you enjoy.'

'Please, Shine. I'm sure there will be a group from the choir going – why don't you call Anna or Mandy?' Angie's biggest fear is that she will bore Sinéad to death and scare her away for good. Her second biggest fear is that if she agrees to go out, Sinéad will bring other people along – Anna or Mandy from the choir, or the belly dancing girls, and they might want to know why she had dropped out of both groups just before their end of year performances. They might want to have a conversation, and Angie can hardly think of anything to say, after saying hello, even to Sinéad.

'But I don't want to go with them – I want to go with you,' Sinéad insists, reminding Angie of her nephew, the youngest of Peter's kids. I want, I want, I want, and I won't have it any other way. 'So, what are you doing Saturday after your appointment, then?'

'Don't know. Coming home and watching a video or something like that?'

'Not good enough, sister. I'll meet you at 2.00 pm at Museum Station. Bring Jimmy, if he wants to come.'

'But ...' There's no way that Jimmy will go. He dislikes crowds almost as much as he dislikes classical music, which is probably not quite as much as he dislikes Sinéad. 'Only if it's not raining.'

'Deal! You don't have to bring anything, apart from your bum. I'll bring the food, the wine, and a blanket for you to sit your bum on. The whole royal treatment.' Sinéad says, and hangs up before Angie changes her mind.


Sinéad feels as if she's just succeeded in extracting a healthy tooth without anesthesia. Who would have thought it would become so hard to get a 'yes' from Angie? A couple of months ago, the conversation would have been something like this:

'Angie, what are you doing Saturday?'

'Oh, I'm working at the charity shop in the morning, and going out in the afternoon with so and so, but I think I'm free in the evening. Why? What's up?'

'Well, I heard about this Symphony in the Domain and –-'

'Sounds good to me! What time do you want to meet? Should I ring Mandy and Anna from the choir and see if they want to come?'

Sinéad leans on the windowsill of her dorm at the student boarding house, contemplating the rain. Could this Angie be the same one she met at the book club, eight months ago?

*People come into your life for a reason, a season or a lifetime,* says one of those chain letters that make their way around the globe via email. When Sinéad received this message from her sister in Ireland last year, she liked it so much she printed it and stuck it to the pin board above her desk, where it still is. With Angie in her mind, she turns her eyes to the yellowing page on the corkboard.

'When someone is in your life for a REASON,' the fading words of *Author Unknown* tell her, 'It is usually to meet a need you have expressed. They came to assist you through a difficulty, to provide you with guidance and support, to aid you physically, emotionally or spiritually. They may seem like a godsend, and they are! They are here for a reason you need them to be.'

Whenever Sinéad reads this she thinks of Angie, whom she met shortly after receiving the email from her sister. Angie became Sinéad's godsend, her guardian angel – although she was more like an angel in training, a little naive for someone her age, but tremendously eager to learn and to experience everything, finding the simplest things (a picnic at Bondi beach, a ferry ride from Circular Quay, a singing rehearsal) exhilarating. And even though she was married, she seemed to have all the time in the world for Sinéad.

Now Sinéad has a renewed resolve to stay in Australia: she can't leave Angie like this, even though she has a husband to look after her. Sinéad is well aware of Jimmy's dislike for her, but she's not going to let that undermine her determination.

Sinéad remembers a conversation she had with Angie in late August the previous year, when Angie was still at the height of her exuberance.

'Jimmy thinks you're a bad influence,' Angie said, shrugging her shoulders. She was sitting at the table in the common kitchen at Sinéad's boarding house, talking nonstop while Sinéad cooked Irish stew. The last stretch of winter was still lingering; it was cold outside, and at 5.30 pm it was already dark. Angie pointed to Sinéad's ankle. 'It must be the tattoo.'

'It's not the tattoo, but what the tattoo means.' Sinéad said nonchalantly, tasting the stew for salt. Her tattoo, the lower case Greek letter lambda, had been internationally recognised as a symbol for gay and lesbian rights since the 1970s – at least in the part of the world she came from.

'But Jimmy doesn't know what it means. It's just that he can be very conservative, and has some funny ideas about women with tattoos, women who drink too much, you know, stuff like that.'

'No wonder he hates me! Not only do I have a tattoo and I like a drink or two, but I'm a lesbian to boot. A conservative husband's worst nightmare.'

'He doesn't know you are a lesbian. I didn't tell him.'

'Angie, anyone who pays a bit of attention can work out that I'm, um, queer.'

'I didn't,' Angie said, defensively. 'Until I asked you about the tattoo and you explained.' Sinéad had short, spiky hair, but other than that, she was every bit as feminine as any other heterosexual girl Angie knew. When Angie had mentioned this, Sinéad clarified that she was a lesbian, not a tomboy.

'Anyway, I have the feeling that Jimmy sees me as some kind of threat, even if it's subconscious. He strikes me as a lad with intuition. Can you pass me your plate?' Sinéad asked, ready to dish up.

'What, he thinks you'll try and corrupt me? Ha! Don't be ridiculous!' Angie said, pretending to throw her plastic plate at Sinéad, like a Frisbee. Sinéad had dropped her wooden spoon, splattering the linoleum with sauce.

'Shit, Angie, look at this mess,' Sinéad said, frowning but smiling, as she kneeled on the floor to wipe the sauce up with a cloth. 'I know it's ridiculous, but Jimmy might not understand that I'm not in the least attracted to heterosexual women, much less if they're married. No offence, Angie – you know I love you to bits.'

Sinéad set the steaming plates on the table and gestured for Angie to sit down. She filled her mug with the last of the beer she had used for the stew, and poured orange juice into Angie's glass.

'Anyway, maybe Jimmy just doesn't like me, full stop.'

'The funny thing is, even though I know Jimmy would hate it, I always wanted to have one,' Angie said, taking a spoonful of stew. 'Shine, this is delicious!'

'Hang on– you always wanted to have one of what?' Sinéad asked. Angie often jumped from one subject to another and sometimes Sinéad found it difficult to follow.

'A tattoo, silly. I've always wanted one, ever since I was a kid. A ladybird.'

In the few months since that conversation, Angie has changed beyond recognition. Sinéad knows what it's like to be depressed, although not as severely as Angie is. Angie had been there when Sinéad needed her, and now Sinéad wants to reciprocate.

When Angie finally gave in to Norah's plea to seek professional help, Sinéad recommended Dr Suenho without hesitation.

'How do you know of her?' Angie asked.

'I saw her for three months at the uni's counselling service.'

'But ... what did you need to see a psychiatrist for?' Angie asked, baffled, for Sinéad seemed the most balanced person in the world to her. Sinéad explained.

'I'm so sorry, Sinéad!'

'Sorry for what?' Sinéad asked.

'For not even noticing that you were feeling low when we first met. I should've been paying more attention.'

'It doesn't matter, Angie. You still helped me more than you can imagine. And you'll like Dr Suenho. I think – no, I know that she can help you.'

At Dr Suenho's rooms, Angie's voice quivers when she starts to read out loud verses from her old scrapbook, while Dr Suenho makes notes. The poem she has chosen has been dedicated to her father.

> I pierced the fabric of silence
> when I awoke one night, screaming your absence
> finding your name nailed
> to the four corners of my death.

Early in the session Angie confessed to Dr Suenho that she hasn't even attempted to open the book on how to beat the blues. Feeling guilty, she made the effort to find her old poetry scrapbook, which was inside a musty cardboard box in her garage, together with some of her high school reports and short lived teenage diaries.

The scrapbook's pages still give off a faint smell of mildew, even though she's left it out on the balcony for a couple of days. The humid weather hasn't helped; this is the first sunny morning after three days of intermittent rain.

Nature has contrived so that Angie has no excuse to get out of her date with Sinéad this afternoon: it's a gorgeous summer day, perfect for an outdoor concert and a picnic in the park. Although Jimmy has declined the invitation to come, he enthusiastically helped Angie pack a cushion to sit on, sunglasses, sun tan lotion, bottled water and a hat, before they left for her appointment with Dr Suenho.

'I wrote these poems fifteen years ago,' Angie says, handing the scrapbook to Dr Suenho. 'Do you think I was depressed then, and didn't know it?'

While Dr Suenho flips through the pages of the book, scanning Angie's poems, Angie remains silent, suddenly swamped by doubts similar to those she felt a week ago, sitting on this chair in this very room.

What am I doing here? Can Dr Suenho help me? It's been a week since she doubled the dose of the antidepressants, and nothing's changed. I caught Jimmy staring at me as I swallowed the pills this morning, and I could read in his eyes his scepticism, his distrust of drugs and anything or anybody associated with them. After all, I got depressed this second time while still taking antidepressants.

Angie opens her mouth to voice these qualms to Dr Suenho, but the ideas seem unable to find their way out, as if the neurons that convert thoughts into words have been completely short-circuited.

The sky is perfectly clear outside; sunlight pours through the window warming Angie's body, but – as Krishnamurti would say – her mind remains clouded and her heart cold.

Silence stretches for what seems to be an awfully long time, but according to the wall clock above the door only five minutes pass. Presently, Dr Suenho shuts the scrapbook, creating a puff of stale dust, and takes off her glasses.

'I would like to propose a scenario to you, Angie. A theory that might give us something to work on,' she says, clearing her throat.

'When you were seven years old you lost your aunt, whom you were very close to. You saw your mother severely depressed, for months on end. And as if this weren't enough, your father, whom you adored, left without an explanation. It is my belief that you were affected by these traumatic events more than you or anybody around you realised at the time. You became mildly depressed at that point and never fully recovered. Because it was not a crippling depression, it remained undetected, and in time become so deeply entrenched that you came to see it as your "normal" disposition. Do you follow?'

Angie nods, mesmerised. If this is true, Sinéad had been right, that night at the party. Angie has been living a borrowed life, a lesser life than the one she was meant to have, for over two decades. She had only started living her real life last year. And what a life it had been.

'Yes!' Angie agrees, adamantly. If Dr Suenho had been seated closer, she would have seen a fleeting spark in Angie's eyes.

'Last year, the antidepressants cleared the depression you've been suffering all this time,' Dr Suenho continues.

'Yes!' Angie repeats – it all makes sense now.

'... But instead of returning you to what once had been your 'normal' state, they thrust you straight into a hypomanic episode. This *Elena* you told me about is no other than your manic alter-ego.'

'No,' Angie murmurs. The theory, which began so well, is now falling apart at the seams. 'No.'

Dr Suenho interprets Angie's puzzled look as a sign of incomprehension. She produces a marker from her desk drawer, and walks towards the whiteboard on the wall behind her. She's wearing a grey pleated skirt reaching almost down to her ankles, and a white linen shirt, buttoned up all the way to the neck. Her hair is in the same style it was the first time Angie saw her, gathered in a bun above the crown of her head. She reminds Angie of the nuns at her Catholic high school, except for her hands. Her nails are long, manicured and polished a deep maroon, and several of her fingers are adorned with rings, among them a wedding band.

'I can see, reading your poetry, that you are very good with metaphors,' Dr Suenho says, as she draws a box and divides it into four horizontal sections. She labels each section: B2, B1, G, L1, like a building. If Angie wasn't totally bewildered before, she is now.

'Here's a metaphor for you: imagine this is a two-storey building with two basement levels. The ground floor is your optimal level. The lift – which represents your moods – has been stuck at B1 for many years. After dropping to B2 last year, it suddenly shot straight to the first floor without stopping at street level, thanks to the antidepressants.' She draws arrows going up and down the building. 'Fortunately,

it stopped there, before it reached the rooftop. Without rail-
ings, the rooftop is not a safe place; many people fall when
they stand too close to the edge. Some people even jump,
convinced that they can fly.'

'No,' Angie says, louder this time. The word comes out
like a frog's croak. 'I agree with the first half of the theory,
but not the other half. What I found last year was my normal
state of mind, the one I've been missing all these years. You
know, the ground floor.'

Angie wants to explain to Dr Suenho that she has read
the list of signs and symptoms of mania, and although she
has experienced most of them (heightened senses, decreased
need for sleep, increased energy, euphoric feelings) she still
can't accept them as symptoms of an illness. These changes
were her way of expressing the happiness she felt at having
found her true, long-lost self. She slept less and had more
energy because she wanted to make up for all the years
she had missed. Her senses were not "heightened"; they
were simply unclouded, after having been marred by a mild
depression for over twenty years. Twenty years lost! What
a tragedy, Angie thinks.

Everything makes perfect sense in Angie's mind, but it's
useless to try structuring an argument: the words dance in
front of her eyes, disconnected and in the wrong order. The
words and the language that she loves so much have turned
against her.

Suddenly the wall clock stops ticking, and a dense fog
fills the room. In fact, it's no longer a room, but an endless
dry plain. Angie stands alone in the middle of this wasteland.
Looking down, she can't even see her own feet.

Elena, Angie calls, and she can hear her own quivering
voice, even though no sound comes out of her mouth. Help

me! Tell Dr Suenho what you told me the other night; tell her about the epiphanies, the exultant singing, the gliding through the night, the radiance of the lights, the bursting with excitement. Show her, get inside her head and show her, like you showed me.

But Elena is not there, and the only thing that reaches Angie through the thick mist in her mind is the echo of her unstructured thoughts. Left to her own devices, Angie tries to string the elusive words together. She opens her eyes, to find Dr Suenho looking at her expectantly from across the room, waiting.

'You said ... you said last week that mania is a state of euphoria. But I looked the word euphoria up in my etylo – etomo ...' Angie stops to untangle her tongue. 'Etymologic dictionary, and it derives from the Greek euphoros, which literally means 'being healthy', or 'bearing well'. How can this be the sign of an illness? Couldn't it be an expression of happiness instead?'

'I see that you like dissecting words, Angie. But if you had referred to a dictionary of psychology, you would have found that euphoria is defined as an exaggerated feeling of wellbeing, an unnatural state of elation.'

Angie listens with pursed lips. She had known she couldn't win the argument, but at least she had tried.

'I have another word for you to look up in your etymological dictionary,' Dr Suenho says, smiling while she scribbles on a yellow post-it-note. 'Euthymia.'

She hands the sticky note to Angie, who looks at her blankly.

'I believe that's the word, and the state of mind we're looking for. And the only way we can find it is by monitoring your medication very closely, making sure the dosage is just strong enough to get you out of the hole you are in and safely onto the ground floor.

When Angie walks out of the cottage she finds Jimmy fast asleep under the shade of a jacaranda, sitting on a carpet of purple petals with his legs crossed, leaning back against the tree's trunk. He's looking so placid in his sleep, and breathing ever so softly, that he makes Angie think of the image of Buddha meditating.

On their first date, as they walked through the Botanical Gardens on their way to Circular Quay, Jimmy had pointed towards a fig tree labelled Ficus Religiosa, and explained that it was under a similar tree that Gautama Siddartha had attained nirvana some two and a half thousand years ago. In 1922, Jiddu Krishnamurti, determined to follow in Buddha's steps, found enlightenment under a pepper tree in Ojai, California. Jimmy's aspiration was to achieve the same one day, perhaps under a eucalyptus in the backyard of the house he would one day own.

Angie kneels on the grass next to her husband, wondering what happened to the young mystic she met over ten years ago. Back then she often didn't understand half of the things he used to go on about, but he sounded so together, so profound and mature for his age.

Angie and Jimmy had known each other for several months before they started dating. Angie was working at the counter in a Quick-Pic photo lab in the city, which had agencies all over the CBD, at newsagents and chemists. Jimmy was still doing his offset printing certificate at nights, paying his way by working as a pushbike courier, picking up film and delivering photos to all the agencies. Back then, he was a lot trimmer, with a head full of golden brown hair, and sported a "mullet" style haircut.

Watching him through the glass shopfront, Angie thought he looked rather fetching in his black tracksuit, helmet and sunglasses, fearlessly negotiating the city traffic. He was intrepid for someone who was afraid of dying in a car accident, but of course, he didn't tell Angie of his fear of driving until later, when he pointed out that riding a pushbike and driving a car were two very different things.

It was only after Jimmy quit his courier job and started his printing apprenticeship at the newspaper that he asked Angie out. She fell in love with him on their first date – she had always thought him attractive, but never before realised how insightful he was.

It had not been a free-falling in love, with sparks of passion burning her heart; it had been more like feeling a gentle breeze in her chest, a sense of peacefulness and ease she had not experienced in any of the few short-lived relationships she'd had before. She was twenty years old, Jimmy was twenty-three.

Within a year they were married and had bought an apartment in the southern suburbs, close to Norah. They couldn't yet afford the house with the eucalyptus tree in the backyard, but that was next on their wish list, followed by two kids, a car and a pup.

One day, a couple of years into their marriage, Jimmy packed up all his books and videotapes on the teachings of Krishnamurti, and took them to the library without explanation.

'I'm not surprised,' Jimmy's mother, Gwyneth, said when Angie told her. 'A few years ago, he did the same with his bibles – he had several versions of the Word – and all the teachings of Christ. He donated them to my church.'

Ever since, Jimmy has focused on his work, taking on as much overtime as possible, so they can pay off their mortgage sooner and move on to the next item on their list faster. He no longer wants to attain enlightenment, but financial freedom, having added "investment property" to their list. He even gave away his pushbike, to Tiger.

'What happened to you, Jimmy?' Angie asks aloud, under the jacaranda tree. 'What happened to us?'

'Shit happens, and then you die,' Jimmy murmurs, philosophically, without waking up.

Angie can't help but to smile at this, shaking her head.

౼

That evening, walking alongside Sinéad after the Symphony under the stars, Angie realises that apart from Tchaikovsky's 1812 overture, she has no recollection of any of the other works that were played.

One thing she is sure of: if this had taken place a few months ago, when Elena was still in her body, the experience would have been very different. Listening to the music with her eyes closed, she had pictured herself crying with emotion, waving a sparkler in the air with one hand, the other arm around her dear friend's shoulder, both of them singing along with the orchestra at the top of their lungs. She remembered, but could not experience, the feeling she had felt in several occasions last year, of being in complete communion with the night, with the world, with each and every one of the strangers around her.

Tonight, unable to feel anything, Angie sat on her cushion until her joints became stiff, doing her best to smile every time she caught Sinéad throwing a concerned look in her direction. She ate a little salad, nibbled on the nuts, and drank a glass of the wine that Sinéad had brought. She didn't touch the chicken, the fruit, the cheese or the crackers. Sinéad had produced a banquet out of her backpack, and she had to pack most of it away again at the end of the night.

'Earth to Angie,' Angie hears Sinéad call. They've been walking for two blocks in silence, and they are about to reach Angie's train station, Museum. Sinéad seems too small for the heavy backpack she carries, with enough food in it for two days. Angie is hugging her cushion against her chest, as if bracing for a plane crash. 'Hey Angie, it wasn't so bad, was it?'

'No, it was good to get out,' Angie says, not very convincingly. She adds, hesitating, 'I just … didn't want you to see me like this.'

'What? Do you think I am just a fair-weather friend, who only wants to see you when you're buoyant?' Sinéad asks, feigning outrage. 'Anyway, you look fine to me. You just need a bit of sun, you're way too pale, and you need to eat more. You've lost a lot of weight.'

'Yeah, but I still could do with a couple less kilos,' Angie says, sighing.

'Watch out. You don't want to develop an eating disorder right now,' Sinéad says, turning serious.

'My God, Shine. Do you think – ' Angie covers her mouth with her hand.

'No, not really. Just wanted to shake you up a bit. But you need to look after yourself, you hear me?'

At the entrance to the station, Sinéad stands with arms akimbo. 'Remember: you can't get rid of me that easily, sister,' she says, planting a kiss on Angie's cheek, and then she leaves to catch the bus.

Angie follows the crowd of excited concert leavers down onto the platform, wondering if she will ever be able to tell Sinéad how grateful she is for her caring, unconditional friendship ... and even for her stubbornness.

Seconds before her train is due to arrive, Angie sees a familiar face amidst the crowd on the opposite platform. It's Tiger, sitting on a bench, wearing an Indian-style shirt, khaki shorts and sandals, chatting with another guy. Angie should've known he'd be around – such a huge Tchaikovsky fan. Still, what are the odds that they would run into each other amongst tens of thousands of people? As if he knows he's being watched, Tiger turns around and meets Angie's gaze. He jumps to his feet, calling her name across the tracks, but just then Angie's train pulls in, blocking him from view.

Angie jumps on the train with her heart racing, and takes a seat all the way at the back of the carriage. The unexpected sighting reminds her not only of the sobbing and hiccupping scene at the Spanish Tavern last year, one of the most embarrassing experiences of her life, but of something that mortifies her even more – the way her sex drive had jumped through the roof during her euphoric period, and how she had exorcised it by writing sexually charged stories about Elena and Dave.

Elena, the woman Angie had suddenly become – attractive and bewitching, a sexy goddess, and Dave, a poorly disguised version of Tiger.

The very Tiger who has just turned back, shrugging his shoulders, explaining to his friend that he'd thought he'd just seen a girl he knew, but must've been mistaken.

On the train, Angie remembers the morning after Elena appeared in the cheval mirror. She had looked at her image in the same mirror, fully awake, and found that she was glowing. She went out to the shops and caught her reflection in the shop windows, and it was still there, the glow.

As the weeks went by, she began to notice something else: men were looking at her in the street. That hadn't happened before, even when she was younger, single and slimmer. It had always seemed to her that most people walked the streets immersed in their own thoughts, with their gaze fixed on some remote point in space, doing everything possible to avoid eye contact.

'I don't know what you're talking about,' Sinéad had said, dismissively, when Angie pointed this out. 'Men always make eye contact when you do. And women, too.'

But there was a palpable change in the air. Sometimes Angie would be standing in a queue, or waiting for the traffic lights to change, and strangers, usually men, would start talking to her for no reason; about the weather, or the traffic, or a book she was carrying. And she was answering, and striking up conversations with them. Sometimes she would walk with these strangers for one or two blocks, talking about trivial things, finding out what they did for a living, telling them about her studies. Once, a man she had been chatting with on the train gave her his phone number on a piece of paper as he left.

Her shyness had dissipated, and she had found an uncensored, confident voice that connected her with people, even those she'd never met before.

She began flirting, with the strangers, with guys in her university classes, many of whom were much younger than she was, and with her tutors, who were a lot older. It was an exhilarating feeling, especially to see that they were all quite happy to go along with the game, regardless of the fact that she wore a wedding ring. It was a game she had never played before, shy as she had always been, and it was fun.

But you can only flirt so much – after a while, Angie found herself wondering what it would be like to proceed to the next stage of the game. The thought excited her, but she was also aware that she was inexperienced, and scared. On the nights when she couldn't sleep, she started writing down lists of possible lovers, only to rip them up at dawn. She considered calling the stranger she had met on the train, but after a few days ripped up the piece of paper with his phone number on it as well.

In the end, realising it was one thing for her to daydream about having an affair and another to actually do it, she decided to save all her fantasies and energy for Jimmy. She spent her sleepless hours thinking of ways to enhance their sex life, which had become much like the national average: a once-a-week non-event with the lights off.

Jimmy, however, was less than receptive to the changes she wanted to bring into the bedroom. When she suggested they make love with the lights on, he said he was too embarrassed by how much weight he'd gained and wouldn't feel comfortable. Angie's new sexy – and very expensive – lingerie passed unnoticed in the dark. When she tapped Jimmy on the shoulder, with 'that look' in her eyes for the third night in a row, he complained that he was too tired and had a headache.

Angie was bewildered. Jimmy was giving her, one after another, all the excuses that husbands always complain their wives give them when they don't want to have sex.

Unable to subdue her excess energy, Angie found herself feeling restless in the mornings, and took up swimming, to no avail. While counting laps at the local pool, she told herself that if her husband didn't find her attractive, plenty of other men did.

But she couldn't make the next move with any of the other men on her list, which included her history tutor, two guys from her class, the owner of the Italian coffee shop, the coordinator of the book club, and even her gay hairdresser. Though armed with Elena's charm, and still radiating the glow, something inside her head was stronger than her physical urges.

Finally, she started writing the stories – on the restless nights that Jimmy rejected her.

> Feeling awkward, Dave shifted in his seat and just then Elena leaned towards him, as if she wanted to say something but decided not to. Their faces were almost touching, and he couldn't resist the impulse of kissing her on the mouth. Surprisingly, she returned the kiss eagerly at first, but then pulled away.
>
> Next thing she stormed out of the theatre, as if she'd seen the devil incarnate. Dave followed, but she was nowhere to be found. He glimpsed a taxi turning the corner.
>
> He went home but couldn't sleep – as soon as he closed his eyes he was back in the movie theatre, which was now empty except for the two of them.
>
> He was kissing Elena's mouth, her neck, her shoulders, her bosom, and she was responding eagerly and passionately, whispering sexy Spanish words in his ears as she unbuttoned her black velvet dress. She was wearing a black lace push-up bra that made Dave's blood boil.

By making Elena and Dave do in print the things she wanted to do with Jimmy in reality, Angie somehow appeased her burning desire. Dave and Elena made love first in Dave's mind, but later, after months of being besieged by Dave and ignored by Mario, Elena caved in. They did the deed in the theatre, on his bed, in his shower, on the bonnet of his car in the countryside, but invariably, when the two fictional characters reached a climax, Angie felt a guilt-laden anticlimax, as if she had indeed been unfaithful to Jimmy.

Overwhelmed by this feeling, she would erase all the erotic parts of the story, only to write a different version the next time. The untitled, unfinished story replaced her lists of potential lovers, and became Angie's own version of Penelope's shroud, a tapestry of desire and shame woven during the night and unwoven as the day approached.

Of all the things Angie misses from her euphoric time last year, this guilty unease is not one of them. Seeing Tiger in the flesh had been like seeing Dave come to life. The character she had created had suddenly crossed over into the real world, if only for a few seconds, to remind her of the one aspect she hadn't known how to deal with when she 'found her true self' last year.

'I must remember to erase that file,' Angie thinks, still red in the face with embarrassment, as she sinks further into her seat on the train.

# ~ Euthymia ~

## January 30th, 1999

Dr Suenho has recommended I start a diary, where I can record my moods and whatever else comes to mind. Nothing much comes to mind, and my moods are as flat and lousy as they were a week ago. So there you go.

Today Dr Suenho increased my daily dose of antidepressants to 150 mg. That's three times the amount I was taking last year.

## February 6th, 1999

I'm now on 200 mg of antidepressants a day. Jimmy's not happy. And he was even unhappier after I told him about Dr Suenho's theory, i.e. that for the last twenty-three years I've been probably suffering from a mild depression. Bullshit, he said. That's more than twice the length of our marriage. Is this doctor trying to say that the woman he fell in love with and married wasn't 'normal', that he doesn't even know the normal Angie? I guess the answer is yes, if Dr Suenho is right.

## February 10th, 1999

According to Dr Suenho, there's a middle ground that lies between euphoria and despair. She calls that state *euthymia*. I remember the word, because its pronunciation is almost identical to Euphemia, the name of a Brazilian girl who used to work at the Quick-Pic shop with me. Apparently Brazilians love ancient Greek names – Euphemia means 'Well spoken of'.

As instructed by Dr Suenho, I've looked up the meaning of euthymia in Reber's Dictionary of Psychology. It means 'Tranquility, a pleasant relaxed state' – deriving from the Greek roots *eu* = well and *thymia* = spirit.

## February 15th, 1999

Dr Suenho says the journal writing can be very therapeutic, so I'm trying to keep it up, even though I have no inspiration to write whatsoever. I miss my muse, Elena, even if the stories she inspired were rather embarrassing.

Some good news: Sinéad has been working as an office temp since the beginning of the year and she encouraged me to register with her personnel agency. I have a six month assignment at an advertising agency, starting next week. It's only two days a week, typing, but that's probably as much as I can handle at the moment. Jimmy and Mum are very pleased.

## March 1st, 1999

First day of classes at uni. I'm only taking three subjects this semester. Although I'm starting to feel better, I'm still afraid of going brain-dead again in the middle of the term, and prefer not to risk taking a full-time load. If there's one thing I've learnt in the last year, is to be cautious.

I told Jimmy I sometimes feel I'm walking two steps forward and one backwards towards completing my degree. He quoted Confucius: 'It does not matter how slowly you go so long as you do not stop'.

**March 2nd, 1999**

Elena appeared in my dreams last night. We were on a stage in an empty hall. She was teaching me how to dance flamenco – we were both dressed in frill-skirted, bright-coloured Spanish dresses. Then a crowd walked in and sat down to watch us. I stopped in my tracks, as if paralysed. Telling Elena that I was too afraid to make a fool of myself, I practically ran backstage as soon as I could move my legs. She followed me. 'Do not be afraid, Angelica,' she said. 'Remember the old Spanish proverb: "A life lived in fear is a life half-lived."'

When I woke up I remembered that I knew that proverb from somewhere: Baz Luhrmann's film *Strictly Ballroom*. There's a second generation Spanish girl in it, played by Tara Morice. When the story starts she's the geek who never has anyone to dance with, with pimples on her face and thick glasses. By the end of the movie she's blossomed into a beautiful, confident woman who defies her fears of rejection and failure.

I loved that movie.

**March 15th, 1999**

As I settle into my new routine – working on Thursdays and Fridays and attending university on Monday during the day and Tuesday afternoons, I begin to feel cautiously optimistic. Could this be the much coveted euthymia?

Dr Suenho is pleased, but she still wants to see me once a fortnight.

∼

After work, over a cup of coffee, Angie apologises to Sinéad for her recent behaviour.

They are sitting at an outdoor table at Rossini's in Circular Quay, overlooking the ferry terminal.

'What are you talking about?' Sinéad asks. 'You have nothing to apologise for.'

'Of course I have. For not returning your calls, for saying "no" to everything you proposed, for pushing you away. What sort of friend am I?'

'You are a friend who goes through ups and downs like the rest of us. The difference is that some of us are better at acting.' Sinéad says, grinning.

'Tell me about it!' Angie says, throwing Sinéad a meaningful look. Throughout the summer, Angie virtually walked around with a sign bearing the word DEPRESSED hanging from her shoulders. Sinéad, on the other hand, was going through a depression at the time they met but nothing in her attitude or demeanour had betrayed her loneliness, her feelings of failure and displacement.

Angie hasn't told Sinéad about Dr Suenho's suspicion that she might have been suffering from a bout of hypomania when they met, although she feels that if there's someone she could tell it would be Sinéad. She wouldn't freak out as Jimmy and Norah no doubt would. Then again, Sinéad doesn't have to live with her.

'Look at that!' Sinéad says, interrupting Angie's musing. She's pointing at the horizon – the sun is setting behind The Rocks, and the pastel blues, oranges and pinks of the clouds are reflected in the liquid mirror of the sea. It's breathtaking, and passers-by have stopped to admire the view, many of them tourists who promptly take their cameras out of their cases in an attempt to catch the magnificence of the sunset.

'I wish I had my camera,' Sinéad says.

They both stare at the landscape in awe, jaws dropped, for a few more minutes.

'I wanted to ask you to promise me something, Sinéad,' Angie says, after the colours fade, giving way to the night sky.

'Fire away,' Sinéad says, turning to face her.

'If what happened to me last summer happens again, I suspect my instinct will be to shut everybody out, and retreat to my cave, just like I did this time around. Promise me you won't give up on me. Don't let me shut you out of my life.'

'I told you, sister. You won't be able to get rid of me that easily. But if you want me to promise, I promise.'

Angie lashes out and orders two glasses of expensive sparkling wine to seal their pact. She's earning some money now, and can afford small luxuries.

With such a loyal friend, such good wine, such a picture perfect view of the harbour, with the sea reflecting the autumn sunset, how can one help but fall into a false sense of security? For a moment, Angie almost believes that the crippling depression of the summer was nothing but a bad dream.

'To euthymia,' Angie says, raising her glass.

'Who?' Sinéad asks, lifting both her glass and her brown eyebrows.

'I'll explain on the way to the train,' Angie says. 'I need to

get going soon. Jimmy worries when I'm late - he's gotten
used to me being housebound.'

≈

Angie has changed her fortnightly appointments with Dr
Suenho from Saturdays to Wednesdays - her day off - since
Jimmy no longer feels the need to escort her. The following
Wednesday she finds herself thinking about the sunset
episode with more disappointment than wonder, while
sitting in Dr Suenho's waiting room. If this is euthymia, she
thinks, it's a hell of a lot better than depression, but there's
still something missing.

'You know, as stunning as that sunset was,' Angie tells
Dr Suenho when her turn to sit in the patient's chair comes,
'my senses were somewhat muffled. When I thought about it
afterwards, I caught myself longing for the wonderful feeling
that I would've had in the same situation last year, of being
a living part of the sunset instead of just a witness. I miss
that sense of unity and connection, which I can't feel right
now. Not even towards Sinéad, my best friend, or Jimmy.'

'Many bipolar patients quit their medication because
they believe that it muffles their senses,' Dr Suenho explains,
elaborating that these sensorial experiences that Angie is
describing are a product of the heightening of the senses that
hypomania can yield. Bipolar patients are willing to endure
the depressions if that means that they can enjoy the highs.
'Unfortunately, twenty-five to fifty percent of untreated
bipolar patients attempt suicide during their depressions,
and eighteen percent succeed. Tell me - do you think it's
worth the risk?'

Speechless, Angie stares at Dr Suenho with wide eyes.

There's a knot in her stomach, but somehow she knows it's not the stifling lump of depression. She's demoralised, a little shocked by Dr Suenho's bluntness, but not depressed. She takes a deep breath, and another, and feels the knot loosening. Two months ago, she would have been in tears, or hiccupping, or both.

'Angie,' Dr Suenho says, adopting a gentler tone. 'You need to understand that what you are longing for is not a natural state of mind. Dull as it might be, reality is a safer place.'

'So, I have to be thankful for not being depressed, full stop,' Angie says, but her tone is not thankful.

'I will answer that with the title of a book I have right there on my shelf: *I never promised you a rose garden.*' Dr Suenho points towards the book in question, a slim volume by Hanna Green. As far as Angie can see, it's the only fiction book on the doctor's bookshelf.

Angie hasn't read the book, but she remembers seeing the movie, many years ago. It had been the late seventies, when Angie was eleven or twelve. In the movie, Debbie, a troubled teenager, escapes reality by running away to a fantasy kingdom of her own creation. At the beginning this is a safe place, but it later turns ugly, uglier than reality. Her journey of recovery starts when she is diagnosed with schizophrenia.

'Don't sound so disheartened, Angie,' Dr Suenho says, refilling Angie's glass from the jug she keeps on her desk. 'Look at the enormous progress you've made. You've found a job, you are back at university and doing well in your studies. And there's still plenty of work to be done. Perhaps you feel there's something missing because you are now back to what previously was your 'normal' state of mind, which, don't forget, wasn't optimal. Unfortunately, in my profession there are no tests that measure optimum mood levels. I can't take a blood sample and say – "Yes! Angie, you are one-hundred-per-cent now".'

There, Angie thinks but doesn't say, lies the source of Jimmy's hostility towards Dr Suenho and all people in her profession.

Jimmy needs proof and facts for everything in life and Dr Suenho can't offer him what he needs. Once upon a time Jimmy believed in God, but he ended up giving up his faith, much to his mother's disappointment, because there was not sufficient proof. His mother tried to explain, to no avail, that the very essence of having faith is believing in something you can't prove.

Angie realises that this is probably why Jimmy gave up on Krishnamurti's teachings too, because hard as he tried, he couldn't achieve the spiritual conviction that was required to find enlightenment.

And now, Jimmy has been asked for a double leap of faith. He's been asked to believe that his wife is suffering from a real illness, even though it's invisible and immeasurable; and furthermore, he needs to believe that a shrink, who in his mind is no more credible than a witch doctor, can cure his wife of this intangible malady.

'Did you hear me, Angie?' Dr Suenho says, looking at Angie with raised eyebrows.

'Sorry. I was thinking ... never mind. What were you saying?'

'I think we'll leave your medication at the current dose until our next appointment, and then we'll start to decrease it – with the aim of stopping it altogether, by the end of next month.'

'That would certainly make Jimmy happy,' Angie mutters.

'And you, Angie? Wouldn't it make you happier, to be drug free?

'Ask me in a month's time, Dr Suenho. Right now, I'm a bit scared of falling down again. You know, without my crutches.'

Dr Suenho nods, and writes this down in Angie's file.

*Patient compares medication to crutches – still lacking the confidence to stand on her own two feet.*

When it's time to make their next appointment, Dr Suenho informs Angie that she'll be going away for Easter and won't be back until the end of April.

'That means I won't see you for a month. But if there's an emergency, you can call me on my mobile,' Dr Suenho says. 'But I really don't think you'll need it. You're doing remarkably well.'

Lost in thought, Angie is about to open the front door when she remembers she needs to head the other way – she was running late this morning and had decided to drive instead of catching the train as she has always done. The car is in the parking lot at the rear of the cottage.

As she exits via the back door, Angie notices for the first time in the three months that she's been coming to Dr Suenho's cottage, that there's a colourful garden surrounding the back veranda. There are white gardenias, pink azaleas, purple forget-me-nots, and standing tall among the others, a bush laden with beautiful red roses.

∽

Angie and Jimmy take two of Jimmy's nephews to the Easter Show – something they've done for the last two years, while Peter stays at home minding his youngest child.

Jimmy, who doesn't usually like crowds, has a ball spoiling the children. He gets on the rides with them, buys them the most expensive show bags, stuffs them with corn on a stick, hamburgers, chocolate, ice-cream and everything else they ask for. He buys a disposable camera and lets them take pictures of whatever they like –their feet, other people's feet, the muddy ground, and the occasional pig or goat. The four of them stand in the rain to watch the parade, only for the kids to complain afterwards that it was boring.

Jimmy comes alive in a way Angie hasn't seen in a long time. Standing in the rain, watching the parade, he looks like a big sturdy tree with one little monkey dangling from each of its branches. He would make such a good father, Angie thinks. She, on the other hand, gets impatient rather quickly with the kids' demands, and resents their propensity to run off without warning. Twice, to Angie's distress, they nearly lose the children in the crowd, but Jimmy doesn't even scold them.

When they return home, exhausted after handing the children back to their father, Angie jokingly tells Jimmy that when they have their own children, he'll probably spoil them rotten.

'It's different when it comes to other people's children, Ange,' Jimmy says. He takes off his boots and swears under his breath when he discovers there's a hole in the sole of his right boot – that explains why his sock, and his foot, are wet. 'You borrow them, you indulge them, and then you give them back to their parents, who can't afford to spoil them – certainly not Pete.'

Surprised at the antagonism in Jimmy's voice, Angie doesn't reply. She leaves the room and returns with a towel, handing it to Jimmy.

'Anyway, I'd rather not talk about having our own kids,'

Jimmy goes on, drying his feet with the towel. Angie is standing at the doorway, staring at him, but he doesn't lift his
gaze from his feet. 'Until we are sure that your condition is
under control. Have you forgotten about your high chances
of suffering from post natal depression?'

This is the first time that the subject of kids has surfaced
in association with Angie's 'condition'. In fact, it's probably
the first time that Jimmy has actually acknowledged that
Angie has a condition; that it's not 'all in her head', as he
had maintained before.

'No, I certainly haven't, and if I was to forget, I have you
to remind me,' Angie hisses, holding back tears. She storms
out of the room, but Jimmy doesn't follow her. Instead, he
heads towards the bathroom and turns on the shower.

In the kitchen, as she slides a small tray of meat under the
grill, Angie wonders just how the hell they will know when
her condition is 'under control'. Her moods are pretty stable
at the moment, but not even Dr Suenho can guarantee that
they won't go down again in the future. Or up, for that matter.

She drains the potatoes that have just finished boiling,
and picks one up, feeling it burning the tips of her fingers.
She holds it in front of her eyes, as if looking at a crystal ball.
As pain flows from the nerves in her fingers to her brain,
Angie wonders not when, but whether she and Jimmy will
ever have children. He's absolutely right – it's not easy to
think about raising kids when the mother has a condition
that could recur at any minute and render her useless.

In her improvised crystal ball she sees not the future, but
the past: her mother, locked up in her room for months on
end, becoming one with the shadows, and looking through
her seven-year-old daughter as if she were transparent. She
sees the sadness in her father's eyes when he comes to say

goodbye, unable to cope with Norah's condition. She sees the tear marks on Grandma Pearl's cheeks, as she promises the little Angie that everything will be all right.

The pain in her fingers becomes unbearable, and Angie drops the potato. She watches it bounce off the side of the sink and hit the tiled floor. She picks it up, throws it into the steaming bowl with the others, and then furiously mashes them to a pulp, tears streaming down her face. Jimmy likes his potatoes well mashed.

By late April, 1999, Angie's life has gradually fallen into a new routine. Her part-time job at the advertising agency is not very stimulating, but she earns a better hourly rate than she used to when she was managing the Quick-Pic shop. Typing for eight straight hours – with a half-hour lunch break – is something she can endure two days a week, for this sort of pay.

Nobody at the agency knows her well enough to suspect that she has recently suffered from severe clinical depression, and she feels as if she's now living not a borrowed life, but a double life. She's a normal person when she's at work and at university, and reverts to being a convalescent mental patient when she's at home or in Dr Suenho's consulting room. Now that Jimmy has acknowledged that she has a 'condition', he seems to see a trace of it in everything Angie says, does or doesn't do. Even Norah seems to live permanently on guard, watching out for signs.

Eager to allay their fears, Angie tries to be a good wife and daughter, arriving home early most nights, and borrowing Norah's recipe books to expand her cooking repertoire. But much as she tries, her meals are never as good as Norah's – she notices the gusto with which Jimmy eats when they go to Norah's for Sunday dinner, always asking for seconds, whereas he often struggles to finish one serving of Angie's culinary experiments.

Still, Angie can see that Jimmy is pleased that she's working and making a considerable effort, and as long as they stay clear of sticky subjects such as having children, things begin to settle down at home as well.

Her studies are going smoothly, although Angie often needs to read her prescribed readings out loud and more than once, in order to absorb them. Her concentration is still not – to use Dr Suenho's term – 'optimal'. On Mondays between classes, Angie meets Sinéad for lunch. Sometimes they also catch up on Fridays after work, for a quick cuppa or a drink at the Quay. Angie has even rejoined the gospel choir, but despite Sinéad's pleas, she hasn't taken up belly dancing again.

'Why not?' Sinéad asks, with pursed lips. They're having noodles at the cheap noodle bar they go to every Monday, in Glebe. They usually sit outside, watching a parade of fit, trendy people passing by, carrying the brown bag lunches they've just purchased at the organic or vegetarian food shops.

'I suck at it, that's why,' Angie says.

'Well it's a bleedin' shame. Your figure eights weren't too bad and your ladybird looked hilarious when you shimmied.'

Angie laughs heartily and is about to reply when someone taps her on the shoulder. She nearly chokes when she turns around to find Tiger.

'Angie? It is you!' he says, smiling from ear to ear. 'I heard you talking as I was passing by and thought, "Gee, that girl sounds like Angie" but I wasn't sure until you laughed. You look so different!'

Angie has lost nearly a stone thanks to the lack of appetite that accompanied her depression. A few days ago, she visited the hairdresser and asked him to chop off the last traces of the infamous burgundy tint that Jimmy disliked so much. She's never had her hair this short, and the cut has enhanced her natural curls.

Angie forgets to introduce Tiger to Sinéad. She clumsily stands up, nearly knocking over her bowl.

'Long time no see!' Tiger says, kissing her on the cheek. He's looking tanned and fit, and very smart in a dark green suit. 'How've you been? How's Jimmy?'

'Fine, Tiger, we're doing fine!' Angie mumbles, unable to take her eyes off him. It is as if she were seeing a ghost. 'You... you're looking well!'

'Ditto,' Tiger says, and then looks at his watch. 'Look, I'm running late for an appointment, but why don't we catch up sometime? I rang the photo shop months ago and they told me you left. What's your new work number?'

'You rang me?'

'Yeah, I'd promised to ring you with my sh-- ' He stops in mid-sentence, noticing Sinéad and smiling politely at her. He lowers his voice. 'With my doctor's details. Remember? You know me – I'm not the best at doing things right away, but I eventually deliver.'

Angie scribbles the advertising agency's number on a napkin, writing 'Thu / Fri' next to it with a shaky hand.

'I'll call you!" Tiger says, already walking away briskly. Yeah, sure, Angie thinks.

She sits down, still flushed. 'An old friend of Jimmy's,' she explains.

'Well, he's sure a fine-looking lad, and I don't even like lads,' Sinéad says, winking and exaggerating her Irish accent. She waits for Angie to elaborate, but when she doesn't, Sinéad picks the previous conversation up where they left it. 'So, are you positive you don't want to shake some belly next Friday?'

❧

Waiting for Sinéad at the noodle bar the following Monday, Angie finds herself scrutinising the crowd, just in case Tiger happens to be about. When Sinéad arrives, she notices her friend's distraction, and wants to know what's wrong.

Angie tells Sinéad about Tiger and Jimmy's friendship going sour and some minor details about her meeting with Tiger last year.

'I just didn't swallow Tiger's story about Jimmy saying the wrong thing when Liz died. It just doesn't sit right, and it's not like Jimmy to be so thoughtless.' She pauses, having second thoughts. 'I suppose he can be, but not in a situation like that – not when someone's girlfriend had just died.'

'So, you never found out why they fell out,' Sinéad says.

'They both insist that they just grew apart; as people do, but I always thought it was a shame, especially since Jimmy doesn't have many other friends.'

'Sounds a bit screwy to me,' Sinéad says, adding chilli sauce to her already hot laksa. She chews her chicken in silence for a few minutes, as if munching her thoughts. 'I have a theory,' she says in the end. 'But maybe I should keep it to myself – it's none of my business.'

'What? You can't start saying something like that and then decide to keep it to yourself. Go on, spit it out!' Angie says.

'Well, when I saw you talking to Tiger last Monday, you

know, the way you stuttered and flushed ... it was obvious to me that you are attracted to this guy, even if it's not obvious to you.'

Angie is too embarrassed to reply.

'So, maybe Jimmy sensed that attraction, and purposely drove Tiger away,' Sinéad says, taking a spoonful of laksa.

'Hang on,' Angie exclaims. 'That's an interesting theory but it's most improbable. Jimmy's never been the jealous type. And he's not as intuitive as you think. Sinéad, are you alright?'

Sinéad's eyes are watery, and her cheeks are red. Sweat is running down her forehead. Before she can reply, she's overcome by a coughing fit. She points at the chilli sauce, and Angie runs inside the shop to fetch a glass of water.

'Holy Mary, that was hot!' Sinéad says, after emptying the glass. 'Listen, you're right, Angie. I'm no marriage counsellor, and I don't even know Jimmy that well, let alone Tiger. Forget what I said, okay?'

Angie doesn't forget. That night she wakes herself up, covered in sweat, consciously escaping from a dream involving Tiger, Jimmy and herself, all lying on the grass together. Jimmy is peacefully asleep on his back between Angie and Tiger, while they play a game of chess on a magnetic board placed on Jimmy's chest, which moves up and down at the rhythm of his breathing.

Tiger looks as he did about seven years ago, when he was teaching Angie to play chess. He's wearing a torn singlet, his unkempt blond hair falls down to his shoulders, and he's badly in need of a shave.

Still, he's a damn fine-looking lad.

# ~ She's back ~

Dr Suenho would be amused if she wasn't so concerned, after listening to Angie's uninterrupted attack of verborreah. Before Angie even opened her mouth, Dr Suenho had feared the worst, noticing the change that had come over her patient during the month that she'd been on holidays. It isn't so much her new haircut, but the makeup, and the provocative red top and tight jeans she's wearing which are clearly one size too small. Her top is short enough to reveal the tattoo of a ladybird sitting just above Angie's belly button.

For the last forty minutes, Angie has been jumping non-stop from one subject to another, and is currently rambling about wanting to free the 'dark angel' inside her, who has always been suppressed.

'I'm tired of decorum, you see?' Angie says, speaking at one hundred miles an hour. 'I've lived my entire life trying to be sensible and proper, and have denied the existence of the goddess that lives within me. When will she have a chance to get out? Jimmy isn't interested in getting acquainted with my sexy goddess. He's satisfied with things the way they are, but I'm not. Where and how, then, am I supposed to explore these aspects of myself if not in my own bedroom, with my husband?'

She stops for a couple of seconds, to catch her breath, but not long enough to let Dr Suenho get a word in.

'Yet at the same time, I'm afraid of what could happen if my dark angel gets out of control. I feel as if I have two powerful forces constantly fighting inside me, you know? The sensible Angie, who can be a bore, and Elena, who can be as dangerous as she is seductive. I'm afraid of becoming either extreme, but don't they say that one can't live in limbo for ever? Sooner or later, one has to choose a side – '

'Angie,' Dr Suenho is forced to interrupt when they have less than five minutes left. 'Listen to me very carefully. We're going to reduce your medication. As from tomorrow I want you to take only 150 mg a day. The week after, go down to 100. Then you need to come back to see me again. You are hypomanic again, Angie. You know what this means, don't you?'

'Yes,' Angie says, 'This confirms your diagnosis, that I'm bipolar, manic-depressive, whatever you wish to call it. Don't look so worried – it's not so bad. I'm back to being the life of the party, and I love it!'

'Angie, there's a big difference between the way you perceive yourself and the way others perceive you. You may think you are the life of the party, but the other people at the party may be looking at you, thinking "What a *fruitcake!*" You don't want that, do you?'

Angie doesn't answer, although she's clearly making an effort, pressing her lips tight together.

'There's a book I want you to read.' Dr Suenho scribbles something in one of her post-it notes. 'But you must promise me you'll read it.'

'Yeah, sure,' Angie replies, sticking the note inside her jeans pocket. 'I'll fit it in between my lecture notes, three uni assignments and the two novels I've already borrowed from the library.'

'And please bring back the book I lent you on how to beat the blues – I have another patient who needs it more than you right now.'

Before Angie leaves, Dr Suenho says, 'Once you are off the antidepressants, we have to switch to a different type of medication, specific for bipolar mood disorder. We'll discuss that next time.'

On her way to the car, Angie pulls the crumpled post-it note out of her pocket. It reads: *An Unquiet Mind: A memoir of moods and madness*, by Dr Kay Redfield Jamison. She crams it back in her pocket and promptly forgets that it's there.

As soon as she gets in her car, she takes a small notebook with a fuchsia cover out of her handbag, and a pen.

It's the diary she has been trying to keep for the last two months.

**May 5th, 1999 – 12. 30 pm.**

Today, at age 31, I've been officially diagnosed as suffering from bipolar mood disorder - Type II. The term 'suffering' perhaps applies to the depressions, but when you are feeling the way I feel right now, you can hardly call it a suffering. 'Enjoying' is a more appropriate word. Enjoy it while it lasts.

So, *she's back*. She's back, and she's more exuberant than ever, because now she knows more about her powers as well as her weaknesses, and is determined to make the best of whatever time she has. A month, maybe two – four at the most.

And I let her seduce me; I breathe her in, let her take possession of my body, take possession of my brain, slowly, smoothly, relentlessly, as if in a lover's game, because I know that it will be different this time. I too, know exactly what's going on, and I am in control.

'Hi Elena,' I tell my reflection in the rear-view mirror. She looks back at me, smiling, her hazel eyes ablaze. We both say in unison, 'I have been waiting for you.'

# PART 2:
# BECOMING ELENA

*Knowledge is power*

- Francis Bacon

# ~ Foes and Allies ~

You tell yourself that you are in control, but you do not realise how weak you are. All I have to do is wait, knowing that sooner, rather than later, you will walk into my trap willingly – you will fall for me like the sailors who followed the chant of the sirens, aware that it would only lead them to their doom.

Not in vain did you name me after Helen, the queen with 'the face that launched a thousand ships'. You read that phrase before, many years ago. It was in high school, in a play by Christopher Marlowe. Back then, you did not know that it meant 'shining light'.

You will follow my scent and my radiance, with your eyes half-closed, entranced. Once you are hopelessly tangled inside my web, I will reveal myself to you in all my beauty, and you will never want to leave.

I am Elena, the Goddess of Light.

You, Angelica, are my vessel.

## Post-consultation tape – May 14th, 1999
## Patient: Angelica Fletcher

Patient's speech accelerated; thoughts unfocused, jumps to and fro between unrelated subjects maintaining they are all connected; elaborates complicated yet disjointed theories about anything and everything. Spends large amounts of money on a variety of articles she's convinced are absolutely necessary, such as aromatherapy kits which she hasn't opened, designer lingerie that she doesn't wear and books in foreign languages she believes she'll be able to read with the aid of a dictionary.

Confident she will achieve high distinctions in all subjects at university. Also reports that work is going well although she is uncertain about her future with the company when her contract runs out in three months.

Although restless, patient does not exhibit any signs of psychosis or paranoia, and is still functional both in her studies and at work. She is well aware that she is going through a second bout of hypomania.

I suggested she bring her husband to the next session, as he would undoubtedly have many questions to ask about the condition and the treatment. Patient tells me she hasn't 'got around' to telling her husband or any other member of her family about my diagnosis, but assures me that she will – in due time.

Unable to discuss lithium therapy (patient arrived twenty-five minutes late). Issued another prescription for Temazepam. Reduced antidepressants to 50 mg starting tomorrow – to be discontinued altogether within eight days.

❧

When Jimmy arrives home one night in May, he finds a note on the table reminding him that Angie is at choir rehearsal and won't be home till ten. There's some frozen pizza in the fridge, if he wants to heat it up. Jimmy feels the knot he's had in his stomach for a few weeks tighten. Is this déjà vu, or is his worst nightmare recurring?

His wife is out there again, just like last spring. Driving that bomb of a car around, with the Irish girl, taking on more than she can handle, behaving as if she too, like Sinéad, were twenty-one, with no husband or responsibilities. Last year he had thought this behaviour had been a momentary lapse, that it would pass, and it had. As stark as Angie's recent depression had been, Jimmy had to admit that he found the depressed, lifeless Angie much easier to handle than the loud, provocative stranger who had moved into his house, into his bed, last spring.

Now the flamboyant Angie has moved back in, and Jimmy is beginning to fear that there might not be enough room for the two of them in the apartment. But he won't be the one to leave, he can't.

Many years ago, when he found out about the way that Angie's father had abandoned his wife and daughter, he promised himself that no matter how bad things got, he would never leave his own family. He had already done it once: at eighteen, he left his parental home, turning his back on his mother's drinking problem and his father's violence.

Jimmy doesn't feel like eating frozen pizza. Yesterday, when he had dinner at Norah's, she mentioned that she would be cooking barramundi tonight, knowing how much Jimmy likes it. As he walks into the bedroom to change, he sees a piece of paper on the carpet, folded in half, standing neatly on its edges like a little white tent. He picks it up.

*Bipolar disorder involves cycles of mania and depression*, the first line reads. *This is a list of signs and symptoms of mania, to assist with recognition and diagnosis.* The list covers, one by one, all the behavioural changes that came over Angie last spring, and again last month, preceded, both times, by a period of severe depression.

'Why?' Jimmy asks aloud, and for some reason, he looks at the ceiling, as if looking into the heavens, questioning the God he doesn't believe in. 'Why do I have to discover this by chance, like I did with the stories? Why couldn't she trust me enough to talk to me about it? Don't I deserve to know what the fuck is going on? It's my life too!'

Sitting on the edge of the bed, he realises that he's made his hands into fists and has inadvertently crumpled the piece of paper. He smoothes the sheet out as best he can, and carries it to the study, where he turns the computer on, connecting to the Internet. With trembling fingers, he types bipolar disorder + mania in the search field.

Norah has just finished eating dinner by herself. Just as well Jimmy hadn't come over – the barramundi was overcooked and dry; definitely not her best. She should have done it in the grill, as usual, instead of baking it. She is about to throw the leftovers away when her phone rings.

It's Jimmy. His tone is flat. 'I hope I didn't wake you up,' he says.

'Jimmy! You didn't. It's only nine o'clock! I had just finished eating dinner,' Norah says, and then she asks, automatically, as she has done so many times in the past year, 'Is there something wrong with Angie?'

'No. Yes – it's complicated. Listen, Norah, there's something I want to consult you about, before Ange gets home at ten. But I don't really want to do it over the phone, and I want to be here when she arrives.'

'I'll come over, Jimmy. I'll be there in ten minutes,' Norah says, feeling queasy all of a sudden.

Angie and Sinéad have decided to join a group of choristers who, for the last few weeks, have been going out for dinner after rehearsal.

'We're doing 'around the world in eighty restaurants,' Mandy explains to Sinéad as they leave the auditorium where they practice. 'Tonight it's Afghan.'

'I've never eaten Afghan food,' Sinéad says, pulling Angie by the sleeve. 'Can we go, can we?'

'Sure, but can I borrow your mobile?' Angie asks Sinéad. The twenty-first century is around the corner and Angie still doesn't have a mobile. 'To call Jimmy and tell him I'll be later than I said?'

'Sorry sister, but the battery is dead,' Sinéad says.

'I didn't bring mine,' Mandy says, apologetically.

'Why don't you just get one, Angie? They're good for emergencies.' Sinéad says.

'Jimmy doesn't want me to have a mobile. He reckons he's got enough bills to pay as it is.' Angie says, sighing. 'He never misses a chance to remind me of my spending.'

They try the payphone on their way to the parking lot, but it's out of order.

'We'll have to eat and run,' Angie says.

Fifteen minutes later they find themselves at a small Afghan restaurant tucked away on the second floor of a bright pink building, together with another eight choristers and the conductor. Before they know it, it's after ten, and they're still eating and drinking and laughing. Angie's light-headed and giggling.

Someone next to her comments, in a deep baritone voice, that he hopes she's not driving home in that state – it's Con, the choir conductor, and he doesn't believe Angie when she tells him that she hasn't touched a drop of alcohol all night.

'It's a natural high,' she tells him, but he wants to smell her breath, to be sure, and Angie exhales close to his mouth, with her eyes closed.

'Okay, you pass,' Angie hears Con say. 'Now, can I get you a soft drink, or perhaps a light beer?'

'Lemonade will be fine, thank you,' Angie hears herself say.

When she opens her eyes, she has the distinct feeling that she's observing this scene through a two-way mirror. She's outside the group and yet wholly connected to each and every one of these people without the need for words. She can actually sense the development of the fabric that binds human beings together taking place, despite the variety of the other chorister's backgrounds, ages and interests.

She can physically sense Con's attraction to her, like an elastic band pulling him towards her as he comes back from the bar. She feels a pleasant current rippling through her gut when their fingertips meet as he hands her the glass. She catches a glimpse of his wedding ring, and it doesn't bother her in the least.

She can sense that young Charles, sitting opposite, is in love with Mandy, although he will probably never tell her, because Mandy has a boyfriend. She realises that Sinéad, although laughing, is rather melancholy inside – longing for someone in Tyrone, a girl, with whom she has shared many a night like this.

Dangerous liaisons, steady relationships, lust, passion, separation, unrequited love. The stuff that makes the world go round, and Angie is experiencing it all at once.

Then Angie feels a tear in the fabric, and spots a young girl at the other end of the table, whose name she doesn't know. The girl, stocky, blonde, with a birthmark beneath her right eye, is new to the choir and she's eating in silence, looking painfully out of place, although no one else seems to notice.

She reminds Angie of her old self, of how she had been before Elena came into her life: the way she would sit in a corner at gatherings and functions, feeling self-conscious. She remembers the shyness, the uneasiness she felt as she tried to blend in with the furniture, looking at her watch every five minutes, impatiently waiting until it was time to go home. Hoping and at the same time fearing that someone would notice her.

Angie's connection to this girl is so strong that she feels like crying. She's about to get up and approach her, to ask her name, make her feel welcome, tell her she knows exactly how she's feeling, when Sinéad taps her on the shoulder and whispers in her ear that it's late, that they'd better get going.

'I don't want you to be in trouble with daddy on my account,' Sinéad says.

'Daddy must be asleep by now,' Angie answers as she gets up, waving the group goodbye and giving Con a parting wink.

After dropping Sinéad off, Angie winds down the car window and takes a deep breath, filling her lungs with the night air. With winter around the corner, the breeze is cold and refreshing.

Life is good, all is well, she reassures herself, sweeping to the back of her mind nagging thoughts about her increasingly frequent arguments with Jimmy, and the way she has been avoiding Norah's gaze lately because her eyes are full of worry.

With the radio blaring, the cool wind whistling in her ears, the streetlights flying past, Angie is aware that her senses are enhanced and she knows very well why: it's all to do with chemistry. If this is, as Dr Suenho says, the product of a chemical imbalance in the brain, well, the hell with balance! She wants to stretch this magical feeling out as long as possible and takes the long way home instead of the motorway.

When she arrives home, Norah and Jimmy are waiting for her. Norah is at the table, holding a cup of tea with both hands, and Jimmy is sitting on the sofa next to a pile of computer printouts. They look at the wall clock as Angie walks in. It's 11.30 pm. Norah's eyes are red, as if she has been crying, and Jimmy looks exhausted. He has black rings under his eyes, is still wearing his work clothes, and looks paler than the crumpled piece of paper he holds on his lap.

'What's the matter?' Angie says, closing the door behind her and leaning on it. 'Did someone die?'

'Have you any idea of the time, Angelica?' Norah blurts.

'I went for dinner with some of the choir guys after rehearsal, and--'

'One day we're going to have to pick you up from the emergency room at the hospital,' Norah interrupts, her voice trembling. 'I dread it every time you take that car out. I infinitely regret having given it to you.'

'What, you want it back now?' Angie says, incredulous. 'Mum, you watch too much E.R. Honestly, I can take care of myself; I'm a big girl!'

'You're not behaving like one, Angie!' Norah snaps, and begins to cry. This is not how she had intended to handle this situation. She should've gone home, let Jimmy take care of things. But Jimmy had asked her to stay. He too, was afraid of stuffing things up. Norah glances at Jimmy and he nods, mouthing the words, 'It's okay.'

'I would appreciate it, mum, if you didn't treat me like a child in front of my husband.' Angie looks in Jimmy's direction, expecting some reassurance, but Jimmy remains impassive towards her. 'What's this? The inquisition? If Jimmy had let me have a mobile phone when I asked for one, I could've called.'

'Ange,' Jimmy finally says, much calmer than Norah, 'You must understand that we worry about you because we care about you. You must trust us, so that we can trust you--'

'Stop trying to channel Krishnamurti and get to the point, Jimmy,' Angie interrupts, so rudely that Norah gasps. 'You want me to give the car up, is that it? Don't you two have something better to do than sit here and plot against me?'

'Angie, you're being paranoid,' Norah says, trying to stay calm. 'It's not about the car, and we are not plotting against anybody.'

'Then I'll tell you what this is about!' Angie says, her face red with anger. 'You can see that I'm happy, and you are jealous of me, both of you, because neither of you have ever allowed yourselves to be truly happy. You can see that I'm breaking free from your grasp, and you can't stand it.'

'Angie, please sit down,' Jimmy says soothingly, ignoring Angie's cutting words. She obviously doesn't know what she's saying. He pulls a chair out from the table for her and places it in the middle of the room. He hands Angie the creased piece of paper that he's been clutching all this time. Angie recognises it immediately – it is the list of signs and symptoms of mania given to her by Dr Suenho. She had kept it tucked away in the book she had returned to the doctor this morning. Angie stares at it blankly, unable to understand what it is doing in Jimmy's hands.

'I found this list on the bedroom floor when I got home,' Jimmy says. 'I printed out all I could find on the Internet about bipolar mood disorder, and your mum and I read a great deal of it tonight.' He points at the pile of paper on the sofa. 'We could've done this together, Angie, the three of us. You could've told us, or your doctor could've told us, and we would've worked on it together. We still can, of course.'

Angie's legs turn to jelly and she falls, like a lifeless puppet, into the seat that Jimmy has readied for her. The palpable feelings of communion she perceived only a few hours ago at a dinner table full of near strangers are all but gone. Here she is, with the two people closer to her than anybody else, the two most important and influential human beings in her life, and she cannot feel the slightest connection to them.

'How long have you known, Angie?' Norah asks, emulating Jimmy's soothing tone. She makes it sound as if Angie has been diagnosed with a terminal disease.

'You don't understand,' Angie says, shaking her head. 'That's why I didn't even try to explain it to you. I'm not crazy, I'm not manic. I'm hy-po-ma-nic, and it's harmless. I feel good, better than ever, and happy, and exultant, and that's all there is to it. But if I had told you, you would have panicked, like you're doing now. You wouldn't just let me be, you would try to change things, to change me.'

'What does your doctor say, Angie?' Norah persists. 'Did she mention medication? Lithium?'

At the mention of the word lithium Angie ceases to hear Norah's words and can only hear Elena screaming inside her mind.

Lithium! Run, Angelica, run! These people are convinced that you are mad, they want to sedate you, to turn you back into a zombie. They want to obliterate me from your life.

Angie gets up, grabs her car keys off the table and runs towards the door.

'No, I won't let you turn me back into a zombie. I've been there, twice, and I'm never going back!'

'Ange, wait!' Jimmy says. 'Where are you going?' He moves towards her.

Norah cries out, too, standing up and reaching out to her daughter, but she trips on the leg of the table and lands on the carpet with the tablecloth tangled around her. Her empty teacup and all the bits and pieces that were on the table end up scattered on the floor.

Jimmy stops to help Norah, and Angie escapes, deadlocking the door behind her. Swearing under his breath, Jimmy finds his keys and unlocks the door as Norah straightens the tablecloth. He doesn't bother to go outside. He knows his wife is already gone. Norah looks at him, desolate, and starts muttering a prayer.

Angie drives and drives, crying, turning corners, crossing bridges, up the hill and down the highway. Eventually she realises she's lost. Lost inside a labyrinth of endless streets and houses and boulevards and driveways. It's past midnight, it's dark, it's cold, and she's lonely.

She slows down and when she reaches the end of a cul-de-sac, she stops the engine. She must be near the water – she can smell sea salt in the damp, chilly breeze. The full moon reveals itself from behind a cloud – a smiling woman's face. It speaks to her with a Spanish accent.

Never mind them, Angelica. They are only human, and it is in human nature to be reluctant to change. They just want things to go back to the way they were, and you and I know that they will – but in our time, not theirs. Now, go find that beach!

When Angie returns home around 1.30 am, carrying her shoes under her arm, her bare feet peppered with sand, Norah has gone and Jimmy is asleep on the sofa. As soon as she closes the door Jimmy wakes up. He opens his mouth to say something but doesn't. His eyes, though a little bloodshot, scream relief.

'I'm sorry I didn't tell you before,' Angie says, sitting on the chair that is still where Jimmy put it, in the middle of the lounge.

While paddling on the beach, listening to the waves, following the path traced by the moonlight, Angie had come to understand that she needs to enlist her family and her doctor as allies. In order to do this, she will need to make some concessions – or at least appear to. Her thinking was sharper than usual, like her senses.

Forcing herself to speak clearly and slowly, Angie explains to Jimmy that Dr Suenho was only able to confirm the diagnosis about a month ago. Seeing that during her depressions Angie has never been suicidal, and so far she has never been manic, but only hypomanic, Dr Suenho diagnosed her with Bipolar Type II – the mildest form of the disorder. If Jimmy and Norah want to look it up on the internet, it would be best if they'd look up the right type.

'Dr Suenho asked if you wanted to come to the last session,' she goes on. 'I didn't think you would, knowing how much you dislike psychiatrists. But I should've asked you.'

'Ange,' Jimmy says in a tired, croaky voice. 'I never want you to become a zombie again. I'm just glad there's a logical explanation for what's been happening to you – other than you being possessed, which is what your mum and I were beginning to think.' He pauses, knowing that this will make Angie smile. 'I know we can work this out together. If you want me to come and see your doctor with you, I will; if you don't, I won't.'

'Let's go to sleep. It's been a long day,' Angie says, in a voice as weary as Jimmy's. She goes to the kitchen, and fumbles in the pantry. Hidden inside a plastic container there is a bottle labelled Temazepam. She opens it and takes two pills – she could do with some rest tonight.

## Angie's Diary, May 22nd, 1999

In the spirit of doing more 'family things' with Mum and Jimmy, the three of us went to see an amazing movie yesterday, the one everyone has been talking about since it was filmed in the streets of Sydney last year: *The Matrix.*

Actually, I had the chance to be an unpaid extra in the film. It happened when I was heading to the State Library one Sunday, to do some research for uni. Pitt Street was closed off around Martin Place, and there were signs posted that said something like, "If you cross this point, you are giving consent for your image to appear in a motion picture." But I chickened out, especially since there was a crowd of people blocking the way.

When we saw the movie, Jimmy was mostly impressed by the martial arts scenes. After all, it was *Kung Fu,* the seventies TV series starring David Carradine, which originally got him interested in eastern culture. Mum confessed that she slept through most of the movie, but the little she saw was too violent.

I seemed to have been watching a totally different movie. Forget about the kung fu or the violence, or the fact that I could have been part of *The Matrix*: the characters were speaking directly to me, telling me about the unlimited potential of the human mind, daring me to follow the white rabbit and to challenge the restrictions that we impose upon ourselves. It reminded me of a Richard Bach book I loved as a teenager, although at the time I didn't fully understand it: *Jonathan Livingston Seagull*. How Jonathan's flying instructor pushed him (a humble seagull) beyond all limits imaginable.

A year ago, I would have barely grasped what Andy and Larry Wachowsky (the creators of *The Matrix*) were trying to say in their movie, just like I failed to comprehend Richard Bach all those years ago. But I can understand their meaning perfectly now, thanks to the new clarity of my thinking. It's all a metaphor – the real flying happens inside our minds, where there are no boundaries or gravity.

## May 28th, 1999

Dragged Sinéad to see *The Matrix*, before they take it off the big screen. It wasn't her cup of tea but I had to share it with her. When the lights came on, all she said was 'Holy Molly! What was all that about? The Second Coming or what?' Again, I was a tad disappointed ... of all people, I thought she'd understand. But later thought about it and yes, it is about a Second Coming of sorts – Sinéad was brought up as a strong Catholic, so she interpreted it according to her own background. Neo, the main character, was a reluctant messiah after all. Which reminds me, Richard Bach also wrote a book about a reluctant messiah – it was called *Illusions*. Maybe there is a connection; everything is connected, I can see the connections so clearly now.

Now that it's no longer a secret, I told Sinéad about my condition, over coffee after the movie. I didn't think she would freak out, but you never know. She didn't. She told me that there's no-one in her family who hasn't been diagnosed with some sort of disorder. Even she, who up until last year was the sanest among her relatives, has now had a taste of depression. At least I'm under the care of an excellent doctor, she said, and made me promise I would keep my appointments 'religiously'.

Didn't tell her I missed today's appointment. I was at the movies with her, when I should've been at Dr Suenho's.

# ~ Tiger ~

Angie is busy typing at the agency when her boss, a woman with false nails and a permanent frown, comes to her desk personally to tell her that she has a private phone call on line five.

'Hey Angie! It's Tiger. Just thought I'd call to see how you are, like I said I would.'

'Tiger! What a pleasant surprise!' Angie exclaims. Instinctively, she looks at her reflection in her computer monitor, and with her left hand tidies up her hair. But her heart isn't racing, and her fingers are not trembling, as they were only a couple of months ago, when she last saw Tiger. 'Listen, I can't talk much 'cos they pay me by the hour and dragon-lady here never takes her eyes off me. But it's high time we got together. So much has happened since we last caught up!' She doesn't give Tiger the chance to get a word in. 'Hey, I haven't been to the movies for a couple of weeks. Do you fancy one next Tuesday?'

'Sounds good to me. Which movie?' Tiger says, feeling a bit disoriented, because although it's Angie's voice at the other end of the line, it doesn't sound like Angie at all.

'Your pick,' Angie says. 'You usually pick good movies.'

'Well, there's a new Australian film on at the Dendy. It's

called *Terra Nullius* and it won a couple of awards. It's probably about native title, you know, Aboriginal land rights.'

'Sounds good to me.'

'Listen,' Tiger says, hesitant. 'What about Jimmy?'

'What about him? Do we need his permission?' Angie says,
lowering her voice to a whisper. 'It's only a movie.'

'Of course. I just meant ... how is he?'

'Oh, he's fine. I think. Frankly, I hardly see him these
days – he's working even longer hours than before. So, it's
a date then.'

'Sure. Where do you want me to pick you up Tuesday
night?'

'No need, I'll be driving,' Angie says.

'We do need to catch up!' Tiger exclaims. 'I didn't even
know you had a driver's licence. About time you guys got
a car!'

On Tuesday, they meet at the bar at the Dendy cinemas in
Martin Place, half an hour before the session starts. Angie
shouts Tiger a glass of Riesling and has one herself. She's
wearing a lot of make-up and a black outfit more appropriate
for a dinner party than a movie. Tiger hasn't had the time to
change, so he's still wearing a suit and business shirt with
a Looney Toons tie.

Bubblier than her drink, Angie talks nonstop about her
book club, her choir, her university studies, her best friend
Sinéad, and she doesn't mention Jimmy even once. She's
going so fast that Tiger has trouble understanding what
she's saying. What's even more confusing is that she herself
seems to lose track of her own thoughts, becoming constantly
distracted by the lights, the music, the waitress's earrings

and in particular, Tiger's tie. She finds it so hilarious it sends her into a fit of laughter. She reminds Tiger of someone, but he can't think of who it is.

'Angie, slow down, I can't keep up with you,' Tiger says, when it's almost time for the movie to start. And then, half-joking, half-serious, 'Are you on drugs or something?'

'The only drugs I've ever taken are antidepressants. But I've been off them for weeks,' Angie says, nonchalantly.

'You didn't stop suddenly, did you? You have to come off those things gradually!' Tiger knows all about Zoloft, and Prozac, and Aropax, and Effexon.

'Don't worry, I'm under the supervision of a very good shrink,' she says, using the same word he's always used.

Tiger looks at her with big round eyes. 'Shrink? You?'

'Yep. The same one who diagnosed me with bipolar mood disorder a couple of months ago. C'mon, everybody's gone in,' she says. Downing the last of her drink, she races to the theatre. Tiger stays on his stool for a moment, in a state of shock. Just then, the penny drops and he realises who Angie reminds him off – not physically, but in her behaviour.

Gwyneth Fletcher. Jimmy's mother, in her late-thirties, a glass of bourbon in her hand, laughing drunkenly and flirting with every man in sight – even with her son's teenage friend.

*Terra Nullius* is in fact *Terra Nova* and it has nothing to do with Aboriginal land rights. It's about a single mother whose child is taken away from her after being diagnosed with mental illness.

'I'm so sorry, Angie, I totally fucked up,' is all Tiger can say when the film is over. 'Of all movies I had to pick this one.'

'Why do you apologise? It was a damn good movie,' Angie says. 'It's about time they started to make more movies about mental illness. Remember when homosexuality was taboo? Now every second movie is about gay relationships.' She starts laughing.

'What's so funny?' Tiger asks.

'I'm thinking about of *The Crying Game*, one of the first movies we saw that tackled transgender relationships. You and I went to see it when I was still living down the road from you. The twist at the end left us both in shock, remember?'

Tiger remembers. It would have been the early nineties, and they had gone to the movies without Jimmy, because he had fallen fast asleep waiting for Tiger, who was running over an hour late in picking them up. By the time Angie and Tiger arrived at the movie theatre, the only film showing was *The Crying Game*, which neither of them had heard anything about. They decided to take a chance, and walked in totally unprepared for what was in store.

'We always used to discuss the movies that we'd just seen. But after this one you drove me home without saying a word,' Angie says. 'Jimmy was where we left him, snoring on the sofa.' She gives Tiger a nudge and stands up. They are the only ones left in the theatre. 'Anyway, stop worrying and take me somewhere to eat. I'm starving!'

On the way out, she continues. 'I'm not schizophrenic, like the woman in the movie we just saw. I'm bipolar. I don't hear voices. My moods go up and down, like a yo-yo,' Angie explains, using the same simple terms that she had used to explain to Sinéad. 'I'm up at the moment, and I feel great, I look great. Don't you think?'

'You're certainly nothing like you were last time I saw you, Angie.' Tiger says.

He doesn't want to say that she looks a bit over the top. Now that he knows, he would say that she looks, in fact, manic.

Tiger suggests a Lebanese restaurant in Surry Hills. They decide to take his car.

'What the hell happened to your car?' Angie says. Tiger's executive sedan is covered by dents, visible even in the poor light.

'The first time in my life I buy a brand new car, and it gets hit by the fucking hailstorm,' Tiger says, referring to the worst hailstorm in Sydney's history, which had caused millions of dollars' worth of damage back in April.

'Let me guess: you weren't insured,' Angie says, and Tiger nods, looking at the pavement. 'Oh, Tiger. Some people never change.'

Suddenly, she's in stitches. Her laugh is definitely manic – high pitched and loud – but it's also infectious, and before he knows it Tiger is also laughing at his misfortune, uncontrollably, seeing the irony of it all. They laugh, leaning on the dented bonnet of his car, until they're almost in tears.

At the restaurant Angie does all the talking again, and Tiger scrunches his face in an effort to follow. She hardly touches her food. No wonder she's lost so much weight, he thinks – even her breasts have shrunk.

The first time she mentions Jimmy is when she looks at her watch and gasps – it's nearly ten.

'Is that the time? Shit! I've got to make tracks. Jimmy doesn't like me driving late at night – well, he doesn't like me driving at all, but least of all at night.'

'I take it that he hasn't learnt to drive yet?' Tiger asks, on the way to his car.

'Jimmy? Ha! He says if he ever wants to kill himself he can think of other ways.'

'Charming, isn't he. He always used to say that. You're right – some people never change.'

Tiger drives Angie back to her car, and tells her to take it easy, promising to call her soon, although this time, he's not sure he'll keep his promise. She opens her arms before they part, taking a step towards Tiger. He instinctively steps back.

'It's only a hug, Tiger. I'm not going to seduce you!' she says, giggling. He lets her hug him.

Driving home, Tiger realises he is as worried about Jimmy as he is about Angie.

You might have your reasons to cut a friendship but it doesn't mean you stop caring about the person.

At the restaurant, Tiger had felt swamped by a sudden dark mood. The movie, Angie's news, the way she had reminded him of Jimmy's mother and of the many nights that Jimmy had come to stay over because things got too rough at home, had all been too much for one evening. But Angie didn't even notice. She never once asked him how he was.

∂

'Did you have a chance to read the brochures I sent you and to discuss them with your family?' Dr Suenho asks Angie the following Wednesday, adjusting the temperature of the small heater that sits under her desk. Since Angie hadn't made it to their last appointment, Dr Suenho had posted her some information about lithium.

Angie has turned up fifteen minutes late, an improvement on her recent record, wearing a red knitted wool dress the same colour as Dr Suenho's poinsettia. It's Angie who points this out, telling Dr Suenho that she's recently read that the poinsettia is native to Mexico. A man called Miguel Poinsettia took the seeds to North America, where it first became known as the Flame Leaf, and later by his name. Did

Dr Suenho know that the bright red petals are not petals at all, but modified leaves?

But today the doctor is determined to discuss medication, and will not be distracted by Angie's horticultural ramblings.

'The brochures, Angie,' Dr Suenho repeats, patiently. She's dealt with people in Angie's state before, and others much worse.

'I had a look at them, and also looked lithium up on the Internet. You can't possibly expect me to consider that option,' Angie says, and reels off a thorough list of the adverse side effects she has read about.

Slurred speech, vomiting, poor coordination, muscle twitching, severe tremors, severe diarrhoea, trouble walking and severe drowsiness are just a few of them.

'Not to mention,' Angie goes on, 'the possibility of life-threatening toxicity.'

'Angie, the ways to monitor the use and side effects of lithium have improved dramatically over the years. Didn't you read that on the Internet?' Dr Suenho says.

'No, but I read heaps of online diaries and forums for people with bipolar. Most of them complain that apart from making them physically sick, lithium affects their capacity to feel emotions. "Flat and colourless" is how they describe their life. But they have to take it, because their cases are much worse than mine.'

'Angie, even though you seem to have the mildest form of bipolar, it could worsen if left untreated. I'm concerned about what could happen in spring. The reasons are not clear, but it's a well-known fact that your illness is seasonal, and fully-fledged mania attacks are more common in spring.'

'Spring is months away. I'd like to cross that bridge when

and if I come to it,' Angie says, with the confidence that hypomania has given her.

Dr Suenho nods, knowing that she can't force her patient to take medication if she doesn't want to; not unless she poses some kind of threat to herself and to others, and this is not the case.

'What about the memoir I asked you to read, Angie? It's very honest and balanced, and also very informed. The woman who wrote is an eminent psychiatrist.'

'I forgot to take the bit of paper with the title out of my jeans' pocket before I put them in the washing,' Angie says, lowering her eyes.

Dr Suenho gets up and takes a book from her bookshelf.

'Here,' she says, handing it to Angie. '*An Unquiet Mind.*'

'Kay Redfield Jamison,' Angie reads aloud. 'I saw her name on the Internet. She wrote another book, *Touched with Fire*, where she studies the link between manic depressive illness and creative genius.'

Angie launches on a lecture examining Dr Jamison's suggestion that Virginia Woolf, Lord Byron, Schuman, and countless other poets, writers, painters and musicians were manic-depressive. They were at their most creative during their mildly manic states, usually in late spring and early autumn, and they polished their work during their mild depressions.

'And I reckon she's spot on. Did I mention to you that I'm writing again? Poetry, short stories, essays ... you name it, I'm writing it!'

'Dr Jamison is an authority on this subject,' Dr Suenho says, remaining focused and firm. 'Will you read this book, Angie?'

Angie remembers that she needs to make some concessions in order to keep her privileges. Her tone is no longer defiant when she says, 'I have one more uni assignment to do. After that, I'll read it.'

Dr Suenho gives Angie a leaflet with information on an alternative drug, to consider instead of lithium. Again, she reminds Angie that Jimmy is welcome to come to the next session. If she's going to go without medication, family support is crucial, and her husband needs to know what is expected of him, and what to expect.

'That might be a little difficult,' Angie says. 'As of last week, Jimmy has taken a second job. He'd been threatening me for a while, saying "I'm going to have to get a second job to support your expensive lifestyle." I thought he was joking, but he wasn't. So he's working the day shift at a print shop, and has taken the afternoon shift at the paper. He gets home at midnight, knackered, sleeps like a rock for six hours, only to get up at dawn to start it all over again. He's even working on Saturdays, although he says this is only temporary.'

'I see. Tell me, Angie: does it bother you what Jimmy said about your expensive lifestyle, and the extremes it's pushing him to?' Dr Suenho asks, pressing her pen against her lips. Angie notices the letters E.S., the doctor's initials, engraved on the pen in a flowery script. It looks expensive. 'Don't you think there might be some truth in what he's saying?'

Angie wants to say, 'I don't need to pay $100 dollars a session to hear what I already hear at home every day,' but somehow she stops herself. She feels the anger rushing up to her face, and the words rushing up to her mouth. She bites her lip. If she hadn't promised Sinéad ...

'I know my spending has increased,' she says instead. 'But not enough to justify Jimmy having to get another job. He's just doing it to make me feel bad.'

On the train home, Angie glances over the leaflet Dr Suenho has given her. If lithium sounded bad, this other medication sounds ten times worse. The section on adverse effects covers over half of the leaflet: aplastic anaemia, severe dermatologic reactions, possibility of activation of latent psychosis, hepatitis, congestive heart failure, thrombophlebitis and other ailments whose names Angie can't even pronounce.

In fact, it is enough to read that 'some of these complications have resulted in fatalities' for her to decide that she may still consider lithium, but she won't be giving this other medication a second thought. She rips the leaflet up and throws the bits away in the first rubbish bin she finds at the train station.

Angie lies on her back on the grass, in a park whose name she doesn't know, waiting for Sinéad to finish work. They're going to a play at the university theatre.

Sinéad is working at a mailing house in Silverwater, stuffing envelopes for the next few weeks, while she waits for a two-month market research assignment that the personnel agency has promised her for the university winter break.

Angie waits, shivering slightly, lying down with her eyes closed, feeling the moisture of the grass penetrating her blouse. She can hear the murmur of the water in the fountain, and the pigeons splashing in it. She can feel the ants, making their way through the hairs on her arm, tickling her skin. She opens her eyes just in time to see an elephant shaped cloud drifting across the sky, disintegrating. One of its ears lingers for a few seconds but inevitably fades. Angie holds her hands in front of her eyes like binoculars, trying, in vain, to hold on to that moment a little longer. A snapshot of a dying sun amidst animal shaped clouds, in shades of pink and orange.

Everything is so amazingly bright – there's an effulgence created by the sunset that makes the contours of the clouds, the trees, the buildings and every element of the landscape glow against the background. Everything radiates life. Until recently, Angie has been blind to this radiance.

The small park doesn't have a sign bearing its name, doesn't have rubbish bins or benches. There is a run-down playground, which has been vandalised: the slide lies on its side, and the swings are missing. The grass is overgrown, and the only thing intact is the fountain, although it is stained by pigeons' droppings. Still, to Angie's eyes, this place is an enchanted garden inexplicably suspended in the middle of industrial suburbia.

'Where is everybody?' Angie asks, aloud – apart from her, there is not another soul around.

'I don't know. Most of them are still working, I suppose,' a familiar voice answers, next to her.

Angie sits up as though she's been struck by lightning, pressing both her hands against her chest. 'Shit, Sinéad, you almost gave me a heart attack!'

'You knew I was here, you silly cow. You talked to me!' Sinéad says, elbowing her friend. She's kneeling on the grass, wearing jeans, a black woolly jumper and a beanie – in this outfit, she looks more like fifteen than twenty-one. Her battered black leather backpack is hanging from her shoulder.

'Never mind,' Angie says, lying down again, her heart still racing. Sinéad lies down next to her, resting her head on her backpack. They stay there for a few minutes, watching the clouds move across the darkening sky. 'Why aren't more people out here, Shine? Lying on the ground, watching nature's show? It costs nothing, and it's spectacular!'

'As I was saying, they are either still working, or battling the traffic on their way home, watching television, feeding the kids, who knows. Who would want to come to a park like this one, anyway? I can see it from the window, over there,' Sinéad points to one of the buildings in front of them. 'And I find it a rather depressing view.'

'Oh well. They don't know what they're missing,' Angie says, ignoring Sinéad's last comment. 'And it's better that they don't, because once you've given your senses the chance to taste life, you will always want more, and when you have responsibilities, kids, a mortgage, a full-time job, there's simply not enough time.'

'Listen, little miss philosopher, we're going to be late for the play; it starts at six-thirty. Even we, who have no kids or a full-time job, don't have much time to waste.' She stands up and offers Angie her hand.

Angie looks at her with slight disappointment but grabs the outstretched hand.

It seems that Elena is the only one who understands what's going on inside her mind. And Angie understands Elena, too. Elena knows that lithium would kill her, and she would never forgive Angie if she let Dr Suenho convince her to take it.

Early one morning, when the midwinter sun hasn't fully risen, Angie jumps out of bed and into the shower as soon as she hears the front door slamming behind Jimmy. It's 6.30 am. She doesn't start work till 9.30, and usually stays in bed for at least an hour after Jimmy leaves. Not today.

From the bathroom mirror, a smiling Elena watches Angie applying her make-up, dabbing perfume behind her ears, styling her short hair, adjusting her long earrings. Elena is pleased.

The transformation is complete.

At 7.45 am, Tiger's phone rings, pulling him out of a nightmare – something to do with his next-door neighbour taking over his place, forcing Tiger to retreat to the laundry room, where he had had to sleep on the cold concrete floor.

'Hi Tiger, it's Angie. I'm calling from the phone box across the road from your place. I knocked on your door but there was no answer. Can I come in?'

'Angie, what are you doing here?' he slurs, thinking that this might be part of his nightmare. Maybe the phone rang in his dream, and he's dreaming that he's awake – it has happened before. 'What's wrong?'

'Nothing is wrong; I just need to talk.'

'Sure, come in; I'll unlock the door.' Convinced that he's still dreaming, Tiger hangs up the phone, stumbles down the corridor, unlocks the door and stumbles back to bed. A few minutes later, he hears the sound of heels on the timber floor, and Angie is soon standing in the corridor outside his bedroom, dressed in a short purple velvet skirt, a black lace top and knee-high black boots.

'Listen Angie,' Tiger says, propping himself up on the bed with one elbow and rubbing his left temple. He has a hangover. This is not a dream – the pain in his head is real enough, as is Angie, still there at the doorway with her head tilted to the side. The last two buttons of her blouse are open, revealing, to Tiger's surprise, a tattoo on her belly. He gestures for her to come in. 'Let me just warn you that I had a very late night, and my head is about to explode, so don't take it personally if I don't sound too hot. Anyway, what the hell are you doing here?'

'When we went out the other night, I never asked you how you were; all I did was talk about me,' Angie says, entering the room and sitting on the edge of Tiger's double bed. 'I just wanted to see that you're okay. I figured that you'd be up by now, don't you start work at nine?'

'I'm okay, Angie, just tired. My first appointment is at ten, so I wasn't going to get up till eight-thirty or so.'

'And your boss is okay with that?'

'You're looking at my boss, Angie. I've been running my own practice for several months.'

'I didn't know that!'

'You didn't give me the chance to tell you. Listen: you do understand that you shouldn't have driven all the way here at this hour, without warning me, don't you?' Tiger tries to sound as gentle as possible, speaking slowly as if talking to a child.

'If I'd warned you, would you have said yes?' Angie asks, raising her eyebrows.

'Nah,' Tiger says, and he can't help but smile.

Angie laughs her manic laugh. 'You see?'

Tiger is fully awake now. He fumbles inside his bedside drawer and takes out a couple of painkillers, which he swallows without water. Angie, after removing her boots, climbs onto the bed next to him. Tiger seizes the sheet with both hands and presses it against his chest, even though he's wearing boxer shorts. He then laughs at his own reaction, shaking his head. This is amusing, after all. He can't understand why Angie or anybody would develop such a fixation on him.

'I just want to talk ... Right now, of all people, I think you'd understand me best,' Angie says, making herself comfortable.

'Well, let's talk,' Tiger says, shifting slightly away from Angie.

Angie's face lights up. She's wearing purple eye shadow, the same colour as her skirt. Her earrings, made of wire and crystal beads, are reminiscent of chandeliers. 'Better still, how about you take the day off and we go for a drive to the coast? South or North – you pick.'

'I don't think so. You're not being reasonable, Angie. What makes you think that you can call in at someone's house at dawn and expect them to drop everything for a drive?'

'I've seen it happen in the movies, many times. And it's not dawn. It's almost eight.'

'In the movies, huh?' He's laughing out loud now. 'I was up till about three this morning, so it's dawn as far as I'm concerned. Anyway, you want to talk; I've got half an hour or so.'

'Me too – I also work, you know?'

She turns on her side, resting her head on her hand, her elbow on Tiger's pillow. She's wearing a gardenia scented perfume. Tiger inches further away, until he's hanging from the edge of the bed, making an effort to keep his balance while Angie, oblivious to his discomfort, embarks on a monologue.

'You say I'm not being reasonable, but hey, what do you expect? I'm high as a kite! I know I have to do something about it, take medication or something, but ... there are things about feeling like this that I don't want to give up. You know, the ability to make connections with strangers, to understand how others are feeling, this sense of communion with the world, with other people, with you.... I don't know why, but I thought you'd understand me better than Jimmy, Mum or even Sinéad.'

'Of course I do. I've felt all those things,' Tiger says.

'How so?' Angie says, squinting at him.

'I've taken ecstasy. That's exactly how it makes you feel. You love everybody; you understand the meaning of life.'

'That's it! The meaning of life, the meaning of everything,' Angie says, kneeling on the bed and waving her arms about. 'See? I knew you'd know. Now, imagine feeling like that for months on end.'

'It would be fucking amazing,' Tiger says, but sooner or later, he thinks to himself, you crash and burn, like you do the day after you've taken ecstasy – and that ain't amazing at all.

'But there's one problem. This is what I wanted to talk to you about,' Angie says, turning serious. 'When I'm like this, my sex drive shoots through the roof and Jimmy seems to be put off by it. I don't understand him; any other man would be thrilled.'

'Well, I can't speak for Jimmy, but don't they say that men reach their sexual peak at eighteen and women at thirty-five, or something like that?' Tiger says, thinking that Jimmy would be mortified if he knew Angie was complaining about their sexual life, to him of all people. 'You haven't even reached your peak and Jimmy has probably been in decline for years.' He pauses, and then goes on, a little hesitant. 'But hey, I'm no expert, in fact, the way my sex life is going, I'm the last person you should be asking. You really need to talk with Jimmy about this.'

'You know Jimmy. He can be so … prudish. Sex is not a subject we've ever talked much about. We 'do' it, but we don't talk about it. But this is making me feel as if there's something wrong with me, as if it was unnatural to feel sexy.'

'No, Angie, it's not unnatural! Didn't you say you're seeing a shrink? He's more qualified to advise you on this.'

'She.'

'Sorry?'

'My psychiatrist; it's a woman.'

'Whatever,' Tiger says. 'You should be asking her these questions; maybe she can see you and Jimmy together.'

'Yeah. As if Jimmy is going to go and talk to a shrink about these things. And in the meantime, I'm going to implode.' Angie says, her eyes getting teary.

Tiger's alarm clock goes off. It's 8.30. Saved by the bell, he thinks, and jumps out of bed with an enthusiasm he's never displayed before at the prospect of going to work.

'Angie, I'd love to stay and talk about this all day, but I've got to go; I'm sorry!'

'Sure. Off you go, then,' Angie says, wiping a tear away with the back of her hand.

'Don't you have to go to work too?'

'I will – don't you worry about me,' Angie says, looking away from Tiger and giving no sign of going anywhere. She's no longer teary – she sounds angry.

Tiger gets up and goes to the bathroom, taking his clothes with him. When he comes out, fully dressed except for his shoes, he finds Angie fast asleep on his bed. He watches her for a few minutes; suppressing the impulse to run his fingers over the smooth surface of her velvet skirt. He's always been fascinated by the texture of velvet.

Angie is sleeping so soundly that Tiger doesn't have the heart to wake her. Shaking his head, he covers Angie with the duvet and scribbles a note on a piece of paper, leaving it on the pillow. 'Angie, make yourself at home, so long as you shut the door tightly when you leave – the lock is playing up.'

∂

Angie wakes up at 11.30 am. It takes her a few seconds to realise where she is. The curtains are drawn and the room smells faintly of mustiness and after-shave. She looks at the time on Tiger's clock radio and springs up but trips on her own boots and falls flat on her rear, giggling. It's too late to try to go to work. She calls the agency and Cheryl, the receptionist, answers in her telephonic voice, changing to a casual tone when she realises who's calling. They have become very friendly lately, going for walks on their lunch breaks and sometimes for drinks on Fridays, after work.

'We were worried about you,' Cheryl says. 'The ice queen is so incensed that she could very well melt.'

'Please tell her that I'm sick,' Angie lies – she's getting to be pretty good at it. 'I woke up at dawn throwing up, went back to bed and only just woke up again – that's why I didn't call earlier.'

'That doesn't sound good. Take care, will you?'

'Will do,' Angie says, and hangs up.

She then dials Sinéad's number.

'Hello, Shine! You'll never guess where I am!'

'No idea,' Sinéad says. 'But I can guess where you aren't – at work. Right?'

'Right. I called in sick. I'm sitting on Tiger's bed, that's where I am.'

'Sitting on whose bed?'

'Tiger. Remember? The good looking lad I ran into that day at Glebe?'

'Yes, I remember him now. And what in Jesus's name are you doing there?' Sinéad doesn't sound amused.

'Don't worry, he's not here, he's gone to work. Tiger, I mean, not Jesus. I dropped in early this morning just to say hello.'

'Angie, are you mad?'

'Of course. You know I am,' Angie says, and starts laughing.

Sinéad waits until Angie stops chuckling, which takes a little while. She then says, in a very serious tone, 'Angie, that excuse is wearing thin.'

There is a long, pregnant pause.

'Angie,' Sinéad says in the end. 'You're playing with other people's lives, not just your own.'

'What are you talking about?' Angie says. 'It was you who pointed out the obvious attraction between me and Tiger in the first place.'

'Go home now, please,' Sinéad pleads. 'Call me when you get there.'

'Yeah, okay,' Angie says. 'Speak later, then.'

Angie hangs up the phone, shaking her head. The hell she's going home, and the hell she's going to call Sinéad when she gets there. If she wants to hear a sermon, there's Jimmy, Norah, and Dr Suenho to give her one. Although she has perceived a rift between herself and Sinéad deepening over the past few weeks, she had still wanted to believe that her best friend was on her side, that she could share everything with her. How dare she speak to her like that? What does she know of what's happening inside her mind?

She shrugs and starts to walk around Tiger's flat, which is as messy as the last time she saw it. He seems to collect newspapers, take away containers and empty bottles of all kinds – wine, coke, beer, after-shave – which lie about the place together with his clothes and shoes.

One room is reasonably tidy – his living room. She reads the spines of the books in his bookshelves idly. She then moves onto his CDs, which include blues, electronic, psychedelic and classical music. He still has a turntable and an assortment of vinyl LPs. Some of them are collector's items – like Linda Perhacs P*arallelograms*, still bearing its $400 price sticker. His video collection includes *The Crying Game*. Despite the shock it had given him, Tiger must have liked it enough to buy the video.

Angie remembers the long conversations she and Tiger used to have in this very room, about literature, music and films. In particular, they shared a special passion for poetry. Jimmy never cared much for poetry, and whenever Angie and Tiger began to discuss the classics, the romantics, or Tiger's latest experiment, Jimmy would leave them to it and go find something useful to do, such as cleaning Tiger's fridge.

After spending twenty minutes figuring out how to turn on Tiger's preamplifier, Angie starts playing Edith Piaf's *La vie en Rose*. She sits on the sofa, fascinated by the floating particles of dust in the light filtering through the living room window, remembering how she spent hours as a child trying to trap those specks inside empty glass jars.

There are two dirty wineglasses and an ashtray full of cigarette butts on the coffee table – she had thought Tiger had quit smoking years ago, but there was obviously someone else there last night. She lifts the ashtray close to her nose and fills her lungs with the smell of tobacco, and something else, much more penetrating – marijuana. Shaking her head, Angie inspects the butts to see if they are smeared with lipstick, and they are not.

Her rumbling stomach reminds her she hasn't had breakfast. There's nothing in the fridge except beer, frozen pies and a carton of curdled milk, which she empties down the sink in disgust. She finds a couple of shortbread biscuits in a jar and downs them with a cup of black coffee. She then notices something familiar pinned to the corkboard on the kitchen wall, standing out among a plethora of photos, bills, flyers and business cards.

It's Angie's short story, *Avoiding Elena*. She had posted it to Tiger, as she had said she would, a lifetime ago. She had forgotten all about doing it. The pages have gone yellow and are dog-eared. She blushes, thinking of the stories that followed and wondering what Tiger would think if he read them.

There are also a couple of photographs stuck to the board. One is of Tiger's mother when she was young, and the other is a photo of Angie and Jimmy's wedding day. There she is, standing in front of the sign that reads 'Registry of Births, Deaths and Marriages', youthful and radiant in her cream lace dress, holding a bouquet of white roses. A slim Jimmy stands on her right, his arm over her shoulder, with his mullet haircut and a navy blue suit. On her left is Tiger, his then long hair in a ponytail, his silk shirt wrinkled.

For some reason, the sight of this photograph brings Angie abruptly back to her wits. Suddenly, her being here, standing in the middle of Tiger's kitchen makes absolutely no sense. In her mind's eye, she sees a giggling woman with too much purple eye shadow and black-stockinged legs climbing onto Tiger's bed, too self-immersed to notice his uneasiness, and she's terribly embarrassed.

She compares the pride in Jimmy's eyes, captured in the photograph, with the look of bafflement he gives her these days, as he tries to find a vestige of the judicious Angie he married. The girl with the long, curly red hair who wore a sensible cream dress and hardly any make-up to her own wedding.

Outside, a storm has been unleashed, thick drops are tap-dancing on the kitchen window. Angie sits down on one of Tiger's aluminium chairs and bursts into tears.

In the early afternoon, when she's sobbed until her tears have dried up and the storm has subsided, Angie gets in her car and heads home.

By the time the rain finally stops, Elena is fully back in control. Driving along, Angie is so taken by the splendid rainbow that has unfolded behind the fading clouds that she forgets all about the photo, the embarrassment, and the crying.

All she remembers is a verse of Samuel Taylor Coleridge's *The Rime of the Ancient Mariner*, which she read in one of Tiger's poetry collections as she sat in his living room.

Fly, brother, fly! More high, more high!

And pressing her foot on the accelerator, she flies.

There is a part of Angie's consciousness that Elena has not yet taken over. That night, after wandering through the corridors of heavy sleep for a while, Angie, wearing a thick bathrobe, walks into a room with cream marble walls and floors. It's a luxurious bathroom, and three candles float lazily in a bowl next to the sink. There's a marble Jacuzzi filled with steaming water, and as she gets closer she realises that she's already soaking in the Jacuzzi, her head resting against the wall, her shoulders glistening, her naked breasts covered in foam.

Just then the door opens, and in walks Tiger, wearing nothing but a towel wrapped around his waist, his muscular body also glistening, as if covered with oil, and he's carrying two silver mugs on a silver platter. He walks right through the first Angie who's standing near the bath, quietly observing.

'Cappuccino?' he asks, handing one of the mugs to the Angie who is soaking in the water. She smiles and nods with half opened, dreamy eyes. But the mug is empty. Sitting on the edge of the Jacuzzi, Tiger fills his own mug with the foamy bath water and starts drinking.

The moment she realises that she's been soaking in steaming hot coffee, Angie's skin starts to peel off. She jumps out of the Jacuzzi in a panic, pushing Tiger aside and bumping head-on into the other Angie, the one who was observing the scene, blending with her. She runs into the endless, maze-like corridors. There are countless doors and she doesn't know which one to open.

'Ange! Wake up, you're having a nightmare.' Angie hears Jimmy's voice behind one of the doors in the labyrinth. She opens the door and wakes up, feverish and covered in sweat, to find Jimmy's face above her, his hand gripping her shoulder. She hangs from his neck and presses her head against his chest.

'What's wrong?' Jimmy asks, taken aback by the strength of her embrace.

'Make love to me, Jimmy! When's the last time we made love?' she says, almost crying.

'Listen to you, Ange!' Jimmy says, breaking away from her grip. 'It's three o'clock in the morning and I'm dead tired, and you – you've just woken up from a nightmare, and you want to make love? I don't understand you, Angie.'

'No, you certainly don't,' Angie says, and turns her back to him, brooding. In less than five minutes, Jimmy is snoring again, but Angie is too upset to go back to sleep. She gets up and heads to the study. She turns the computer on and starts to frantically type her frustration away.

Sitting on his kitchen table and lighting up a cigarette, Dave smiles as he remembers the events of the day. It had been an interesting day indeed. Elena had surprised him by turning up at his doorstep first thing in the morning, dressed in lace and velvet, wearing the leather boots he had bought for her. After they made passionate love on his bed, she had suggested that they could both take the day off work and go for a drive to the coast. He couldn't remember the last time he'd taken a sickie. Without giving it a second thought, he rang his secretary and asked her to cancel all his appointments for the day.

They drove south for two hours, and had a picnic by the sea. They spent the afternoon talking, walking the streets of small coastal villages, window shopping, and simply enjoying each other's company. Since they started their affair, all their encounters had been secret and rushed, and being out together in public felt unusually liberating. He was glad he had said yes to Elena's idea. Then again, he could never say no to her.

When Angie finishes writing a nine-hundred-word account of Dave and Elena's idyllic day at the South Coast, instead of erasing the story as she used to do last year, she saves it in a floppy disk. Underneath a pile of manila folders in one of her desk drawers, there is a round biscuit tin. In the tin there are several other disks containing the many stories of desire, adultery and deception that she has written in the last few months. She slides the most recent one there, without a label or a date.

# ~ Riding the wave ~

A few nights later, Jimmy finds Angie waiting up for him when he arrives home from work. She's reading a book on the sofa, wearing her winter pyjamas. Putting the book down, Angie asks him to come to a party with her, on Saturday night. The choir is celebrating its fifth anniversary, and they're going to a club for dinner and dancing. He is surprised at being asked – Jimmy has gotten used to being excluded from Angie's social life – but his first reaction is to say no. Nightclubs have never been his scene – and he anticipates being rather tired on Saturday night, at the end of a sixty-hour working week.

On the verge of tears, Angie reminds him that for the past month they've hardly gone out anywhere together. With the insane hours he's working, they often don't see each other for days at a time! Angie has plenty more reasons why Jimmy should go, but before she can cite them all, Jimmy relents – he's too tired to argue.

৵

'This is so not my scene,' Jimmy whispers in Angie's ear on Saturday, as they take their seats; but Angie doesn't reply, busy waving and throwing kisses right, left and centre. She's wearing a bright orange dress, the colour of the Hare Krishnas' tunics, but this is not a tunic: it clings tightly to her body and has a cleavage that leaves very little to the imagination. Angie's proud of her new, slimmer figure, and she likes to flaunt it.

There are another twenty or so people at their table, and all of them, including Con, the choir conductor, seem to be at least ten years younger than Jimmy. At thirty-four, he suddenly feels ancient, while Angie looks perfectly comfortable with this much younger crowd.

Jimmy notices that Sinéad is missing.

'She couldn't make it,' Angie explains.

'Why, because I was coming?' Jimmy asks.

'Not at all. She was going to meet her cousin at the airport. But for some reason, she insisted that I should ask you to come with me.'

After dinner, the DJ announces that for the next hour he'll be playing music from the seventies and eighties, and starts with Gloria Estefan and the Miami Sound Machine. Angie jumps to her feet, pulling Jimmy by the arm, but he holds onto the edge of his seat.

'Ange, you know I can't dance.' Jimmy says. 'And I thought you couldn't either!'

'There's a lot about me that you don't know, Jimmy,' Angie says, shrugging and pulling Con onto the already crowded dance floor. A young woman, who introduces herself as Con's wife Tina, moves to the seat next to Jimmy. She starts telling Jimmy all about her ten-month-old baby, whom she has very reluctantly left with a babysitter tonight. Tina asks Jimmy if he and Angie have children, and when he says no, the conversation dies.

Twenty minutes later, Angie is still twirling around like a gyroscope, barefoot and with her arms up in the air. Con comes back to his seat, sweating and puffing, and tells Jimmy, 'Your turn mate, I can't keep up.'

Jimmy gets up, red in the face, but he doesn't head towards the dance floor. Instead, he walks out. A number of smokers are outside, shivering and chatting in small groups. Jimmy sits on a bench, away from them all.

'It's a bit stuffy in there, isn't it mate?' a silver haired man says, sitting next to him. 'Every time I sit down, the wife makes me get up again, to dance. I'm not as young as I used to be.' He takes a leather pouch out of his jacket pocket and starts rolling what looks like a joint.

'Want to roll one, mate?' the man asks, offering Jimmy the pouch. Noticing Jimmy's suspicious look, he says, smiling: 'It's only tobacco.'

'No thanks, I don't smoke.'

'Oh! I thought you were out here because you did. Do you mind if I do?'

'Be my guest.'

'The name's Richard, but everybody calls me Ricky. We've come from Canberra for my daughter's engagement party.'

'Jimmy,' Jimmy says, and they shake hands. 'Are you at the long table down the back?'

'Yes, we are the noisy ones. But the whole lot of us together couldn't outdo the young woman in the orange dress,' he says, laughing. 'Did you see her?'

'That's my wife,' Jimmy says, matter of factly.

'Oh God. I'm sorry,' Ricky says, looking away. Then, thinking about what he just said, he turns back. 'I mean, I'm not sorry she's your wife; I'm sorry about what I said.'

'I know what you mean. You won't believe this, but she hasn't had anything to drink.'

'She's very ... umm... energetic.'

'She hasn't been herself lately,' Jimmy says, and then adds, hesitantly, 'She hasn't been well, you see?'

'I see. I hope it's nothing serious. Do you want to talk about it?' Ricky says. And he sounds like he means it.

At this, Jimmy finds himself doing something he had thought impossible: pouring his heart out to this stranger, whose face he can hardly see in the darkness, whose surname he doesn't know. Voicing things he hasn't been able to tell his own family, or his own wife, starting with his mother's alcoholism and ending with the recent events.

'Last year, my worst nightmare came true,' Jimmy says at the end of his tale. 'My wife began to turn into my mother!'

Jimmy pauses to make sure that Ricky is still awake. He is, and is looking at Jimmy intently.

'At times I feel like a kid again, watching my mother lose the plot, at others I'm the dad, scolding my daughter for being naughty. I am no longer a husband. She is no longer my wife. On nights like this one, I don't even know who she is. And then she wonders why I'm not responsive in bed. I feel as if I'm sleeping with the ghost of my mother – even though she's not dead.'

'Oh dear. That must be pretty awful.'

'Shit, Ricky, I can't believe I just told you all that,' Jimmy says, apologetically. 'I didn't realise how much I needed to talk about it.'

'It's because you know we'll never see each other again, so your confidences are safe with me. You talk as much as you need to – but I need another smoke.' Ricky says, smiling while he rolls another cigarette. 'Go on.'

'Lately it occurred to me that maybe I was supposed to stay and deal with the situation at my parents' home, instead of escaping like I did. Maybe I was supposed to force Mum to get help earlier. A number of people would've been spared a lot of grief, including her. But I ran away instead, and that's why it's all coming back to me, and this time I have to deal with it. But you have no idea how much I find myself wishing that things would go back to the way they were eighteen months ago.'

'Look,' Ricky says, exhaling smoke, when he's sure that Jimmy is finished. 'I don't know much about manic depression, but I can relate to what you are saying from a different angle. I'm an engineer, you see, and I can tell you that from a scientific point of view, it's quite possible that your situation will settle down in time. You just need to stand back and be patient.'

'I'm not sure I follow, Rick.'

'Let's see,' Ricky says, clearing his throat, as if he is about to deliver a paper at a conference. 'Think of the placid surface of a lake being disrupted by someone throwing a stone in the water. There is a violent disturbance when the stone breaks the surface, and then you get the ripples. The bigger the stone, and the harder it hits, the larger the disturbance. But after a while, the water settles and it's as if the disruption never happened.'

'I appreciate what you're saying, Rick, but I doubt that disturbances in relationships can be as predictable as, err… disturbances in lakes.'

'Oh, but wave propagation is anything but predictable. I guess what I'm trying to say is that once the stone hits the water, there's nothing anyone can do to stop the ripples. You just have to ride the wave, until it settles of its own accord.

Because it will settle, Jimmy, one way or another. Every disturbance does.' He pauses for a few seconds, finishing his cigarette.

'You're right,' Jimmy says. 'My mother eventually settled.'

'See?' Ricky says, raising his eyebrow. 'Sometimes it's better to let things be, because no matter how hard you try to be in control, there will always be factors outside your power.'

'You have no idea how much I value what you just said, and your willingness to listen. I wish we had more time.'

'Maybe another day, Jimmy, if our paths cross again.'

'Next time you can tell me about your troubles,' Jimmy says, starting to get up.

'It's a date!' Ricky says, following Jimmy.

The men return to their different tables, without having exchanged phone numbers or emails, without empty promises to keep in touch.

Angie is back on her chair, her fringe stuck to her forehead, a look of concern in her eyes.

'There you are! I was worried thinking that you'd decided to go home. I haven't danced like this since my high school days; I just couldn't stop!'

'It's okay. Actually, I'm glad we came,' Jimmy says.

'How nice of you to say that just to please me,' Angie says, patting Jimmy on the hand. 'Anyway, I promised Mandy we'd give her a lift home, and she wants to go soon.' She points to a young brunette across the table, who waves at Jimmy.

While the girls talk nonstop in the front of the car, Jimmy, who had been more than willing to take the back seat, reflects on his conversation with Ricky.

Just sit back and be patient, Ricky had said; but Jimmy decides that, as comforting as Ricky's theory was, he isn't one to sit back. Yet, he hasn't been dealing with the situation either, he has been escaping from it, just like he did in his mother's case.

He had promised himself he would never leave Angie no matter what, but in a way, he already has.

After they drop Mandy off, Jimmy asks Angie when her next appointment with Dr Suenho is.

'Wednesday week. Why?'

'Can you change it to a Saturday? I'd like to come with you,' Jimmy says.

'But you work on Saturdays.'

'Not anymore,' Jimmy says, already feeling better.

❧

Jimmy is taken aback by how much Dr Suenho reminds him of his grandmother, Ruth. In fact, the resemblance is uncanny. The blue eyes, the pink cheeks, the spectacles, the slim pointy nose, the long grey hair neatly tied in a bun, even the way Dr Suenho nods empathetically at Angie, who seems to be on the verge of tears. His Nan used to nod like that when Jimmy's mother came to her for counsel when Jimmy was a child.

For the first half of the session, Jimmy sits next to Angie staring at the doctor with fascination. Angie does most of the talking – she's speaking about a book that Dr Suenho lent her. Her tone is one of vexation at first, but progressively turns anxious.

Jimmy had seen the book on Angie's bedside table: *An Unquiet Mind*. His heart had sunk when he read the subtitle: *A memoir of moods and madness*. On the front cover, at the centre of what seemed to be an abstract painting in black, grey and purple brushstrokes, was a photograph of the author as a young woman, taken against the light. Behind a curtain of long blonde hair, her face was distorted by an exaggerated grin, with teeth clenched and eyes tightly shut.

Jimmy found it hard to believe that it was the same person as the attractive, middle-aged woman depicted in black and white on the back cover, looking serene and reflective, her head tilted to the side and resting lightly on her index and middle fingers.

Angie had been trying some new clothes in front of the mirror, and had caught Jimmy's reflection as he studied the back cover of the book.

'When I'm finished with it, Mum wants to borrow it. After that, you're welcome to read it,' Angie had said, looking at him in the mirror.

'Sure,' Jimmy had muttered, quickly putting the book down.

In Dr Suenho's office, Angie's voice is rattling with emotion as she recalls passages from *An Unquiet Mind*.

'What about the time Dr Jamison was stopped by police, for drink driving, when in fact she was suffering from lithium intoxication? Or the way she threw books at walls because lithium blurred her vision so much that she couldn't read them? Or the time she almost overdose on lithium?'

'All that is true,' Dr Suenho says, in a soothing tone. 'But isn't it also true that towards the end of the book, Jamison admits that when her doctor finally manages to find her optimum dose, lithium allows her to lead a normal life?'

'I didn't get to that part. I couldn't go on reading that book, it scared me too much.' Angie says. 'You can't possibly say that my case is as acute as hers. You can't put me through the same ordeal.' Angie turns towards Jimmy, giving him a heartbreaking look. Tears are running down her cheeks.

'I'm not going to put you through anything, Angie,' Dr Suenho says, handing Angie a box of tissues. 'I'm simply offering you choices. Doing nothing is among your choices. It's not the one I'd recommend, but ultimately, it's up to you.'

Jimmy puts his hand on Angie's knee and squeezes it gently.

'Doctor,' Jimmy says. 'Could you explain to us exactly how lithium works in the treatment of Angie's condition?'

'I'm afraid its exact form of operation is not really known; it simply works, in most cases, to treat and prevent both depression and mania,' Dr Suenho says.

'I beg your pardon?' Jimmy says, with an incredulous tone.

Since the day, two weeks ago, that he decided to come and see Dr Suenho with Angie, Jimmy has tried to keep an open mind about both shrinks and lithium therapy. Angie had a lot of praise for her doctor, but she had nothing good to say about lithium. Until recently, all that Jimmy had known about this substance was that it was used to make rechargeable batteries.

In preparation for today's session, he had consulted an online dictionary of biology. What he read about lithium had not helped; particularly the references to it causing toxicity, cancer and birth defects. Jimmy had expected that Angie's doctor would be able to throw a little more light on the subject.

Dr Suenho, seeing that Jimmy's not impressed by the lack of a scientific explanation, puts her notepad down and picks up her black marker. Walking to the whiteboard, she writes 'John Cade' on it, explaining that Lithium was first used in the treatment of manic depressive illness by an Australian doctor named John Cade back in 1949.

'Unfortunately, Cade's experiments were rather ad hoc and he didn't keep proper statistics. It wasn't until the seventies that lithium became widely used thanks to the more methodical studies done by a Danish psychiatrist,' she says, writing the name Mogens Schou on the board. 'Schou ended up receiving all the credit for the discovery.'

She goes on to say that Dr Cade accidentally discovered that the urine of patients suffering from mania had a toxic element. Trying to pinpoint the toxin, he broke down the components of urea until he found a soluble salt, lithium urate. When he injected guinea pigs with it, to see if it caused toxicity, he discovered instead that it had a calming effect. After testing the lithium on himself for side effects, he began to use it with his manic-depressive patients with a high rate of success.

'That's all I can tell you, Jimmy,' Dr Suenho concludes, putting the marker down. 'It's like electroshock therapy. EST is still used today, because it's the only treatment that works for some cases of severe depression. No one knows how or why it works, it simply does.'

'Thanks Dr Suenho, that was very educative. Wasn't it, Ange?' Jimmy says, nudging Angie. She nods adamantly, her cheeks sparkling with tears. Jimmy turns back towards Dr Suenho.

'Still, it's clear that the prospect of lithium therapy is distressing Ange, and I'm not that comfortable with the idea myself. So, for the time being, and while we think about it, I'd like to support her decision to ride the wave without lithium.'

'In that case, I must emphasise that it's vital for Angie to continue seeing me every fortnight.' Dr Suenho says. 'And don't hesitate to contact me immediately if you detect any significant changes in Angie's moods, as the signs are often more obvious to other people than to the patients themselves.'

'Agreed, Ange?' Jimmy asks his wife.

'Agreed!' Angie says, sighing with relief.

Who would have thought, Angelica, that it would be Jimmy who would help us win this battle against the shrink? It is true that we should have expected him not to trust the medicine she recommended, when she could not even explain how it works. But we never expected him to come out with an expression like 'riding the wave'.

What a fitting metaphor. Riding the waves, Angelica, that is what we have been doing. Surfing, hand in hand, through a sea of new experiences, flying high above the water at times, and at others sinking into the depths of the ocean, defying the storm, exploring a range of emotions, colours, feelings and landscapes whose existence you did not even know of until last year.

Still, we must not give in to complacence. We have won this battle, but the war is far from over.

# ~ Wild ride ~

It's Friday and Angie is late for work for the second day in a row. The previous day she hadn't been able to find her car keys. After turning her place upside down, she realised that she'd locked them inside the car. It took her so long to remember where she kept the spare keys that she was nearly an hour late for work, and her boss hadn't been impressed.

Today, she leaves home earlier to make up for Thursday's lateness, but when she gets into the car and tries to start the engine, she discovers that the battery is dead. She must have left the lights on all night. Not for the first time. Hitting her forehead against the steering wheel, Angie swears under her breath. 'Shit, shit, fuck.'

These things are happening way too often. At first she laughed them off, but now she's becoming as impatient with herself as Jimmy is. He's constantly having a go at her, telling her that she'd misplace her head if she didn't have it screwed on. Lately, he's started leaving post-it notes stuck to the front door reminding her to turn the lights and the computer off before she leaves. He has also pointed out that she is swearing like a sailor. Angie, his old Angie, he had said, rarely said the "s" word, and would never utter the "f" word.

'I rang the NRMA and they said they'd be here in fifteen

minutes at most,' Angie explains to her boss over the telephone.

'I suppose we'll see you when you get here,' her boss says, with an audible sigh at the end.

No sooner has Angie hung up than the NRMA man arrives. It takes him less than five minutes to set everything up and jumpstart her car. Angie looks at her watch; it's only 9.30 am. If she hurries, she can make it to work before ten, when her busiest time starts. That should please Madam.

Speeding through the hilly back streets with the windows wound down, Angie suddenly recalls the Mad Mouse rollercoaster ride her father once took her on at the Royal Show in Adelaide. This is just as thrilling. She would've been seven then, as it was not long before he left. He had gone to Adelaide to close a deal with a winery and had taken his family with him. Angie had insisted on going on the rollercoaster – she'd never been on one. The carriages only took two people, and Norah had been relieved that there wasn't enough room for her, as she suffered from motion sickness.

'C'mon, ladybird, it's just you and me then,' Angie's father had said, lifting Angie up and depositing her in the carriage. They had screamed and screamed as they went down the slopes with their stomachs jumping all the way to their throats and the wind roaring in their ears. For a few minutes, if felt as if they were both seven years old.

Ridiculously pleased to have that feeling of exhilaration back, Angie takes her foot off the brake as she's going down a hill, to see how much faster she can go. She shouts 'Whoooaa,' at the top of her lungs, and races up the next hill.

Faster, Angelica! We can ride much faster than that. Elena's voice rises above Angie's screams of excitement.

Angie goes to press her foot down on the accelerator, but

in her light-headedness she brakes instead. The wheels lock and the car swirls 180 degrees, the brakes shrieking. Angie's exhilaration turns to panic as she tries to regain control of the wheel, with the landscape spinning around her. Finally the car comes to a stop at the bottom of the hill, facing the wrong way.

Breathing hard, Angie looks around with wild eyes. The car could have overturned. Another vehicle could have appeared on the other side of the road and they would inevitably have collided. She could have died. Someone else could have died.

Nearby, a woman peers over her fence, shaking her head. She's bringing her clothes in from the line as the sky is hanging menacingly low. A dog barks. A solitary car materialises at the top of the hill and descends slowly.

'Whoever gave you a license should be sued!' the man shouts as he swerves around Angie's car.

Shuddering, Angie pulls over to the side of the road and leans her forehead on the steering wheel. A part of her mind begins to understand why her condition can be life threatening. It's the part of her psyche that Elena hasn't been able to usurp, the part that made her cry at Tiger's place, the part that causes the nightmares, the part that makes her feel guilty because she has been hiding things from Dr Suenho and from Jimmy.

Elena stirs inside her, sensing that she's losing her grip over Angie.

Angie remembers what happened all those years ago at the Royal Adelaide Show. As soon as she got off the Mad Mouse and set her feet on firm ground, she had fallen down on her knees. Bending over, she had thrown up so violently that her parents had to take her back to the hotel, where she laid in bed for the rest of the day with a terrible case of motion sickness. She remembered the first part of that memory, one of the last recollections she had of her father, but she had forgotten, until now, the nasty end of the tale.

Too shaken to drive all the way to work, Angie parks the car at the nearest train station and catches the train, just as the grey skies open up and the rain begins to fall.

From behind the reception desk, Cheryl gives Angie a worried look when she walks into the office at ten-thirty.

'Angie, are you okay? You're pale as death!' Cheryl says.

'Thanks! Had a bitch of a morning, but you just made me feel a whole lot better.'

'Oh dear! I'm just being honest. In fact, I think we better cancel our date for drinks tonight. You look like you need to get some rest, and you won't have any of that here. Wait until you see your in-tray. And,' Cheryl says, lowering her voice, 'the ice queen said she wanted to see you the minute you walked in.'

'Maybe I'll need that drink after she's finished with me,' Angie says, trying to sound cheerful. Heading to her boss's office, she feels as if she's marching to the abattoir.

The ice queen is colder than ever. She doesn't even ask Angie to sit down.

'Angie, as you are no doubt aware, your six-month contract finished in July, but we've been keeping you on because Cindy extended her maternity leave until October. I'm afraid, though, that we can't keep you any longer. You've become far too unreliable in the last month or so, and your attention to detail and accuracy also leave a lot to be desired. Not to mention your punctuality.'

She hands Angie a piece of paper, which Angie assumes is her notice. It isn't. It's a media release Angie typed the day before, and it's riddled with errors, which have been circled with red pen, no doubt by the queen herself.

'I've spoken to the personnel agency this morning, and they will be sending someone else as of next week.'

Angie stands speechless in front of her boss's desk, clutching the appallingly typed media release. She has never been dismissed from a job in her life. In all her years in the work force, Angie Fletcher has been renowned among her employers and colleagues for the very qualities that the ice queen has just said she lacks: punctuality, accuracy, and reliability. 'One word would sum up all of Angie's attributes,' her last employer had written, in the reference he gave Angie when she left the photo lab last year. 'Professionalism.'

Back at her desk, Angie stares at the black cursor pulsating on the blank page of her computer screen for a long time, trying to find the motivation to start typing, and to keep on typing until the end of what will be her last day at the agency.

What's happening to her? When did she cross the bridge from being the personification of professionalism to being so utterly incompetent? All this job had required of her was that she turn up for work on time and type accurately.

'How did you go with the ice queen?' Cheryl asks, peering over Angie's partition. She's on her lunch break, eating a banana. Angie looks up, unable to answer. Cheryl answers her own question. 'It can't have gone that well. You look like you are about to cry.'

'It's nothing,' Angie says, swallowing the lump in her throat. She didn't make a scene in front of the ice queen and she won't make one now – this is the time to prove that she still has at least a scrap of professionalism left in her. She looks at the ceiling, blinking several times. 'I've got something in my eye, that's all.'

'I see,' Cheryl says, depositing her banana peel in Angie's bin. 'Listen, I still think we better cancel drinks tonight. You really are looking a bit tired.'

'You're right. I'll have to stay back, anyway, to get through all this,' Angie says, pointing to the pile of paper in her tray. For all it's worth, she will not leave tonight until it's all done, and she will check everything twice to make sure there are no mistakes whatsoever.

'We'll have drinks next week then,' Cheryl says, and goes back to her desk.

That night, when nearly everyone has gone home for the day, Angie packs the few personal things that she has brought to this office in a small black cardboard box she found in the stationery cabinet. A personalised mug, a pencil holder, a few classical CDs. Next Thursday someone else will be sitting in her chair and in two weeks nobody will remember her, not even Cheryl. Unfortunately, it will take Angie longer to forget the first job she has been fired from.

Angie wants to call Sinéad, tell her about the terrible day she's had, but she feels she has let her friend down in yet another way. It had been Sinéad who had recommended Angie to the personnel agency that found her this position.

&

Norah arrives home at about eight o'clock, laden with groceries, to find Angie sitting on her veranda, waiting in the dark. Her hair and shoulders are damp from the rain, and on her lap there's a black shoebox.

'I've been waiting for forty-five minutes!' Angie snaps, without even saying hello.

'How was I supposed to know you were coming?' Norah

says, putting the bags down on the floor so she can open the door.

'Come in and get dry, you're going to catch a cold. Anyway, to what do I owe the pleasure of this spontaneous visit?'

Norah can't remember the last time Angie dropped in unannounced. She hardly sees her daughter these days – and with Jimmy working double shifts, she hasn't seen much of him either.

'I've just had the worst day,' Angie says, following Norah inside the house, carrying the box under her arm and leaving it on the kitchen counter. While Norah unpacks her groceries, Angie starts to pace around in circles, waving her arms. 'The car wouldn't start this morning, I was late for work, my boss told me not to come back next week, I stayed back late, and when I got home, desperate to have a bath and get into bed, I found that I'd locked myself out. I came to get the spare keys.'

'Your boss asked you not to come back next week?' Norah repeats, as if that were the only thing Angie had just said. And then, pointing to the box that Angie has left on the kitchen counter, 'and you still went and bought yourself yet another pair of shoes?'

'What?' Angie says, stopping in her tracks.

'Your husband is killing himself working to cope with all your expenses, and even on the day that you lose the little income you had, you go and buy yourself another pair of shoes?'

'What are you, Jimmy's accountant or something?' Angie exclaims. This is the last straw.

'Someone has to look after him,' Norah says, giving her back to Angie to put some cans away in the pantry.

At that moment, Angie ceases to see Norah and her surroundings – all the frustration, fright, anger, disappointment and humiliation of the last twelve hours melt into one. All she can see is red, and bitter red bile comes out of her mouth.

'And what do you know about looking after a husband?' she hisses in a tone that Norah has never heard before. Norah turns around, looking at her daughter with wide eyes. Angie goes on, in a trembling, hysterical voice. 'If you'd looked after your own husband, he wouldn't have left us the way he did. He'd still be around, and I wouldn't have grown up without a father. So don't you try and lecture me about how to look after Jimmy. I'm sure I'm doing a better job than you did with dad.'

Norah gasps, and collapses into one of the kitchen chairs, too shocked even to cry. After all these years, the truth has come out. Her daughter blames her, has always blamed her, for driving her beloved father away.

Angie takes a few steps towards Norah, covering her mouth with both her hands.

'Mum...' she mutters. 'I'm sorry, I didn't--'

'That's enough, Angie,' Norah says, standing up, tall and dignified. She holds her hand in front of her face to stop Angie from getting closer, just like Neo in *The Matrix* did when he stopped bullets in mid-air. 'Don't you say you didn't mean it, because you did. If you knew the whole story, if you had ever bothered to ask, you'd feel very differently. But I'm not going to even attempt to give you any explanations now, given the appalling way you've been treating me. I'm your mother, and you owe me a little more respect.'

'But I-- ' Angie begins, then realises that she can't unsay what has been said. Worst of all, she can't *unfeel* what she has just discovered she's always felt.

Norah gestures towards the door. 'I would like you to leave now. Your spare keys are hanging from the key holder over there.'

Before leaving, Angie picks up the black box, and opening it, she spills the contents out over the kitchen counter.

'It wasn't even a new pair of shoes. It's the few things that I'd taken to the office. I brought the stupid box because I wanted to return your CDs.' And she leaves, grabbing the keys on the way out, leaving the mug, the pencil holder, the soundtrack of Amadeus, a collection of Chopin's preludes, and *The Marriage of Figaro* behind.

On Saturday, when Jimmy comes back from the newsagent with the Herald, he's also carrying a note addressed to both of them.

'It's from your mum – she left it in our letterbox. She's going to spend a few weeks at your grandmother's and wants us to water her plants.' Jimmy says, leaving the note on the table. 'Unusual for your mother to make such an impromptu trip. I hope your grandma is okay.'

'Grandma's fine,' Angie assures him. 'Mum had been planning to go visit her next month, but something obviously sped up her plans – probably last night's argument.'

Over breakfast, Angie had explained to Jimmy that her employment at the advertising agency had been cut short and that she would speak to the personnel company first thing on Monday to see if they had something else. She had also mentioned that she had had a disagreement with her mother, without elaborating on the details.

Contrary to what Norah had anticipated, Jimmy didn't seem too worried about the abrupt ending of Angie's contract.

'Oh well. It was only a two-day-a-week typing job, Ange,' he said, to Angie's disbelief.

It was only as he had been walking out the door to get the paper that he had voiced what he really thought.

'Perhaps when the university semester ends, you can start looking for full-time work.' He had closed the door behind him before Angie could reply.

A few days later, a letter from Norah arrives in the mail, addressed to Angie. Angie finds it in the letterbox when she comes home from university, at about four o'clock in the afternoon. It's several pages long, written in Norah's round longhand.

Norah has used the stationery that Angie gave her last Mother's Day: smooth, cream coloured paper, with a border of golden staves peppered with musical notes.

12th August, 1999

Dear Angie,

I'm writing this sitting at your grandfather's desk. The lemon trees outside the window are looking cold and bare, but inside it's nice and warm, with flames crackling in the fireplace. Anyway, I'm not writing to tell you about the lemon trees or the fire.

After last Friday's episode I decided to come and spend some time in the safe haven of your grandmother's home. I'm one of those daughters who turn to and not away from their mothers when they need healing. We have spent the last few nights talking until the early hours of the morning, and I have come to the conclusion that it is time I clarified a few things with you. I've waited for too long for the 'right' moment and it has never arrived.

But first, I want to know what has happened to my daughter. Who was that person, screaming at me the other night? Who was that woman who took me lingerie shopping the other day, and was blatantly flirting with strangers in front of me? Was that the daughter I brought up in the very best way I could?

How much of this is your illness, and how much is the real you coming through? I read that one of the characteristics of bipolar disorder is that during the 'highs' you lose your inhibitions. This means that the things you say, hurtful things like what you said to me the other night, are what you really feel, but would not normally say aloud. So, now I know where I stand with you – but you ... you don't know how wrong you are.

I always knew you had lots of questions about your father's leaving, but you never asked them. I assumed you preferred not to know. I realise now that you came to your own (wrong) conclusions a long time ago, and didn't think it necessary to seek clarification.

So, where to start? Let's go back to the inhibitions. This person, this uninhibited woman you have become, liberal, flippant, overtly sexual, reminds me a lot of your Aunt Jo, and I don't like it. She was the sort of woman who had no scruples about sleeping with married men. And you know what? With your hair short and curly the way you have it now, and the provocative way you dress these days, you even resemble Jo physically, more than you ever resembled me.

I am afraid for you, Angie, of what you might do.

Last year, after I told you that Jo killed herself, I waited for you to ask me the reason, but you never did. Perhaps you didn't care or perhaps it's part of your character, not to ask questions whose answers you know are going to hurt. But here it is, anyway: when Jo left for Milan, she was pregnant, and the father of the child was a married man with whom, she told us in her suicide letter, she'd been trying to break up for a long time but couldn't. An addiction, she called him. By escaping to Milan she wanted to start a new life, just her and her baby, but then she had a miscarriage and when she lost her baby girl she couldn't go on living, and ... you now know the rest.

What you don't know, Angie, is that the married man she was having the affair with was your father. There, I said it. The secret I've been guarding all these years, to protect you, yes you, because of the way you cherished your memories of him, the way you adored him as a child, the way he adored you in return. Why, you even decided to bear a permanent tribute to your father on your own skin! I wonder what he would think of that, of you having a tattoo of his pet name for you.

Believe it or not, I was also protecting him, because God knows he paid the price for his mistakes. Not only did he have to carry Jo's death in his conscience for the rest of his life, but he also had to give you up, the apple of his eye, his Ladybird, and that must have been his greatest punishment.

I would never have known but for the fact that he couldn't live with the guilt. When he found out what had happened to Jo, huge chunks of hair fell from his head – he went almost bald overnight. Good catholic that he was, he confessed his sins to me after Jo's funeral, before he left. Perhaps now you will understand why I had the nervous breakdown, as we called it in those days. Contrary to what everybody assumed, he didn't leave me because of the breakdown. The breakdown happened because he left.

Your father said that Jo seduced him. They had run into each other during one of his interstate trips, had a few drinks, and one thing led to another. He had tried to break the affair off several times, but Jo would threaten to tell me, and she even threatened to kill herself! She wasn't well in the head, he said. He had been afraid she would actually carry out her threats, which she did in the end. That was his version of the story. We never heard Jo's true version. The secrets, the lies, they were necessary, was all she said in her letter.

So, now you know that you father didn't leave me because I didn't look after him – God knows I was a very devoted wife. But now that I think about it, you may be right after all – if I had been better, you know, 'under the covers', perhaps he wouldn't have gotten involved with Jo in the first place. But I couldn't compete with her. She thrived on the sexual liberation of that era, while I remained caught in the previous generation's conservatism. Funnily enough, until recently, you were also a very conservative girl, and as such, you married a man with similar values.

The day that you took me lingerie shopping, you, my once conservative daughter, spent a fortune on things that I thought only prostitutes wore (I still wonder why you took me instead of your friend Sinéad). My hair stands on end as the similarities between the 'new' you and my dead sister become more evident.

In trying to organise my thoughts and my memories to write this letter, what your father said about Josephine 'not being well in the head' kept coming back to me. Now that I think about it, in the last few years of her life, her behaviour was rather odd. The way she couldn't keep a job or a relationship, the way she couldn't manage her money, the way she drank and partied as if there were no tomorrow, the way she dressed, the way she would be exuberant for months and then turn suddenly demure for the next few. How she changed boyfriends, her promiscuity, not to mention her illicit affairs, her suicidal tendencies, other things we don't even know about. And I've come to the conclusion that your aunt was suffering from the same condition that you're suffering, and because it remained undiagnosed, it spiralled out of control.

In the book you lent me I read that although they

haven't yet found a 'bipolar gene' to prove conclusively that bipolar disorder is genetic, research done on the family histories of people with this condition indicates that it's inherited. What will become of you, Angie, if you continue to refuse treatment? You are both fortunate and unfortunate in having been diagnosed with this illness. Unfortunate to have it in the first place, but fortunate to know that you have it, so you can do something about it before it's too late.

I only say this because I love you. For the last year or so we haven't been able to communicate face to face. You seldom come to see me these days and when you do, it's to mistreat me. I don't know how much more of that I can take, hence I'm telling you these things in a letter. It's up to you what you do with this knowledge.

God bless you and guide you always; you know where I am if you need me.

Mum

Sitting at her dining table, Angie braces herself for the downpour of emotion no doubt about to hit her, but nothing happens. It's only after she reads Norah's letter a second time that the storm is unleashed. She starts weeping so violently that her whole body shakes, and her tears smear Norah's words.

She weeps for her father and Josephine, for her unborn sister... for her poor mother. Aunt Jo and her baby dead, Angie's father as good as dead, and Norah wounded for life – all casualties of the same disease that is threatening to ruin Angie's own life. Just as Josephine had seduced her own sister's husband, Angie – no, not Angie but Elena – has been intent on seducing her husband's best friend, without considering the consequences.

Not satisfied with having an affair with Dave in the pages

of Angie's written fantasies, Elena won't stop until Tiger, the flesh and bone Tiger, has also succumbed to her charms.

'That excuse is wearing thin,' Angie hears Sinéad say, inside her head. Or is it Dr Suenho? It's an indistinguishable voice, perhaps the voice of her conscience. 'It's time you owned up to your actions. There is no Elena – it is you, it has been you all along, and you know it. Fortunately for you, Tiger either has more willpower than your father did, or he simply doesn't find you attractive.'

Hearing this, Angie is overcome by a bout of frenzy. She starts walking around the table, holding her head with both hands. She calls her mother's name, her aunt's name, and then realises that she can't think of her father's name, the name that hasn't been spoken by her or anyone around her for almost twenty-four years. When she's completed one turn around the table she goes around again in the opposite direction, until she remembers.

It's Reginald. Reginald J. McMillan. The 'J' stands for Jacob. McMillan is Angie's maiden name. She repeats it over and over again.

Reginald Jacob McMillan, the cheating husband. Reginald McMillan, the man who slept with his wife's twin sister. Reggie McMillan, the man who drove five hours to say goodbye to his beloved seven-year-old daughter, wearing a baseball cap to hide the bald patches caused by remorse.

Angie picks up the phone, starts dialing her mother's number, but remembers that Norah's not home. With shaky hands she looks up Grandma Pearl's telephone number in her address book, but then decides that this is not something she can talk about over the phone. She wants to ask for forgiveness, to cry on her mother's shoulder, to ask all the questions she has never asked. She looks at her watch.

It's not quite five o'clock; she could make it to the Sapphire Coast before midnight.

She scribbles a message for Jimmy and leaves it on the table – 'Gone to my grandmother's – will call you when I get there.'

Still distraught, she throws the letter, her address book and a change of clothes into an overnight bag, climbs in her car, and starts driving against the afternoon sunlight. She has never driven all the way to her grandmother's, and it's not long before she takes a wrong turn. Also, she notices that a white car has been following her, ever since she left home. There's no doubt about it; no matter how many turns she takes, the white car remains tenaciously behind. She remembers seeing this car before, parked outside her place. Someone is following her, and this is not the first time. A private detective? A stalker?

For a moment, she forgets about the letter inside her bag, busy trying to lose her stalker in the traffic – she's scared, but also excited. She drives to a busy road, in the opposite direction to the one she should be travelling in, and begins to shift lanes to confuse him (she's sure it's a him although it's hard to see). At the same time she tries to find a sign with a street name so that she can work out where she is, shielding her eyes with one hand to protect them from the blinding sunlight.

Too late does Angie realise that a van has suddenly stopped in front of her to turn into a laneway. She slams on the brakes, making them shriek, but the wheels lock and the car helplessly slides towards the back of the van in slow motion. Angie braces herself for impact. The white car behind brakes in time, swerves around them and continues on its way, a young woman behind the wheel.

Angie collides with the van. Her body jerks forward with the impact and is then pulled backwards by the seatbelt. Angie sits still for a moment, leaning back in her seat. The first thing she thinks is that the damage to her car can't be too bad – fortunately, she wasn't driving very fast, and the impact hadn't felt that strong. The second thing she thinks is that Dr Suenho had once said that paranoid delusions, such as the idea of being followed, are signs that hypomania has progressed into the next, more dangerous stage.

The van's young driver taps on Angie's window, gesturing for her to drive to the side of the road, so that they can exchange details. Getting out of her car, Angie starts crying and shaking. She tells the young man repeatedly, that she's never had an accident before, that she doesn't even know what to do, that she didn't even see his blinker because the sun was blinding her.

The van has a scratch above the bumper bar, and the number plate is slightly bent. The driver, seeing Angie's distress, is very sympathetic. He thinks that it will only cost a couple of hundred dollars to repair his vehicle, that it may not even be necessary for her to access her insurance, and it's definitely not worth calling the police.

Norah's old car, on the other hand, looks a lot worse than Angie had initially thought. The van's tow bar has made a big hole at the front of the car, puncturing the radiator and concertinaing it against the engine. Sitting by the side of the road, it looks like a mortally wounded animal, bleeding green coolant on the ground.

After the van drives away, Angie walks two blocks to the nearest public phone, and calls Jimmy on his mobile – he's working till eleven.

'I had a car accident, but the important thing is that I'm

okay,' she says, quickly, between sobs.

'You know, Ange, ever since your mother gave you that car, I've been fearing this call ... ' Jimmy is saying when the line drops out.

Angie only has enough change for one more phone call. She gives herself a few seconds to calm down and prepare to receive the full blow of Jimmy's wrath. Taking a deep breath, she looks at her surroundings, and recognises the shopping mall where she's standing. She's managed to drive to Rozelle, and she's less than ten minutes away from Tiger's place. She decides to call him instead, on the off chance that he will be home at 6.00 pm on a weekday.

Tiger happens to be home, although he was about to get in the shower, change and go out to the local pub to meet some friends. When he picks up the phone and hears Angie crying, telling him she has just had a car accident round the corner from his place, and that she has no idea what to do, he says: 'Stay right where you are, Angie; I'll be there in fifteen.'

Tiger soon arrives in his dented executive car, still wearing his business clothes. In a matter of minutes, armed with his mobile phone, he organises for a tow truck to take Angie's car to a local panel beater, calls them to warn them that it's coming, and contacts Angie's insurance company. Once the car has been towed away, he drives the distraught Angie to a cafe where he buys her a coffee, and lets her talk and sob to her heart's content.

'I know it was my fault,' she cries, embarking on an incoherent spiel similar to that she gave the van driver, 'but I was lost, and the sun was in my eyes, and the white car behind, and the van, stopped without warning, and I slammed on the brakes, but the car slid, and slid ... and there was nothing I could do ...'

'It's okay, Angie. They say that any crash that you can walk away from is a good crash. Besides, the police didn't get involved, so you haven't lost any points.' Tiger tries to console her, to no avail.

'It's not even my car, it's not even my car,' she keeps repeating, blowing her nose on serviettes while her coffee goes cold. The car is still in her mother's name.

When she's calmer, Angie tells Tiger about Norah's letter, and Norah's fears that her illness might end up getting out of control, like Josephine's had. Tiger orders another round of coffees and they talk for the next hour.

At about eight, he drops Angie at her place.

'Thanks for all your help, Tiger,' Angie says, feeling strangely relaxed. Norah's letter, the accident and everything else seem somewhat distant, as if they had happened a long time ago. She has finally resigned herself to the fact that she will have to go on medication, and this decision has brought her some peace of mind. 'You've been so patient with me. I never apologised to you for my recent loopy behaviour.'

'You have nothing to apologise for, Angie. No offence, but if I was to run a loopy behaviour contest among my friends, you wouldn't win first, or even second prize. And today, accident or no accident, you seem a lot more – sober, for lack of a better word. Anyway, it's good to see the old Angie back.'

'I wish you could stay to help me diffuse the situation a bit. Jimmy's going to go ballistic. Thank God my mum is not around tonight. It's her car, you know?'

'You know I can't stay, Angie. It would only make things worse. But you'll be right. Surely Jimmy and your mum understand that accidents happen. Goodbye, Angie,' Tiger says, leaning over to give Angie a kiss on the cheek.

She turns around to face him, and her eyes are filled with tears.

'What's the matter?' Tiger asks.

'I don't know why, but I have the feeling this goodbye is for good. Anyway, it's probably better that way.'

'What are you talking about, Angie? You can call me any time you need me. I've told you that before.'

'I'll try not to. Thanks again, Tiger – and goodbye,' Angie says. She gets out of Tiger's car and walks into the house without looking back.

~

'You call me to say you had an accident, and then you hang up on me?' Jimmy says to Angie as soon as she walks in. He's eating beans on toast, still dressed in his work clothes: a grey jumper, jeans splattered with ink, black steel-capped boots.

Angie starts. She hadn't expected him to be home, not for another few hours. She thought she'd have some time to prepare for his arrival, although she had been unsure whether he'd be furious or sympathetic – it was a bit hard to tell with him these days.

He had been so supportive about her reluctance to take lithium, and yet had taken to leaving her notes reprimanding her for silly things like forgetting to turn the lights off. He had been almost dismissive when she told him about losing her job, but tonight, when she needs support, he's livid.

'I was talking to myself for five minutes before I realised you weren't even on the line. I waited for you to call me back, worried sick about you, and nothing. I called home an hour later, nothing. So I came home early to check that you've made it home safely and instead of finding you I found a note saying that you've gone to your grandma's. To your grandma's, for God's sake! Don't you know how far it is? You've never driven that far before!'

'I didn't hang up the phone. You dropped out! I told you I was okay. And I only had enough change for --' Angie tries to explain but Jimmy interrupts her.

'You hung up on me, Angie, no use denying it. You hung up because you knew I would tell you what you need to hear but don't want to - that you shouldn't be driving in the state you are in, that you are a menace to yourself and others. And haven't you heard of people walking away from a crash only to collapse later?'

Angie sees that there is no use in trying to explain the circumstances to Jimmy. He's convinced that she had the accident because she was driving recklessly or speeding maniacally, and because her judgement was, and is, impaired. And he's not completely wrong. No one in their right mind decides to drive such a long distance in the state of mind she had been in. No one in their right mind becomes convinced that they're being followed just because a car remains behind their own for a few blocks.

Mentally and physically exhausted, Angie leans on the door and slides down until she's sitting on the floor, a heap of incongruent emotions, feeling the last of Elena's spirit fleeing her body, leaving her hollow and limp. Holding her head with both hands, as she had earlier in the afternoon, she starts to cry; the peace and composure she felt only a few minutes ago are completely gone.

'Yes, you're right, Jimmy. You win, I give up, I need help. I need medication because I'm not responsible for my actions any longer, and I'm a menace to others and myself. I thought I could beat this on my own, but it's taking control of me, of my life, of my actions, and I can't fight it any longer. You win, I lose.'

Jimmy looks at his defeated wife, sitting on the floor, bawling like a baby, and he doesn't know what to say. Finally, he takes a step towards Angie, offering his hand to help her up.

'Nobody has won, Angie,' he says in a much calmer tone. 'I'm sorry for being such an arsehole. It wasn't the best way to show you that I care, that I was genuinely worried about you. Let's order some pizza and you can tell me what happened.'

Over dinner, Angie tells Jimmy everything, starting with last week's near accident, then going onto her poor performance at work, the true nature of her argument with Norah, the letter, her father, Josephine, the white car. The only detail she omits is that she had chosen to ring Tiger with the last of her change because she knew he'd be more sympathetic. She remembers what Tiger said: telling Jimmy would only make matters worse.

After washing the dishes, Jimmy goes to bed, saying that he needs a good night's sleep. It will take him a while to digest all the information that Angie has given him, and to understand how a man could betray his wife with her sister – her twin sister, for God's sake. It's almost incestuous. He's still shaking his head when he closes the bedroom door.

Sitting cross-legged on the sofa, not in the least tired, Angie spends a long time feeling infinitely sorry for her husband. It was hard enough for him to have unwittingly married a nutcase. Now he has discovered that her entire family is completely screwed up. It's no wonder he gives mixed signals and is inconsistent in his responses. It is a wonder that he's still around.

Shaking her head free of these thoughts, Angie decides

that she will wait until Norah returns to speak with her face to face, but there's one person she wants to speak with tonight.

She dials Sinéad's number. As soon as she hears her friend's sleepy voice at the other end of the line, she starts to unravel the whole story once again, beginning with her dismissal from the agency last week. This time she doesn't cry; she has run out of tears. When she's finished, it's Sinéad who's almost crying.

'Holy Mary,' Sinéad says. 'Oh, Angie, you've had such a horrible couple of weeks! I wish I'd been there with you, when you needed me. When you started avoiding me I realised you thought I was a judgmental bitch, and it's true I probably sounded like one. I just didn't want you to end up doing something you'd regret later. I'm sorry to have hurt you.'

'I'm the one who needs to apologise. To you, to mum, to Jimmy, to Tiger, to everybody. What a mess I've made of things.'

'Enough of apologies. The important thing is that you've made up your mind about treatment, like your mother said in her letter, before it's too late.'

'I think it might be too late already, Sinéad.' Angie says. Her voice breaks this time.

'What do you mean?'

'Another depression is around the corner. It's inevitable, unstoppable, and I can't run away from it. And, to be honest, this time I'm not sure I can survive it.'

'Don't give me that defeatist bullshit. Of course you can, and you will!' Sinéad says, resolutely.

# ~ Postcards from the dark side ~

**From Dr Suenho's records, 20th August 1999**

Patient soft-spoken and subdued, clearly on her way down. Admits that she's been experiencing paranoid delusional thoughts – had been convinced she was being followed while driving, which resulted in her having a relatively minor but traumatic car accident.

After uncovering some issues in her family's past (which seem to confirm my suspicions that bipolar disorder runs in her family), patient has agreed to lithium therapy. She would like to start therapy when the university semester finishes, just in case the side effects of lithium affect her concentration and attention span and interfere with her studies. She says that she couldn't bear to fail at university as well as at everything else.

**Letter from Jimmy to Norah, 27th August 1999**

Dear Norah,

I'm sorry you couldn't talk with Angie when we spoke on the phone the other night. She has been going to bed rather early. I don't mean to worry you, but I think she's going downhill again. The doctor had to put her back on the antidepressants. She has agreed to start taking lithium, starting in November. I'm still wary about that particular treatment, and have asked her doctor to please take one more look into the alternatives.

Anyway, the reason I'm writing is that the car insurance company finally got back to us regarding the assessment. I'm afraid your old car has been written off. Attached is the cheque for $2,500 that they sent; it's in your name, since the car insurance was still in your name. It's not bad, I guess, considering that the car was twelve years old and you were only offered $1,500 when you wanted to trade it in, before you decided to give it to Angie.

Angie and I would like you to have the money, as we will not be replacing the car. Maybe you and your mother can go on a holiday or something. I seem to remember that Pearl wanted to visit the Great Barrier Reef.

Looking forward to seeing you soon,
Jimmy

## Angie's diary, September 3rd, 1999

So, the spring has finally arrived, and instead of being high as a kite – as Dr Suenho feared – I'm back in the pits. To top it all off, I managed to write the car off, and I hadn't realised until now how much I've come to depend on it. I'm housebound, motherless, jobless and more isolated than ever.

Went to the physio the other day – I have a nagging pain in my shoulder, as a result of the accident. I was lying down on her massage table, and she was rubbing my shoulder when, just making conversation, she asked me something like 'And how's life been for you lately?' Next thing I was bawling my eyes out and she didn't know what to do. I'm so embarrassed I don't think I'll be going back.

**From Dr Suenho's records, 10th of September, 1999**

Patient evidently depressed. Prone to tears and unable to concentrate on her studies. Disappointed in herself and distressed because she believes that she is letting everybody down. Afraid that the damage she's inflicted on some of her relationships is beyond repair. She thinks that she has completely alienated her mother and it won't be long before the same happens with her 'long suffering' husband.

Increased medication to 100 mg a day.

**Angie's diary, September 24th, 1999**

Mum's back and she was over the other night for dinner. At the sight of her, tanned from her holiday in Cairns, I burst into tears. Couldn't say any of the things I wanted to say. Ended up locking myself in my room, crying. Jimmy told me that she went home without eating.

Sinéad visits regularly. Sometimes she stays for dinner. She and Jimmy are getting along better. I see them talking, but can't hear what they're saying. They belong to a different dimension.

The personnel agency has managed to get me a placement until December. It's at a marketing company. Packaging material for a nation-wide promotion. I spend three mornings a week by myself in a storeroom, counting leaflets. Stuffing them in envelopes and sticking on labels. Even this menial job can be hard some mornings. But it's better than staying home staring at the walls. Have to catch the train and a bus to get there. Takes me over an hour each way. It would only take twenty minutes driving. I miss the car terribly.

In the afternoons I turn up for class and sit there like a

zombie. Can't participate in any discussions. Haven't been doing my readings or assignments for weeks. It doesn't help that I chose a course in Third World politics. Couldn't have chosen anything gloomier than that. Stupid, stupid me.

Just re-read what I wrote. Even in this diary, I only seem to be able to write basic, short sentences. That's when I manage to write anything at all.

Four words, which Sinéad thinks come from the bible, keep me going.

*This too, shall pass.*

### From Dr Suenho's records, 15th October, 1999

Patient didn't stop crying throughout the session. Has been unable to complete her assignments at university and requested that I write her a letter certifying that she has severe depression, in order to obtain special consideration. Issued certificate and increased dose of medication to 150mg a day.

I gave her information on a drug we have not considered before, sodium valproate, an anticonvulsant which has been successfully used in the treatment of manic depression as an alternative to lithium. Patient will need medical tests to check that she doesn't have a tendency to liver disease or ornithine transcarbamylase deficiency, which would prevent her from taking this medication.

### Angie's diary, 30th October 1999

This comes from the sodium valproate information leaflet that Dr Suenho gave me:

Sodium Valproate is used to control epilepsy. It may also

be used to control mania, a mental condition with episodes of overactivity, elation or irritability. It belongs
to a group of medicines called anticonvulsants. These
medicines are thought to work by controlling brain chem-
icals which send signals to nerves so that seizures do
not happen.

**From Dr Suenho's records, 15th November 1999**

Patient still depressed but stable. She has been granted
special consideration at university and has been given until
the end of the year to complete her assignments.

After lengthy consultation with her family she has agreed
to start taking sodium valproate, starting immediately on
200mg a day.

## ~ The Law of Gravity ~

By late November, Angie's mood begins to improve with the help of the treatment. Sinéad and Jimmy work together to help Angie finish her university assignments, while Norah resumes the housekeeping role she took the previous year, helping Angie with the cooking and the cleaning.

Norah doesn't mention her letter or its contents, remembering what she told herself last year, when she burnt Josephine's suicide note: some things are better left alone. Besides, Jimmy has filled her in on the circumstances of Angie's car accident, and Norah is aware that the letter could very well have been its cause.

While staying at Pearl's, Norah had gone to mass with her mother every Sunday, and one of the Pastor's sermons had made a deep impression on her. He had talked about reconciliation, and had said that sometimes it's necessary to accept the fact that certain disagreements may never be resolved, that once something has been broken it might never be the same as before. Once you acknowledge this, it becomes easier to reconcile and to forgive, or at least to move on. 'Reconciliation,' he had said, 'does not mean restoration.'

Norah no longer wishes for things to go back to the way they were before the awakening of Angie's latent demons.

She just wants to reconcile. Angie hasn't asked for forgiveness, but she's pleasant enough when Norah is around, always thanking her for her help. She is also very distant, but Norah tells herself that Angie has been somewhat distant from everybody, even Sinéad. It's evident to Norah that even though her daughter is much better, she's still not completely recovered.

Norah, like Jimmy, has warmed to Sinéad, having seen her dedication to Angie. Not only has Sinéad helped Angie complete her university assignments, but she's also determined to help Angie find a part-time job, as the end of her casual employment at the marketing agency is imminent.

❧

Sinéad arrives at Angie's place one Monday afternoon in early December, with the local paper under her arm, saying that she has seen an advertisement for a job with 'Angie's name written all over it'. While Angie boils the kettle to make tea, Sinéad spreads the paper out on the dining table.

'It's managing a section in a specialised bookshop – collectors' books. It's only a few stops down your train line, so you can easily get there by public transport,' Sinéad says, running her finger down the newspaper page until she finds the advertisement in question. 'It asks for experience in retail management and customer service, and "a passion for books". It's perfect for you!' She pauses, as if having second thoughts. 'Pity it's full-time. But, if they really, really like you, they might be willing to make it a job-share position.'

'Actually, Jimmy has been hinting for months that it would be good for me to go back to full-time work,' Angie says, without much enthusiasm. She sets a tray with a steaming teapot, a plate of biscuits, two mugs, sugar and milk down on the table. 'I don't think he can cope working double shifts for much longer, and he's intent on sticking to our original plan of paying off our mortgage in ten years, even though our circumstances have changed.'

'When are the ten years up?' Sinéad asks.

'Next year.'

'But – what about your studies?'

'It's probably better that I go back to studying part-time, taking one or two subjects at the most. I never, ever want to repeat my most recent experience – I feel I've cheated, with you and Jimmy practically writing all three assignments for me.'

'Rubbish!' Sinéad says, making a dismissive gesture. 'We just gave you a hand putting them down on paper – you had done all the research already.'

'Anyway, show me that ad again. I guess it would make Jimmy happy if I made the effort to apply.'

Two days later it's Sinéad who ends up writing Angie's application for the job at the bookshop. The applications close at the end of the week and after struggling for hours, Angie has been unable to compose a decent letter. On the way home, Sinéad personally drops the envelope into the express-post box.

One week later Angie receives a call from a woman with an Italian accent, asking her to attend an interview the following Monday, at the Southern Cross Bookshop. It is two blocks away from the train station, next to the medical centre. Angie will be seeing Joe Speranza, the owner.

When Angie hangs up, she's more terrified than excited. What will she do, what will she wear, what will she say? She hasn't been to a formal job interview for years, and in her current state, she's afraid of making a fool of herself. Sinéad, on the other hand, is beside herself when Angie tells her over the phone.

'I told you this job had your name on it!'

'You applied for it. You should go for the interview.'

'I would, honestly. I'd love nothing more than to have a job at a bookshop. But I can't work full-time on my student visa.'

The entire interview, much like everything else in her life right now, is a blur in Angie's mind. Most of what was said, what was asked, and the last name of the man who interviewed her, elude her. On the train home, she remembers vaguely that the pay and the hours had seemed reasonable, the location convenient, and the job, within normal circumstances, well within her capabilities. She recalls a conversation about books and authors. She remembers mentioning that she had read Italo Calvino's *If on a winter's night a traveller,* for one of her university subjects. Joe – whatever his surname was – had been impressed.

One thing she remembers clearly: that she had kept thinking how much she'd love to work in this place, but had been completely unable to convey her enthusiasm because her thoughts were inarticulate and her tone monotonous.

By the time she arrives home she's certain that this was her worst job interview ever.

That night, Jimmy gets home and finds Angie still awake, staring at the ceiling from the bed. He asks her how the interview went, and she tells him that hopefully in the New Year, she'll feel well enough to apply for jobs.

'At the moment it's a useless exercise, Jimmy,' she says, wiping away a silent tear.

'Don't punish yourself, Angie. We'll manage.' Jimmy

says, turning the lights off. It is so much easier for him to be supportive of the meek and defeated creature who lies next to him in the darkness than it would have been with the overconfident, aggressive Angie of a few months ago. He can't say that he has gotten used to the fluctuations in Angie's personality, even though he's seen her through two full cycles.

At around midday on Christmas Eve, Angie is writing a list of ingredients for the dessert that she wants to take to Norah's the next day, when her phone rings.

'Merry Christmas, Mrs Fletcher!' says a familiar voice with an Italian accent. 'This is Joe Speranza. My wife is typing your letter of offer and I wanted to see that it would be suitable for you to start the first week of January,' he says, and pauses. 'If you decide to accept the offer, that is.'

'Thank you, thank you! I most certainly accept!' Angie exclaims, incredulous. A surge of delayed enthusiasm ripples through her body. Then she tells him, her voice quivering with emotion, 'This is the best Christmas present I could receive!'

As soon as she hangs up, Angie dials Sinéad's number, cursing under her breath at having said something so cheesy to her future boss. When there's no answer, she remembers that Sinéad has gone home for the holidays and won't be back until February. So Angie rings Jimmy instead, to tell him the good news.

'That's great, Ange! Call your mum and tell her – you'll make her day,' Jimmy says.

Angie calls Norah and leaves a happy message on the answering machine.

That night, Jimmy and Angie go to mass with Norah, just as they have done every Christmas Eve since they were first married. At mass Norah cries tears of relief, looking away so that Jimmy and Angie don't see her. Jimmy holds Angie's hand, and for Norah's sake, pretends that he's comfortable in church – it's Christmas Eve after all, and things are looking better.

Angie sits through the service, so deep in thought that she hardly hears the sermon or the hymns. She's thinking that if there's something she has learnt from the rollercoaster ride of the last two years, it is the basic principle of gravity: everything that goes up, will eventually come down. And in her case, it also works vice versa. With the same certainty with which she has expected her elation to wear off in the past, she knows now that no matter how paralysing her depressions are, they too, will pass.

The clouds of depression are lifting again. Whether it's thanks to the combined medication that has finally kicked in, whether it is the change in her circumstances, the new job, the spirit of Christmas, the unfailing support from her best friend, family and doctor, or something else all together, Angie doesn't know. All she knows is that she has managed to survive yet another cycle of her illness.

'Yes, but for how long?' the voice of inevitability hisses from the back of her mind, but Angie has started singing 'Joy to the world' at the top of her lungs, and can't hear it.

# PART 3:
# FINDING ANGELICA

*Not until we are lost
do we begin to find ourselves.*

- Henry David Thoreau

# ~Dreamchild ~

It's mid-April, 2000, and the countdown for the long awaited Sydney Olympic Games has started. There's a buzz of excitement everywhere she goes, yet Angie doesn't feel enthusiastic. For several days now, she has been having a recurring dream in which she's pregnant. During the night she conceives a child (she has the strong feeling it's a girl), feels her kicking and moving inside her abdomen and soothes her by gently massaging her stomach. She experiences morning sickness and cravings, feels her womb expanding, her breasts growing heavy, the skin on her belly stretching, the veins on her legs swelling.

Every time she has the dream the pregnancy advances further, but invariably she wakes up alone, lying on a hospital bed, with the certainty that not only the foetus is gone, but also her entire reproductive system. Nothing but pain fills her empty abdomen, as she lies there, unable to move, cry or scream. The pain is as real as the physical symptoms of the pregnancy had been. Blood flows between her legs, staining the white sheets. There's so much blood that it goes right through the mattress and Angie can hear it dripping down onto the white tiled floor.

It is still dark outside when Angie wakes up in her own

bed, gasping for breath, feeling tearful and agitated. Jimmy is asleep by her side, facing the window, snoring softly and looking quite comfortable, even though in her anxiety she's pulled all the blankets away from him. After making sure that there's no blood on the sheets, Angie grieves the loss of her dreamchild in silence.

But … why such dreams now? Her moods have been stable since the beginning of the year, thanks to the medication. She hasn't suffered any of the major side effects she had read about and feared, except a significant weight gain, which she's not happy about, but can live with. Her new job at the bookshop is going well, and Jimmy is pleased that she's earning a full-time income again. They're even going away in a few days' time, a whole week in the country. A well deserved holiday after two years of turmoil.

A distinct sense of things returning to the status quo has reigned in their home for the last few months, and Angie doesn't want to tamper with it by telling Jimmy about the recurring nightmare. Besides, Jimmy is not part of the dream in any way.

It's not even five in the morning and it's unusually warm for this time of the year. Angie is feverish and covered in sweat. She switches on the ceiling fan and watches it spin for a while. All she wants is some sleep. Dreamless, untroubled sleep. While she drifts in the space between awareness and oblivion, her semiconscious thoughts keep returning to the subject of babies.

Jimmy and Angie had first started to talk seriously about having a baby back in 1997, and had decided that if it didn't happen earlier 'by accident' they would definitely have their first child in the year 2000, the year Jimmy anticipated the mortgage would be paid off. A millennium baby – that is, if the world didn't come to an end at midnight on the 31st of December, 1999, as so many people, including Jimmy's mother, had predicted.

Despite all the paranoia about the end of the world, the Y2K bug and the debate about whether the new millennium started in 2000 or 2001, the new year arrived amidst spectacular fireworks and the earth continued to spin, just like the ceiling fan above Angie's bed.

The year 2000 brought Angie a new, enjoyable job, financial and mental stability, brought her also to the last stage of her university degree, but it didn't bring the millennium baby.

'And ... what does Jimmy say about your dream?' Dr Suenho asks. Angie is lying down on a psychiatrist's couch in Dr Suenho's room, but it doesn't look anything like the last time she was here, two months ago. For starters, there has never been a couch in this room before – so Angie has never had to lie down.

In an effort to show Jimmy that she was doing well enough not to need a psychiatrist, Angie stopped visiting Dr Suenho in February, after they had evaluated the success of the medication.

Yet, here she is lying on a leather couch at Dr Suenho's. There's something much more peculiar about the room than the presence of the psychiatrist's couch: the walls and furniture are made of glass. There is also a huge transparent ceiling fan, humming softly. From the corner of her eye, Angie can see the contents of Dr Suenho's desk drawers. Post-it-notes, paperclips and highlighters are perfectly organised in a plastic tray. There are keys, a tape recorder, tapes, AA batteries and an open packet of rice crackers.

Dr Suenho is waiting for an answer, her hand resting on the desk, holding her favourite fountain pen, the one engraved with her initials: E.S.

'Angie?' Dr Suenho calls, tapping her pen softly on the glass desk. 'What does Jimmy say about your dream?'

'Jimmy says this dream probably means that I am afraid of miscarrying,' Angie blurts. 'Or perhaps of being pregnant altogether. But the more I think about it, the more convinced I am that he's the one who's afraid: afraid of fatherhood, of the commitment and responsibility that comes with it.'

Angie gasps; amazed at hearing herself say this with such conviction. She hasn't even discussed the dream with Jimmy.

'And there's the matter of your condition, isn't there?' Dr Suenho remarks, writing some more cryptic signs on the ruled pad. Angie notices that even the fountain pen is transparent – she can see the blue ink inside it.

'Well, yes.' Angie carries on, trying not to be distracted by her see-through surroundings. 'My condition has given Jimmy a very good excuse to avoid having children. The few times we've spoken about it in the recent past he has blamed it all on me and my condition. He says that I might not be emotionally and physically fit for the task. I always end up in tears, so we've stopped discussing the subject altogether. But now, now that I've made so much progress, that I'm feeling stable--'

Angie can't complete the sentence, afraid that she'll start crying. One thing Angie knows for sure is that every time this dream recurs, a part of her being dies with the baby. This idea reminds her of one of her favourite short stories, Borges' *The Circular Ruins*, which she read last year for one of her university subjects. In the story, a magician dreams another being, piece by piece, and conjures him into reality.

She opens her mouth intending to voice these thoughts; they seem to be worth some of Dr Suenho's expensive fountain pen ink. But Dr Suenho is becoming transparent too, like a ghost, and Angie stares at her with her jaw dropped.

'Maybe,' Dr Suenho says with a fading voice, apparently oblivious to what's happening to her, 'the dream has something to do with your aunt's baby girl, who was actually your half-sister as well as your cousin, and who died before she was born.' As she says this Dr Suenho disappears altogether; everything in the room follows her except the fan which, since the ceiling is transparent, appears to be hanging from a lilac sky.

Angie wakes up with a start for the second time this morning, at 5.45 am. The fan is still spinning beneath her lilac-painted bedroom ceiling. Her imaginary conversation with Dr Suenho is ringing in her mind – she can still hear it, almost word for word. She shakes her head, trying to dismiss the whole dream as nonsense. An office made of glass. Dr Suenho fading away. Jimmy afraid of having children. Ha, ha, ha.

Angie remembers what Jimmy said to her one night, when they had been dating for a month or so. They had returned to her house following an afternoon of bike riding, and after he had kissed her goodbye at the door, his lips salty with sweat, Jimmy had said: 'You know, Angie, if everything works out between us, I'd like you to be the mother of my children.'

Angie had looked at him in astonishment, unable to reply, trying to work out whether he was pulling her leg or not. They had only been going out for a month!

'Not straightaway, of course. A few years down the track,' he added in all seriousness, seeing the bewilderment in Angie's eyes. Then he climbed on his bike and rode away.

Something else reverberates in Angie's mind this morning, as soon as the memory of the dreamchild comes back to haunt her. The part of the story *The Circular Ruins* that talks about the dreamed being awakening inside the dream.

Suddenly, Angie starts shivering as she visualises her own dreamchild opening her eyes and begging her for help. The all too familiar butterflies living in her stomach, who have been in a state of hibernation for the last few months (not the colourful butterflies of exhilaration but the other ones, the black ones that herald anxiety), wake up and start flapping their bat-like wings.

Industrious spiders inside her brain busy themselves weaving strings of irrational thoughts.

What if this child wants desperately to be born, wants to cross over from the dream world into consciousness, and she's failing her every time? Why doesn't she give up? Why does she keep trying even though Angie seems to be, just as Jimmy says, too physically and emotionally fragile to carry out this task, even in a dream?

And then, there are the more rational questions: does this dream mean that she's afraid that pregnancy will trigger another episode of mania? She's read, on the internet, about one US study in which a whacking seventy-four percent of bipolar women who were being successfully treated for their condition had their symptoms recur immediately after childbirth.

Angie reaches out towards Jimmy. She wants to wake him up and tell him about the nightmare, but she withdraws her hand before it touches his shoulder. She considers calling Dr Suenho, making an appointment for the next available Saturday but she discards this idea too.

Despite the nightmares, she feels stronger. She knows she can make it on her own this time around. She might need to give Sinéad a call, get it off her chest, but that's all. Maybe not even that. Why alarm Sinéad, even? The dream, the anguish and the feeling of loss will subside; the nasty butterflies will go back to sleep. She knows this with the same certainty that she knew her last depression would clear.

In one of their last sessions, Dr Suenho had congratulated Angie for making it through yet another cycle of her illness – hopefully the last – and told her it was largely due to her remarkable resilience.

Angie had left that session holding her head up high, making a note of the term Dr Suenho had used. *Resilience*; a word that conjured both buoyancy and toughness, the strength not of a rock but of an elastic band that can bend and stretch without breaking. She has called upon it many times, reminding herself that even though it may not appear so, she can be, and she is, strong, adaptable and resilient.

The clock radio goes off at 6.30 – time to get ready for work. Angie turns it off before Jimmy wakes, and resets it for 9.00, when he is due to get up, long after she's gone. She washes her face and scrutinises her features in the mirror. The rounder, fuller face that looks back at her is indisputably that of the pre-Elena Angie: free of makeup, with shoulder length ginger hair and a judicious look in her hazel eyes.

After breakfast, dressed in a two piece suit, she swallows two purple pills and a little yellow capsule labelled 'Monday' and hurls herself into the cloudless, mild autumn day. As the intensity of her dream dissipates and the splendour of the morning takes over, she begins to feel lighter and bubblier, looking forward to all the things she needs to do today.

You cannot see what you are doing Angelica, can you? You are killing me. You have erased me from your day-to-day life, from your mirror, from your eyes. You are muffling my voice with drugs. Worse still, the hateful shrink, who is to blame for all this, is now invading the only realm where I was still having some success in reaching out to you – your dreams.

The more you ignore me, the more my light fades. I need you to take a good look at me, Angelica, to clap your hands and say that you believe in fairies, that you believe in me, before I cease to exist.

In the meantime, while I still have strength, I will push this doctor away from your unconscious – she will fade, together with her sensible dream interpretations, like she did this morning.

And you will dream about me, Angelica, you will mourn my imminent death over and over again, until the time comes when you stop denying my existence and deliver me back into your life.

∾

While Angie glides into the dreamless sleep she wants so much, shortly after settling down in the train with her book opened on her lap, Jimmy gets up before the alarm goes off and starts planning his day under the shower.

For the last two months, Jimmy has been learning the art of digital typesetting, having reached the conclusion that the traditional printing trade is a species facing extinction. If he wants to continue working in the graphic arts industry, he needs to update his skills – so he spends a couple of hours every morning practising on the computer at home.

While making his coffee, Jimmy notices that there's a plastic bag on the counter. It's Angie's lunch. Jimmy hesitates for a few minutes, contemplating on the one hand the plastic bag on the counter, and on the other, the neat plan he has already laid out in his mind for the hours ahead. He decides, in the end, to do something out of character, maybe because he's been reading a book that Norah gave Angie for Christmas, *The Road Less Travelled*, which Angie shoved in the growing 'self-help' section of their bookcase.

He will walk the path less travelled today, and instead of spending the morning in front of the computer, he will visit his wife's new workplace, meet her workmates and treat her to lunch before heading off to his afternoon shift.

Angie is ridiculously pleased to see Jimmy. Smiling from ear to ear, she takes him around and introduces him to the other two girls who work there, and even to some of the regular clients. The shop is bigger than Jimmy imagined. It has two levels: on the ground floor they sell new books and the place is buzzing with customers. Upstairs, Angie's domain, is dedicated to second-hand books, collectors' volumes and rare editions. This section reminds Jimmy of a library; it has an atmosphere of serenity. Soft, unobtrusive classical music plays in the background and a few people scrutinise the shelves in silence or sit on chairs leafing through the books they have picked.

After they buy lunch at the milk bar, Angie takes Jimmy to a park nearby, to show him the tree under whose shade she often sits to read at lunchtime. The tree is one of the largest in the park and its long twisted branches extend several metres across. It has red bristled leaves and the bark is smooth on the upper part of the trunk.

'This tree is magnificent!' Jimmy exclaims, looking at the tree in awe, and then scanning the ground around it.

'I thought you'd like it. It looks like a tree conducive to enlightenment! Do you know what kind it is?' Angie asks. She knows that trees have always fascinated Jimmy.

'It's a red oak tree,' Jimmy says without hesitation. 'And looking at the amount of acorns on the ground, it's between fifty and a hundred years old.'

'How can you know that?' Angie sits down under the shade of her tree and takes a bite of her tuna and curried egg sandwich.

Jimmy explains that oak trees only start producing acorns after their twenty-fifth year, but their largest production is between fifty and one hundred years. After that, they start to slow down again. He sits next to Angie with his legs crossed and puts a hand on her knee.

'I like this place, Ange. This tree, this park. And the bookshop. I'm glad I came, I'm glad that you are ... back to normal again.'

'Well, I'm glad you're glad,' Angie says with a trembling voice, and then lies on the ground, resting her head in Jimmy's lap. They spend an hour in the park, eating sandwiches and talking about oak trees, birds and rare books.

For that hour it feels to Angie as if they have been transported back to the time when they were dating and used to go for picnics at the Botanical Gardens or for long bike rides in Centennial Park – a time before Angie was diagnosed with a mental illness, before she knew that her father had been her aunt Jo's lover and that Jo had not died of pneumonia.

A time long gone, before certain things became too difficult to discuss with her husband, before she became afraid of going to sleep at night, before her dreamchild loomed in the darkness waiting for her time to die.

❧

That afternoon, Norah arrives at Pearl's timber cottage after a five-hour drive. When she last spoke to her mother, two days ago, Norah had hardly been able to understand her, the way Pearl had been coughing. In the end, Pearl had admitted that she'd been 'a little under the weather' for a couple of weeks. For Pearl to make such admission, it was no doubt something major. After cancelling the pupils she was scheduled to teach on Monday and Tuesday, Norah packed an overnight bag and departed early on Monday morning.

'The G.P. reckons it's bronchitis. Always making a mountain out of a molehill, them doctors!' Pearl says, making a dismissive gesture in the air while boiling the kettle for tea. The smell of freshly baked blueberry muffins fills the house. 'It's just a little cough. I'm taking lemon lozenges.'

'You can't treat bronchitis with lemon lozenges, Mum!' Norah scolds her.

'I told you, it's not bronchitis,' Pearl says as she surrenders to a coughing fit.

'You should come and stay with me for a while, Mum. You can see Angie. You haven't seen her since Christmas and you wouldn't believe how well she's doing now! I'm sure she would like to come and see you, but it's harder for her to get around now, with her new job and without the car --'

'I know you're lying,' Pearl interrupts, throwing Norah a menacing look.

'What makes you say that?' Norah says, astonished.

'You're telling me good news but you sound miserable. Now stop putting on a brave face for my sake and tell me what's wrong with Angie.'

'Oh Mum!' Norah says, covering her mouth with her hand.

Pearl removes the whistling kettle from the stove and sits down on the sofa next to Norah, who's produced a baby-blue handkerchief out of her pocket and is pressing it against the inside corner of one eye and then the other.

Norah tells Pearl that Angie is doing great, really; she has a very good doctor and her medication is working well. So if she sounds sad, it's not about Angie but about what's happened between Angie and her.

'Things started to go pear-shaped when I told her about Jo's suicide. And the way she treated me last year, when she went haywire – as if I'd become her worst enemy! I knew that telling her about her father and Jo would only make things worse, but I had to tell her, Mum. All these years resenting me, whilst glorifying his memory!'

Norah is interrupted by Pearl's coughing, and pauses while her mother fishes a lozenge out of her apron's pocket and shoves it into her mouth. Pearl gestures with her hand for Norah to go on.

'I kept telling myself that she wasn't well, and when she got better things would get back to normal. But now that she's better, there's still a shadow in her eyes when she looks at me. Sometimes I think she hates me.'

Pearl moves closer and pulls Norah's head against her shoulder. Pearl's shoulder is firm and springy, like an orthopaedic pillow. It's also drip-dry, and smells of lavender scented fabric softener.

'C'mon Norah, your brain is working overtime again, reading too much into things. Angie doesn't hate you! And that shadow may have nothing to do with you.'

'I know it does. My motherly instinct tells me.'

'Fair enough. But remember, this has been a pretty wild ride for Angie as well as you. That shadow will take a while to clear, but it will clear – you just need to give it time. Trust me. Pull yourself together now, pet. You need to save your energy for your poor sick mother!'

Norah can't help but laugh at Pearl's last comment.

'See? That's better. That's my girl,' Pearl says smiling.

❧

Sitting at the station after missing her train home that night, Angie suddenly remembers something Dr Suenho told her last year when she first began to have anxious dreams, one dream in particular.

Angie kept dreaming that she was running late for an important appointment, and missed the train. Sometimes she got on the train, but it broke down before it reached its destination. Once, the train departed, but the last carriage, in which Angie was sitting, was left behind.

Dr Suenho said that this type of anxious, recurring dream was quite common in manic and hypomanic patients whose minds were restless at night. Dreaming that you keep falling from a great height was another variation.

'Try this,' Dr Suenho had advised. 'As soon as you wake up, and while you are in that semiconscious state of mind, close your eyes again and visualise a resolution to the dream. For instance, imagine that you walk out of the station after missing your train and there's a taxi waiting for you. Or better still, you could fly all the way to your appointment and get there with plenty of time. Remember: things like flying can happen in dreams.'

Angie resolves that if the dream child comes back tonight, she will do just that: visualise the pregnancy reaching completion and a healthy baby girl being born. For the first time in over a week, she looks forward to going to sleep.

No, Angelica, no! You do not understand. You must not give birth to me in the dream world. I must be born into your waking life. Things must go back to the way they were last year, when we had the time of our lives!

Just as Angie suspected, once she comes up with a solution, the dream doesn't recur. The following few nights are mercifully uneventful and so are the days in between. On Friday night, she finally catches up with Sinéad for a movie and dinner. When they meet outside the movie theatre, Sinéad clings to Angie as if they hadn't seen each other in years, although it's only been a few weeks.

'I've missed you, big sister!'

'Ditto!' Angie exclaims, kissing her friend on the forehead. 'How about we skip the movie so we have more time to eat and talk?'

'Sounds like a plan!' Sinéad says. 'There's this café in Leichhardt that makes the best baked ricotta cheesecake in Sydney. It's only a few stops away by bus or we could even walk there.'

They decide to walk – the weather is mild, the night is starry, and if Angie is going to try this legendary cheesecake she needs to burn a few calories first.

'How is the book club?' Angie asks over dessert.

'Ruben, the coordinator, keeps asking me about you,' Sinéad says, taking a spoonful of creamy cheesecake with her eyes closed. 'He said you could be a nuisance sometimes, but he missed you. What does Ruben call you ...' She scrunches up her face, thinking. 'Oh yes. Chatterbox. Where's that chatterbox, Angie, he asked the other day. Everybody misses you, Angie. Me too.'

Angie smiles. 'I just don't have the time, Shine. I'm back where I was two years ago, working full-time, studying at night, and without a car to get around. The good news is that I love my job. So, what are you reading at the club?'

'Oh, it's a book about three generations of Italian women, written in the form of a diary. It's called *Follow Your Heart*.'

'You guys are reading a book called *Follow your Heart*?'

'Yes, I had my doubts. But it's deeply insightful. You'd like it, being so close to your mum and your grandma. I'll lend it to you when I'm finished.'

'And your work? How's that going?' Angie asks, changing the subject before Sinéad enquires about her mother and grandmother. She hasn't spoken with Norah in a while, and hasn't seen her grandma since Christmas. She makes a mental note to call Grandma Pearl. Jimmy, who speaks with Norah more often than Angie does, has told her that Pearl has been unwell.

Sinéad has been working at the university's student information office two days a week since the beginning of the semester. When asked about her job, she sighs.

'Got paperwork coming out of my ears – graduation time. But I need the money.' She pauses, and her eyes light up. 'Hey? They don't have a vacancy at your bookshop, do they? I've always wanted to work in a boutique bookshop like yours.'

'Afraid not, Shine!' Angie says, shaking her head. 'But I'll keep an eye out for you.'

'I imagine you meet a lot of interesting people, and get to read a lot of interesting books.'

'You're not wrong. I just finished reading a book a customer recommended, called *The Master and Margarita*, by Mikhail Bug-- no, Bulgakov.'

'Never heard of it. Sounds Russian.'

'That's right. There's a cat that talks and walks on its hind legs, and one of the characters is the devil himself! Apparently it's a political satire full of hidden meanings about Stalin's regime.'

'Very intriguing.'

'Truth is, I was too busy trying to keep up with the multiple plots, the huge number of characters and their unpronounceable Russian names to discover the underlying connotations. But I still enjoyed it.'

'A book like that would lose me in no time,' Sinéad says. She's finished with her cake and is now licking the spoon.

'Yeah, my head's still spinning, but at least I managed to read it from beginning to end. When I was low, I couldn't even finish a newspaper article. When I was high, I was devouring books, but couldn't remember their titles the next day.'

'So, how does it feel to be normal again? Sinéad asks, putting her spoon down. She has been wanting to ask Angie about her mental health, but didn't want to bring the subject up, thinking that perhaps Angie would like to have a normal conversation, about food, books, work and other trivial things, without the term *normal* becoming the topic. What's normal anyway? Is she herself normal? Is anybody?

Sinéad remembers what Angie said last year, when her husband and her mother kept seeing symptoms of her illness in everything she did and said. 'Don't they understand that there's more to me than my condition?' Sinéad had promised herself back then that she wouldn't bring up the subject of Angie's condition unless Angie did, and now she has.

'It's been so long since I've been this normal,' Angie replies, playing with the crumbs on the table, 'that normality feels weird. Not bad, or wrong, just weird.'

The friends are silent for a moment, staring at their empty

dessert plates. It's after 10.00 pm, and they are the only two patrons left at the café. The background music has been turned off, and the waiter is setting up the tables for the next day. The clatter of dishes being washed can be heard from the kitchen. It's Angie who speaks first.

'I once told Dr Suenho that all I wanted was to have a normal life again. She answered with a question: "Have you ever had a normal life, Angie, and most importantly, would you really want to have one?"'

'You know, I was just thinking along the same lines ...' Sinéad says, once again amazed at Dr Suenho's wisdom.

'I guess she was saying that it's okay to be different, as long as you are at peace with yourself.'

'That's right! And are you?'

'Not yet, but I think I'm a lot closer than I was two years ago, before all this happened. The track is a bit hazy sometimes, but at least it's the right track.'

**Easter Holiday, Day 1**

Cleaned the flat thoroughly, although it's to remain empty for a week, because Mum will come to water the plants and no doubt will be conducting an inspection.

We had a pleasant train trip, though it was nearly six hours. Slept most of the way. Arrived at Wauchope station at 5.00 pm. Sean, our host, was waiting for us there to drive us to his country retreat near Port Macquarie.

This is what Jimmy wanted – a place where we could escape from the stress of our busy lives while avoiding the tourist crowds. Our two-bedroom cabin has a log fire. Ordered Italian takeaway, unpacked and went to sleep. Great day!

## Easter Holiday, Day 2

We slept in, had breakfast delivered to our door in a basket: juice, croissants, cereal, and freshly laid eggs. Chickens everywhere, also rabbits, cockatoos and a dog named Ellie. There's a solar heated spa, a swimming pool, and a recreation room with billiard table, table tennis, magazines, books, VCR and a piano. No other guests at the moment.

Had a spa in the afternoon. What a dream! To float aimlessly on the water, looking at the cloudless sky and the trees, thinking that yes, life can be this easy, peaceful, slow, simple in its beauty.

Ate the leftovers from last night's takeaway on our deck, by candlelight. Two dogs (Ellie and a friend) watched us intently, hoping to get fed. Watched *12 Monkeys* on video, followed by *Loch-Ness* on TV, drank a couple of glasses of port, went to sleep around 10.30 pm.

## Easter Holiday, Day 3

Slept in till 9.30 am! Had a big breakfast and got a lift into town. Took photos of the Hastings River with its almost impossibly clear water.

They have a pretty good movie theatre, but there was nothing on we wanted to see. Went for a long walk instead. We climbed a bit of a hill, puffing. At the top we had a discussion – quasi-argument – about how unfit we are and how much we need to lose weight, each one accusing the other of not doing enough about it. I didn't want to bring up the fact that my weight gain might be a side effect of my medication.

Bought charcoal chicken and vegetables, took them back to the cabin, had dinner, lit the log fire, took photos of me putting logs in the fire, of Jimmy relaxing next to the fire, of the fire blazing. Jimmy wants to send them to Grandma Pearl.

Watched a documentary about the artificial insemination of koalas and another one about bats being sexual totems in Aboriginal culture. Learnt that the three most important things that make bats attractive during mating season are their scent, singing, and 'knock you over' looks.

Made love, for the first time in weeks, next to the log fire. Must've been those raunchy documentaries.

## Easter Holiday, Day 4

Got up early and had a cab pick us up at 8.30 am to go to the markets. No big deal, only a few stands of second hand clothes, bric-a-brac and Avon beauty products. Still, picked up a few goodies and a Chinese shoulder/neck/head massage. Had breakfast at a café called Savoy and made a dinner reservation for tomorrow night.

Sean picked us up and brought us back to the lodge just on time for my therapeutic massage. I completed the treatment with a one-hour spa session. Even Jimmy got in the water this time.

Had dinner, watched a video. Afterwards we started a game of table tennis, but the conversation quickly turned sour for no particular reason.

The list of subjects we don't seem to be able to talk about without arguing, or to talk about at all, is growing. It now includes:

- Having babies (or not)
- Having sex (or not)
- My tattoo
- My condition

- Our being overweight
- My credit card bill – still high after last year's extrava-
gancy
- Our long-term future, after what we've been through in
the last couple of years.

## Easter Holiday, Day 5

This morning we met the newly arrived guests next door: a
middle-aged man called Ron, his young wife Suzie and two
small children. Ron gave us a lift to Hastings River where
we joined a fishing cruise – his wife stayed at the retreat
with the kids. We returned home about 3.00 pm, had a nap,
and joined them again for a glass of wine outside until the
mosquitoes forced us to look for shelter.

This is Ron's second marriage. On the way to the Hastings
we asked him why he divorced the first time. Leave it to us
to ask such questions of someone we've just met, but Jimmy
recently came up with this theory that people tend to confide
in strangers who they're likely not to see again, and turns
out he's right. Ron told us all these personal things without
hesitation! He said that for eight years, he and his first wife
tried every way possible to have children, including IVF,
unsuccessfully. She became very bitter, and her inability to
have children became the centre of her life. In the end, he
couldn't stand it and he left.

'When you leave your wife for someone else,' Ron told
us, 'it seems to be more acceptable to her than if you leave
because you don't like her anymore. I just didn't like who
she'd become, and she couldn't hack that. She turned her
rage against me, and sucked me dry. I had to sell everything
I owned. But the story has a happy ending: I met Suzie and

now have a lovely young family and a new business.'

Dinner tonight was at Savoy's; a first class gourmet treat. Over dinner, we did a lot of talking. We tackled one of our taboo subjects: my condition and what it has put us through over the last two years. Being in a public place, we didn't get upset or argue.

It became evident that it will take a long time for the scars to heal - provided I don't have a relapse, but our long conversation marked the beginning of the healing.

We watched *Smilla's Feeling for Snow* on video and went to sleep around midnight.

## Easter Holiday, Day 6

After dreaming that I was pregnant again, and gave birth to a fish (at least the dream was funny this time), I decided to bring up the baby issue today. We hired two bikes and rode to the beach, where we had a picnic. Lovely weather, clean sand, clear water, not too crowded – the idyllic holiday setting. If we couldn't talk heart to heart here, then where?

After lunch I told Jimmy about my recurring nightmare, and one thing led to another. We talked, really talked, without either of us getting upset, aggressive, defensive or emotional. Maybe it was the sea breeze, the waves, the voices of children playing, or the holiday mood finally kicking in.

No surprises – turns out that Jimmy is also afraid that pregnancy and childbirth could provoke a relapse.

Returned to our cabin at sunset, played with Ron's eighteen-month-old daughter at the cubby house until her mum took her away; had a game of table tennis and went to sleep at 9.30 pm.

**Easter Holiday, Day 7**

Packed after breakfast. Left our host a box of Easter eggs on the table and got a lift to the train station before midday. Sean said he hoped to see us back again soon and we assured him that he would.

During the trip we continued our talks. In the end, Jimmy confessed, ever so cautiously, that he has been thinking this would be a good time to start trying for a baby. I'll be completing my degree in November and we'll finish paying off the mortgage at around the same time, so we would no longer have any financial or academic pressure.

He only asked one thing: that I go see Dr Suenho first, and ask her opinion on the matter. One year ago, it would have been unthinkable for him to ask for Dr Suenho's opinion on something like that.

# ~ To have or not to have ~

'It's not advisable that you fall pregnant while you are taking your current medication,' Dr Suenho says, after Angie has brought her up to date. 'Unfortunately, it increases the usual risk of physical malformations and spina bifida fivefold.'

With a sinking heart, Angie looks out the window of Dr Suenho's room. The jacaranda tree outside was in full bloom the last time she was here. The now naked branches swing in the early May wind.

'Fivefold,' she repeats. 'What's that? Five in one hundred babies?'

'Two in one hundred,' Dr Suenho says. 'Still, it's considered a high risk. We could look into changing to a different treatment during the critical months.'

'I don't want to change treatment, now that I've finally found one that I'm comfortable with. It's a catch-22 situation, isn't it? I feel well enough to have children thanks to this medication, but this medication is no good for me if I want to have children.' Angie pauses and shakes her head at the irony of it all. 'And there's the matter of my condition itself.'

'Your condition itself?' Dr Suenho asks, looking up from the pad in which she's dutifully recording their exchange.

'I could pass it on to the baby.'

'Or you could have a perfectly healthy baby.'

'Are you the devil's advocate or something?' Angie asks, forcing a smile.

'Angie,' Dr Suenho says. 'It's my duty to inform you of the risks, but nobody can ever be sure that they'll have a perfectly healthy baby and that they will be model mothers for ever after. Sickness happens, circumstances change, relationships break down – there are countless factors at play, independent of your illness.'

Dr Suenho recommends that Angie consult her family doctor and then a gynaecologist.

~

'I strongly disagree with your psychiatrist's advice,' says Dr Hamilton, when Angie and Jimmy visit him a week later. 'It's not worth risking a relapse by fiddling with your medication. You're very lucky to have found something that works well for you.'

'Those were my thoughts exactly,' says Angie. 'But there's the risk of spina bifida–'

'So what are our options, Dr Hamilton?' Jimmy interrupts, shifting uncomfortably in his chair.

'I've had two epileptic patients, on the same medication that Angie is taking, fall pregnant and have healthy babies. With careful monitoring, of course. Last year, I supervised a bipolar patient's pregnancy, while she was on lithium, and her baby was also fine. Folic acid and the AFP test would be a must.'

'AFP?' Jimmy repeats.

'The alpha-foeto protein test. It's a blood test with no

risk to the mother or the baby. If it shows high levels of alpha-foetoprotein, this could mean spina bifida.'

'And what happens if the levels are high?' Angie asks.

'If the results are conclusive, you can choose to terminate,' Dr Hamilton says. Angie gasps, Jimmy starts scratching his head. The doctor explains that even if the results are positive, they are not necessarily conclusive. A further test, called amniocentesis, would then be carried out.

Angie's head is spinning. Dr Hamilton keeps talking, explaining the amniotic fluid test. Jimmy looks at him intently, his chin resting on his fist, but Angie's mind has shut down.

After leaving the surgery, Jimmy and Angie walk home. Both have their heads down and are dragging their feet. Jimmy is the first to speak.

'We haven't even started trying yet, and the whole thing has become bigger than Ben Hur. And after all these tests, consultations and dramas, we may find out that we can't even have kids, and all of this was for nothing.'

And there's the small detail, Angie thinks, but doesn't dare say, that to conceive we need to have sex. Instead, she says, 'Like Ron, you mean.'

'Who?' Jimmy asks, lifting his eyebrow.

'The guy we met at the country retreat, remember? He and his first wife went through all that trouble to have children and couldn't, and in the end that's what killed their marriage.'

'Something like that, I guess,' Jimmy says, 'but we are not them, and it won't kill our marriage. Sometimes children kill marriages, especially when couples have been together for a long time without them.'

'What are you saying, Jimmy?' Angie says. They stop, waiting for the lights to change.

Jimmy looks around to make sure there's no one near them. 'I'm saying, maybe we shouldn't rush into this. We should think about it some more. Maybe you won't have to take this medication for much longer.'

'And we'll wake up one day to find that we're too old to have children. That would solve the problem for us, wouldn't it?' Angie says bitterly.

'Give me a break, Ange! You're only thirty-two! We have years ahead before you are too old. In any case, you could at least wait till we get home to continue this argument.'

Angie bites her lip. She understands now, as they cross the street side by side but keeping a healthy distance between them, why have they procrastinated about having children for so long. It is hard. Bloody hard.

☙

On Mother's Day, Angie and Jimmy treat Norah to lunch at a local café. After they have ordered, they tell her about their recent consultations with Dr Suenho and Dr Hamilton.

'I fell pregnant with Angie six months into my marriage and that was that,' Norah says when Jimmy is finished and lunch is served. She pulls her lasagna apart and picks up some of the minced meat with a spoon. 'Back then, it wasn't something you thought about. It was just part of the cycle of life - you got married, you had children, your children had children, and so on.'

'True, our generation thinks too much about everything,' Jimmy says. He spears a piece of steak with his fork and inspects it closely, shaking his head. He had asked for well-done, not charred. 'But to run the risk of having a severely disabled baby ...'

'*A baby we would love just the same,*' Angie wants to say, but her throat has closed up.

Silence sets in. Angie is having trouble swallowing, and starts fishing olives out of her salad and setting them aside.

'Things have changed a lot since you had me, Mum,' Angie finally says, when her voice comes back. 'Only the other day I read some statistics predicting that almost a quarter of Australian women who are now in their child-bearing years won't have kids, mostly by choice.'

'Where did you read this?' Jimmy asks, raising his left eyebrow as he does when he is only half-convinced.

'A lifestyle magazine at the dentist's surgery,' Angie goes on, with more confidence, 'Many of the interviewees said they couldn't believe that in this day and age, they were still being frowned upon, specially by women who would like to have children but can't.'

'But you can have children, Angie!' Norah says.

'Mum, you're missing the point--'

'I understand how afraid you are of a relapse, but if anything should happen, Jimmy and I are here to help.'

Jimmy doesn't look at Norah in agreement or otherwise; he seems to be absorbed in his own thoughts. Angie seizes the opportunity to change the subject.

'Mum, you still haven't told me how Grandma Pearl is.'

'I haven't had the chance - you've been so busy since you came back.'

'Well, I'm asking you now,' Angie says, thinking that it's going to be one of those days.

'Well, there isn't much to tell. You know your grandma. She's as stubborn as a goat. I couldn't force her to see the doctor, but Betty, her next door neighbour, has my number and promised to keep me informed.'

Norah pauses, placing her spoon and knife on top of her half-eaten lasagna to indicate that she's finished. 'Anyway, your grandma said she'd like to see you, Angie. Maybe you should think about visiting her before the end of the year. I have a bad feeling--'

'Oh, Mum, you can be so negative sometimes!' Angie says, pushing her plate aside. She, too, has lost her appetite.

'Show a little sympathy towards your mum, Ange! It's Mother's Day, for God's sake.' Jimmy snaps, suddenly returning from la-la-land.

Angie blushes. She had promised herself this morning that she would try to make an effort with Norah, today in particular.

'I'm sorry, Mum. Yes, maybe I can visit Grandma on the June long weekend,' she says sheepishly – but the damage is already done, and Norah's eyes are teary.

The voice of inevitability, which Angie hasn't heard in a long time, hisses in her ear. 'I told you it wouldn't last long, this so-called normal life.'

Angie sighs, making a mental note to call Dr Suenho first thing on Monday.

'Up until last month, I always thought that Jimmy and I would have children. It was a fact of life, as my mother put it,' Angie tells Dr Suenho the following Saturday, explaining what Norah had said about the cycle of life.

'And what has changed now, Angie?' Dr Suenho asks.

'Remember my dream about the dying baby?' Angie says.

'I'm afraid I don't recall it,' Dr Suenho says, checking the previous page in her notes. 'When did you tell me about it? Was it during our last session?'

Angie suddenly realises that her conversation with Dr Suenho about the dying baby did not take place here, but in a room made of glass, in another of her dreams. She smiles, thinking that she can't even tell between the real and the imaginary these days.

'Actually, I didn't. It happened during the months that I stopped visiting you,' Angie confesses, and tells Dr Suenho about her dream. She explains that she thought that her maternal instinct was talking to her, telling her that it was about time to start trying for a baby. Jimmy finally agreed, but then, all these complications came up.

'The whole thing became too hard, and I realised that even though I'm more stable, things at home are far from stable. Now I'm thinking that maybe what this dream expressed was my need to fix a rocky marriage. Maybe I thought that a baby would help.'

Angie is amazed at how candidly and calmly she can talk to Dr Suenho about this subject, which has become a minefield at home. In fact, up until this instant, she hasn't been this honest even with herself.

'Angie, it would be unrealistic to expect your relationship to survive the emotional turmoil of the past eighteen months unharmed. But this doesn't mean that your marriage is rocky. Is that really how you perceive it?'

Angie thinks of the list of topics, growing by the day, that she and Jimmy can't even mention without starting an argument. At this rate, they will soon have nothing left to talk about! She recalls the long, deep conversations they had during their Easter holiday. Even then, it had been evident that there was a lot of fear and pain lying beneath the surface. She remembers their lovemaking at the country retreat; it had been their first – and last – sexual encounter in months.

Blushing, she thinks of the biscuit tin inside her desk drawer, filled to the brim with disks holding stories of what could happen when a woman's sexual frustration reaches boiling point. She herself had reached that point, and God knows what would have happened if Tiger had reacted differently to her clumsy, inexperienced attempt at seduction.

Rocky? She thinks. That's a mild way of putting it.

She nods, with her eyes fixed on the carpet. She starts fidgeting with her wedding ring; the skin underneath has suddenly become itchy. There are no tears, though. There haven't been tears for months.

'In that case, I would strongly recommend that you and Jimmy seek marriage counselling,' Dr Suenho says. She doesn't need to delve deeper into the subject – Angie's body language is clear. 'Now that you are psychologically stable, you need to deal with your relationship issues, especially if you are thinking about having a baby. I'm glad you can see for yourself that it isn't a good idea to have a child as a quick fix to an ailing marriage. Not that I perceive your marriage as ailing.'

'Maybe Jimmy could come with me next time. You could help us sort out our issues.'

'I'm not a marriage counsellor, Angie. And as your psychiatrist, I have already established a connection with you. You need a neutral party, who can start afresh with both of you.'

Dr Suenho writes the phone number for a relationships counselling service on a post-it note and gives it to Angie.

'Don't put this one in the washing,' she says, winking.

Angie smiles and slips the note inside her wallet.

⤙

Jimmy has been busy all afternoon pulling apart their computer and putting it back together. When he has installed the programs he needs for his graphic arts training, he discovers the memory is insufficient, and decides to have a go at upgrading it himself. At a critical moment in the process, Angie slams the front door and erupts into the study.

'Jimmy, Dr Suenho says we should think about getting marriage counselling.' She blurts, before even saying hello.

'Marriage counselling? Whatever for?' Jimmy exclaims.

'Whatever for? What do you mean whatever for?' Angie says, dropping her handbag on the floor, among the screwdrivers, instruction manuals, empty packaging and old computer parts. She throws her arms in the air and looks up toward the ceiling. 'I must be so unreasonable. I must be asking for so bloody much.'

'Ange, you are being such a drama queen! Go have a cold shower and talk to me when you've calmed down.' Jimmy says, irritated. The computer bleeps, demanding his attention. There's a message on the screen telling him that he needs to re-start. He presses the enter key.

He can hear Angie only a few paces away from him, trying to slow down her breathing. When he turns around, she's still standing at the doorway, but the look in her eyes has shifted from frustration to helplessness. Jimmy sighs.

'I tell you what,' he says, in a softer tone. 'Remember the long talks we had during our holiday?'

'Yes,' Angie manages to say.

'We could set aside one night a week to go out, to a restaurant. We could talk over dinner, like we did at Port Macquarie. We don't need a middle-man. That's for couples who are in real trouble.'

'Why do we need to go out? We could talk at home – we

could talk right now,' Angie says. She has regained her composure.

'You know what happens, Ange. You get emotional and I get shitty, and we always end up arguing. That wouldn't happen in a public place.'

'Allright, but ... which night?' Angie asks.

Jimmy knows as well as she does that they can't go out during the week, because he works the late shift. They go to Norah's on Saturday nights, and there's only one local restaurant open on Sundays: the Korean place whose food has twice given Jimmy indigestion. They can't change Norah's night – she recently joined the church choir as an accompanist and her rehearsals are on Sunday nights.

'I'd like to change back to the day shift. We don't need the extra money anymore, and I'm thinking about going back to school. I'll speak to the boss next week. Agreed?'

'It's a deal,' Angie says, her face brightening up. 'Why do you want to go back to school?'

'Not school, technical college. I want to do a course in digital printing. Now go change, Ange. Your mum is expecting us in half an hour. I'm almost done here,' Jimmy says, glad that it has taken so little to appease his wife.

### Angie's Diary, June 28th, 2000

Back in May, Jimmy promised he would change his working hours, so we could spend more time together, and discuss our problems over dinner once a week. But his boss asked him to stay on the night shift until the end of the year, and Jimmy said yes. In the meantime, all our unresolved issues keep piling up in the 'too hard' basket, and we are dealing with them by pretending they don't exist.

The days are growing colder, darker and heavier, and I'm terrified of sliding down again. My co-workers and even my clients, who are completely unaware of my mood problems, are inadvertently pointing out the signs. 'Speak up, Angie,' they tell me, because I'm mumbling. 'Angie, you've been very quiet lately,' they say, when I don't talk at all because I can't articulate my thoughts.

'You're like a bloody yoyo,' Sinéad said yesterday, jokingly. At least she made me laugh. Jimmy doesn't say anything – I hardly see him anyway. And Mum ... Mum and I have become more distant than ever.

Do I really want to be writing this down?

I see Dr Suenho every two months, I follow her advice to the letter, and I'm compliant with my medication (That's the medical term: compliant). What else can I do?

One thing is certain: I'm nowhere near ready to have a baby.

**July 3rd, 2000**

Dr Suenho says not to panic – it seems to be a case of the winter blues, rather than a clinical depression. She adjusted my medication, lowering the dose a little.

In the meantime, she asked me to write my own 'fightback' list. This is what I've come up with – more items to come.

- Stay in touch with people – do not isolate yourself.
- Keep active: Physically, exercise; mentally, start a project.
- When you feel worthless, think of your achievements.
- Put things into perspective – don't catastrophise or dramatise them.

- Remember the Spanish proverb: 'A life lived in fear is a life half lived.'
- Turn your negative thoughts around – think of the glass as half-full instead of half-empty.

## July 29th, 2000

I went to the Sapphire Coast for a few days, to visit my grandmother. It has been a regenerating experience.

Whenever I'm at Grandma Pearl's it feels as if I've stepped back in time, to my childhood, when life was uncomplicated, smoother, slower – just like I felt that day in the park with Jimmy under the great oak tree.

Grandma Pearl is good to have around, even though she's full of contradictions. On the one hand, she swears there's nothing wrong with her; she's strong as a bull. Despite the cough she does look well – plenty of colour in her cheeks and meat on her bones. Still, after asking me to swear on Grandpa's grave that I won't tell anybody, especially Mum or Jimmy, she gave me an envelope with an advance on my inheritance: a bank cheque for ten thousand dollars.

I counted the zeros and double-checked that it was really meant to be ten thousand and not one thousand dollars. She laughed, and nodded. Touched both by her generosity and the thought that she might really be dying, I began to cry.

'Stop that nonsense, pet!' She said and hugged me. 'This is to make you smile, not cry. You know how much I love my Norah and your hubby. But if you tell them about the money, they will surely have an opinion as to what you should do with it. This is for you, and I know you'll use it sensibly.'

That night, I thought about some of the things, sensible and reckless, that I could buy with ten thousand dollars. A car, a trip around the world, a liposuction treatment, a diamond necklace, a master's degree ... When I got home to Sydney, I opened a secret bank account and deposited the cheque. I have decided not to touch it until it's absolutely necessary.


## August 31st, 2000

Winter is over and I've survived the winter blues!

More good news: yesterday, Jimmy and I made our last home loan payment. We own our place freehold! We'll even throw a party to celebrate, as the event coincided with Jimmy's thirty-fifth birthday. We've invited all and sundry to a barbecue at Bicentennial Park, near the Olympic village, next weekend.

Mum will be coming, and Sinéad, of course. Mandy from the choir and two of my workmates, Kim and Simone, have also confirmed. Even Jimmy's mum and dad will be making the trip from up north and staying with us for a couple of days. Pete (my brother-in-law), his new girlfriend and his three kids will be there too; also Joe, my boss, with his wife. Sinéad said she'd bring a friend she met at the book club, George (?!) – I seem to have missed out on quite a lot during my winter hibernation.

# ~ Exuberance ~

It's the first day of September, the year 2000. The much anticipated Olympics have finally arrived in Sydney, and the entire city has come alive like never before, bustling with tourists, spectators, athletes, international press, artists and volunteers.

While the Olympic City awakes and begins to stir, Angie dreams that she's heavily pregnant. As she starts feeling the first contractions, a loud shriek wakes her.

It's a cockatoo, perched on the tree outside her bedroom window. Propping herself up on her elbows, Angie looks at the clock: it's 5.47 am. Jimmy is sleeping on his back, breathing peacefully, his fingers interlaced behind his neck. Angie runs her shaky hands across her belly – it's not as flat she would like it to be, but it's definitely not a heavily pregnant belly. There is no pain, no blood, no swelling. Everything is as it should be.

Fully aware, she remembers the technique that Dr Suenho once told her about.

Taking a deep breath and holding it, as if she were about to dive from a cliff, Angie lies down again, closes her eyes and takes herself back to the hospital room, the room with the naked white walls and the white bed linen.

She's lying on the bed. Her exposed abdomen looks enormous, just about ready to burst. Angie is sweating, panting and screaming, but this time she's not alone: there is a midwife at the end of the bed, several nurses moving about, and someone – whose face Angie can't see – is gripping her hand.

'Call the doctor,' the midwife says. 'It will have to be a caesarean.'

Angie passes out for what seems to be both an instant and an eternity. When she comes around, a nurse is placing a baby, all bundled up in pink, in Angie's arms.

'It's a girl,' the nurse says. The baby has porcelain skin and a mat of ginger hair, just like Angie's, on her head. 'She was born smiling.'

Angie wakes up feeling butterflies of excitement in her stomach. She slips out of bed quietly, not wanting to disturb Jimmy. She notices that there is a spring in her step that she hasn't felt since her hypomanic days. It's as if by delivering the baby she has allowed a part of Elena's spirit back into her life. She can feel it bubbling in her marrow and tingling under her skin. But it's also as if Elena has been slightly tamed, as if she herself has understood that in order to prolong her stay in Angie's body, she needs to slow down.

Under the shower, Angie ponders whether she should mention this to Dr Suenho – she may want to increase Angie's medication.

I'll wait and see, she thinks, remembering what her baby had looked like. Perhaps this is not Elena at all, but Euthymia.


That night after work, Angie joins Norah outside Norah's house, where a crowd has already gathered to watch the passing of their local Olympic torchbearer. There's music, balloons, banners, a free sausage sizzle and soft drinks. An enthusiastic group turns up, wearing their best formal outfits and carrying plastic flutes filled with champagne. Angie notices that even Norah has dressed up for the occasion and is wearing her pearls.

Everybody hangs around afterwards. Neighbours who often see each other in the street and never say hello to one another are now conversing as if they were old acquaintances.

'Let's go try those sausages, Mum,' Angie says, taking Norah by the arm. 'And I'll tell you about a dream I had.'

But before Angie can begin her story, the retired couple who lives two doors up from Norah join them by the sausage sizzle. They are working as volunteers at the Olympic Village, and are dying to share the excitement of their first day. Soon there are about a dozen people gathered round, listening and asking questions. Half an hour later, when the sun has set, Norah looks at her watch.

'Gosh, look at the time! *The Bill* is about to start.'

They quickly say their goodbyes, and Angie walks Norah to her front door.

'That was fun, wasn't it, Angie?' Norah says, fumbling inside her bag, looking for her key.

'It was. There are lots of free things happening at the moment: concerts, festivals, exhibitions, you name it. We should go to some of them.'

'Count me in. Ah! There it is!' Norah says, fishing out her key. And then she remembers: 'You said something about a dream.'

'Next time,' Angie says, giving Norah a kiss on the cheek. 'Enjoy *The Bill*.'

᷾

On Sunday, at Bicentennial Park, Sinéad arrives holding hands with her new girlfriend – whose name is not George, but Georgie. She's a head taller than Sinéad, with short blond hair and small round glasses. She wears denim overalls and army boots. Norah is speechless, and so are Jimmy's parents.

'I knew it all along!' Jimmy mutters to himself, without turning his attention away from the barbecue. He's overcome by a sense of relief. He had never thought that Sinéad could seduce his wife, but he had been afraid that one day, she could develop feelings for Angie and this would mark the end of what had become – he had to admit – a very positive friendship. Now that Sinéad has a lover, her friendship with Angie remains safe.

Just then, someone slaps him on the back, snatching him out of his reverie.

'Congratulations, mate! I'm Georgie, by the way. I heard it's your birthday. So, how old are we?'

'Err... Thirty-five,' Jimmy manages to say.

'No kidding! I'm thirty-five next month.' Georgie says.

'Well, you don't look a day older than twenty-five!' Jimmy says. Georgie certainly doesn't look thirteen years older than Sinéad. 'Listen, could you make yourself useful and pass us that meat tray over there?'

'Sure!' Georgie says, smiling. 'Anything else? A beer?'

In one of the shelters, Angie stops slicing tomatoes to hug Sinéad.

'I'm so happy for you!' Angie says. 'We'll have to make a date next week, so you can tell me all about Georgie!'

'It will have to be later this month,' a glowing Sinéad says. 'Georgie and I are going to the Gold Coast for two weeks. We wanted to get away from all the Olympic madness and her sister said we could stay in her beach apartment. Can you believe my luck?'

'Of course! You deserve it. Personally, I wouldn't want to be anywhere else right now, but I'm sure you'll have a great time!' Angie says, and then lowers her eyes. 'I imagine Georgie will be heartbroken when you go back home at the end of the year. I know I will.'

'Hold on, Sis! I haven't told you my other bit of good news yet. I'm applying for permanent residency. Georgie wants to sponsor me. Didn't I say to you last year that you couldn't get rid of me that easily?'

'Woo-hoo!' Angie screams. 'I wish I'd brought some champagne. There's so much to celebrate!'

'We can toast with beer. We have an esky full of it in the boot of Georgie's car.'

～

The Olympics come and go, and so do the Paralympics, yet the festive spirit lingers on Sydney and in Angie. She feels optimistic and exuberant, but not euphoric. She's not even upset by the fact that Jimmy is still working the late shift. Since there's no hurry to get home after work, she's enjoying the post-Olympic atmosphere – going out with two friends she's made at work, Kimberly and Simone, or 'Kim and Sim', as she calls them.

The trio soon becomes a quintet, when Sinéad and Georgie return from their romantic getaway looking relaxed, tanned and even more in love with each other.

Seeing Sinéad so happy with Georgie reminds Angie of her unresolved issues with Jimmy. Feeling optimistic, she decides to do something about tackling her marriage troubles – even though Jimmy has ruled out the idea of relationship counselling, there must be other avenues they can explore.

'Here, it's all paid for, out of my own savings,' she tells Jimmy one Saturday morning as they are having breakfast, handing him a manila envelope. Inside there are two return plane tickets to Melbourne, a voucher for two night's accommodation at the Rydges, and two tickets to a musical at the Crown Casino. 'It was a special show and accommodation package.'

'But we've already had a holiday this year!' Jimmy protests, annoyed at not having been consulted.

'This is not a holiday. It's a celebration. See the date? Twenty-sixth of November. I will be handing in my very last university assignment on the twenty-fourth. We're celebrating the completion of my degree,' Angie tells him, resolutely.

When she puts it that way, Jimmy can't help but agree. It is indeed a remarkable achievement, considering all the ups and downs of his wife's mental health throughout the four years of her university studies. He can't even argue against the trip on financial grounds. They both earn good money now, and without a mortgage they have plenty of disposable income.

That afternoon, Angie lifts her eyes from a crossword puzzle to find Jimmy looking at her intently, with the newspaper he was reading resting in his lap. Before he can look away, she has enough time to discern a mixture of concern and suspicion in his eyes.

'What's wrong, Jimmy?' she asks, putting her pencil down.

'Nothing,' he says, hiding behind the newspaper again.

'C'mon, Jimmy. How can I do something about it if you don't tell me what it is?'

'I don't know what you're talking about, Ange,' Jimmy says, folding the paper. He sounds exasperated. 'Whatever it is, it's all in your head. Maybe you should pay your doctor another visit.' He gets up and heads towards their bedroom. 'I'm tired. I'm going to have a nap.'

'I'm tired too,' Angie mutters, throwing her pencil to the floor. 'But a nap is not going to help.'

∾

'I've been feeling very optimistic for two months now,' Angie tells Dr Suenho a few days later. 'But I can't help thinking that it's hard to tell between a healthy optimism and mild mania. And I know that Jimmy is worrying too, even though he doesn't seem to be able to voice his worries. Instead, he keeps telling me that it's all in my head, just like he did when I first got sick.'

'If I remember correctly, last year I asked you to write a list ...' Dr Suenho says, shuffling papers inside Angie's file, which has become quite substantial.

While she waits, Angie looks at her surroundings. Dr Suenho has moved her office to the more spacious room next door. From here, Angie can no longer see the jacaranda tree through the window. A bonsai tree, sitting on the windowsill and partially obscuring a view of the parking lot, has replaced the poinsettia, which didn't survive last winter. On the pin-up board, next to the picture of the young woman holding a baby, there's a portrait of the same curly-haired child, now about three years old. It's still hard to tell whether it's a girl or a boy, but it has Dr Suenho's eyes.

'Is that your grandchild?' Angie asks tentatively, pointing at the photographs.

'Yes, her name is Sophie,' Dr Suenho says, glancing at the photo and returning to her search.

'She's gorgeous!'

'Here it is!' Dr Suenho says, pulling out a sheet of paper from the file and handing it to Angie. It's a photocopy of a dot-point list in Angie's handwriting. 'Do you remember this list? You should have the original somewhere.'

Last year, when Angie first started to take sodium valproate, Dr Suenho had asked her to write her own personal list of 'signs and symptoms of mania,' and then distribute it to her family and friends. That way all of them would share the responsibility of identifying the symptoms, as the person who suffers from the condition is often the last one to notice.

Angie's list reads:

- overconfidence
- loss of inhibitions (in dress, behaviour and language)
- excessive talking
- insomnia
- lack of focus
- tendency to overspend.

'Tell me, Angie – in all honesty: have you been experiencing any of these symptoms?'

Angie goes through the list. She feels confident, but not overconfident. She has been exuberant, but in the right measure. She feels sensual, but not overtly sexual. She has been sleeping well, no longer has nightmares, and has remained focused in both her work and her studies. If she had been talking excessively, other people, including Dr Suenho, would have pointed it out – they always have in the past. Her credit card is well under control, and the ten thousand dollars her grandmother gave her is still intact, earning interest in her bank account. She is financing the upcoming Melbourne trip with her own savings.

Angie imagines that, like the signs and symptoms of

mania, the face of the illness also varies from person to person. Hers has almond shaped eyes, long dark eyelashes, olive skin and charcoal black hair. Angie has stared at Elena's face closely enough to be able to identify her if she saw her again.

'Have you been experiencing any of them, Angie?' Dr Suenho repeats, pointing at the sheet of paper in Angie's hands.

'No,' Angie says decisively, returning the list to Dr Suenho. 'Not even one.'

'Well, there you have it.' There is pride in Dr Suenho's voice. 'Remember when you first came and we deduced that you might have been mildly depressed for several years? I'd say that what is happening now is that when we adjusted your medication back in July we stumbled across your optimum dose.

'See Angie, you've been mildly depressed, severely depressed or hypomanic for so long, that you are having trouble recognising the real you – the witty, exuberant, confident and capable Angie that you should've been for the past thirty-three years.'

'You mean we've found euthymia?'

'I think we have, Angie! You remember the exact term – I'm impressed.'

'From the Greek roots eu, meaning 'well' and thymia, meaning 'spirit' – "a balanced, relaxed state of mind," Angie quotes, her face lighting up. She wants to throw her arms around Dr Suenho and plant a kiss on her forehead, but a sudden realisation makes her freeze in her chair.

'That's it!' she exclaims. 'The look in Jimmy's eyes. If it's hard for me to recognise the real, euthymic Angie, imagine how difficult it must be for him. How can he recognise someone he has never known before?'

# ~ The disease ~

**Melbourne Holiday, Day 3**

We are going back to Sydney this afternoon, not a day too soon. What I had hoped would be a romantic escape, with candlelight dinners, long conversations and lovemaking, has become the holiday from hell – a long weekend of ill health, misadventures, frustration and bickering. Three days can be a long time under such circumstances and we are both glad it's over.

Two days before leaving, Jimmy brought home a cold. On Friday night, we were both so sick that we thought about postponing the trip, but in the end decided to go. Bad move.

When we arrived at the airport on Saturday we were told that our plane had been overbooked and we'd been placed on a waiting list for the next available flight. We sat at the airport lounge, blowing our noses and sneezing, for over two hours.

When we finally arrived in Melbourne it was almost dinnertime. The hotel's restaurant was fully booked, so we dropped our stuff in the room and jumped on a tram to the city to find a place to eat – but the tram broke down in the middle of nowhere. We had to get off and wait for the next one. Just then, the skies opened up, and of course, we hadn't brought an umbrella, so we got drenched. We finally caught a taxi back to the hotel, ordered room service, and were in bed by eight-thirty nursing our colds.

On Sunday night, we turned up at Crown Casino to discover that our dinner and show tickets were for the previous night. We could still have dinner without the show, but Jimmy was so upset he had lost his appetite.

Perhaps, if we had been feeling better, we would've laughed at this comedy of errors: late planes, broken down trams and date mix-ups. But even though the weather and our health improved slightly over the course of the three days, our moods didn't.

## Monday night, Sydney

On the plane home I asked Jimmy, again, when he would be changing back to the day shift, so we could spend more time together.

'Spend more time together doing what?' he asked.

'Working on our marriage,' I answered, surprised.

At this, he turned around, looked at me straight in the eye, and said, 'Ange, what we have is not a marriage. It's a disease.'

He then moved to one of the empty seats several rows ahead, leaving me on my own for the rest of the flight.

If there's one thing that I've become good at, it is pinpointing turning points in my life. I know, for example, that the exact moment my marriage troubles began, or rather, my awareness of these troubles, was that Saturday afternoon in March 1998, when I wrote the first story about Dave, Mario and Elena.

The morning I gave birth to my dreamchild was another turning point: I had found Euthymia, having lost her nearly twenty five years ago.

Sitting by myself on that plane, too stunned to cry, I knew Jimmy and I had reached a defining moment, even if he didn't know it. The fragile bond that was keeping our marriage together had finally come undone – I actually heard it snap, like a rubber band that has been stretched beyond its limit.

When we arrived at the airport, and while we were waiting for our luggage at the carousel, Jimmy started talking to me as if nothing had happened, commenting on the bad weather in Melbourne and other inconsequential things – but I could hardly hear him. I could only hear the phrase 'what we have is not a marriage, it's a disease' whirling around in my head. I didn't say a word for the rest of the night but Jimmy didn't seem to notice. When we got home I locked myself up in the spare room and cried and cried, like I haven't cried in months.

## December 2nd, 2000

Dear Jimmy,

For months I've been saying that we should do something to address our marriage troubles and you've kept telling me that we don't have any troubles; that it is all in my head. Yet the other night, you defined our marriage as a disease. The word 'disease', the way you said it, sounded worse than an illness. It sounded like our marriage, in your mind, is already dead – 'deceased'.

I know you were referring to my condition, my disease, and the way it has interfered with our relationship and our lives. I know that you want nothing more than to go back to the way things were before the onset of my illness. But even if I wanted to, I couldn't go back to being the person

I used to be, the Ange you married. The thing is, Jimmy, the Ange you married no longer exists.

I have finally found my true identity. This identity incorporates good and bad things: the illness I fear, the depressions I loathe, and the exuberance and confidence I love. I have to come to terms with both the positive and the negative aspects of my new personality, or I will disintegrate again. More difficult, but also essential, is the need to come to terms with the ever-present fear of a relapse.

Understandably, you are having even more trouble than I am coming to terms with all the changes and the extremes that have been imposed on you, and having to battle fears over which you have no control. You can't possibly know how much it pains me having put you through the ordeal of the past three years. To make matters worse, I might have to take this medication for the rest of my days, and might not be able to give us the children we always wanted.

Once, when I told you about the way that my father abandoned my mother and I, you promised that you would never, ever, under any circumstances, do the same. I know that you are a man of your word and feel bound by this promise. Since you will never leave me, it is I who has to leave, even if it's just for a while.

What if you are right and all the troubles are 'in my head'? Maybe I just need to get away and think about things, evaluate our marriage, you know – do what I have to do. Perhaps during that time you can do some thinking too.

I'm going to the Sapphire Coast, to stay with my grandma. I have almost four weeks' annual leave, and I'm taking two weeks unpaid leave. I am lucky that Sinéad has finished uni and jumped at the opportunity to cover for me at the bookshop, while she organises her visa.

Joe was happy with that arrangement and my job will be waiting for me when I get back.

I only ask two things of you: first that you don't try to contact me for the time being (don't worry, mum will keep you updated), and second, that you trust me and believe that I'm doing this in full possession of my senses, after having thought about it long and hard.

I am not mad, not today; quite the contrary. Despite the fear, I have finally found, as the Quakers say, 'peace at the centre'. I would also like to be at peace with you.

Please take care.

Love, Angie

# ~ Follow your heart ~

Reading Angie's letter again and again, Jimmy struggles to remember the exact circumstances in which he defined his marriage as a 'disease'. It had been a thoughtless remark, made in a moment of frustration at a time when he was feeling physically ill with a stupid cold, and he had forgotten all about it by the time their plane had landed in Sydney.

Over the course of the following days and weeks, Jimmy will read Angie's letter many times, and will wonder whether he could have said or done anything to stop his wife from walking out on him, had he been awake at the time.

For when Angie left at seven-thirty on that Friday morning, closing the door gently behind her as she did every day when she went to work, Jimmy was still asleep – completely unaware that there was a taxi outside waiting to take his wife to the airport.

While packing on the Thursday night, Angie had come across the biscuit tin in her desk drawer, containing disks holding enough material for a disjointed novel. She had decided to destroy its entire contents, but then she started wondering if any of the stories would be worth keeping. She had spent close to two hours at the computer, opening each document and reading it, sometimes blushing, at other times weeping. One by one, she deleted most of the stories, but there were a few that she couldn't bring herself to erase.

By the time Angie had reached the bottom of the tin, she had realised that if there was one thing worth saving among the thousands of words she had written, it was Elena and Mario's relationship.

A crazy idea had formed in Angie's head: if she could fix the couple's marriage on paper, she might also be able to find a solution to her own relationship problems. She still hadn't given up hope.

She had saved the few stories she had decided to keep onto a single disk, and had slipped it into her handbag, together with her one-way plane ticket to Moruya, the closest airport to Pearl's place.

After taking her packed suitcase to the garage, Angie had rung her grandmother to confirm the time of her arrival.

'Don't forget that the plane arrives at eleven-fifteen,' Angie had said.

'No worries. Betty is fetching me at nine-thirty – at the speed that she drives it'll take us well over an hour to get to Moruya.'

'Grandma, in all honesty, do you think I'm doing the right thing?' Angie had said, shaken by a sudden wave of doubt. Lacking the courage to ask Norah for her blessing, she had decided to leave her a letter very similar to the one she had written to Jimmy. The penchant for letter writing runs in the family.

'If your heart is telling you to come here, listen to it, pet. You know that you're welcome to stay for as long as you like,' Pearl had answered.

As soon as she had hung up, Angie had gone straight to her bookshelf to find the book Sinéad had given her for Christmas: *Follow your Heart*, by Susana Tamaro. She had turned to the last page, and there it was – what Pearl had just said, almost word by word. It had to be a sign.

The last bit of advice the dying Italian grandmother had written to her granddaughter in America, had been to listen to her heart in silence, and pay heed to what it told her.

Angie had sat still for a long time, with her eyes closed and the book in her lap. She had asked her heart whether she was doing the right thing, and then she had waited, and listened. She had heard the sound of her blood, like waves, pulsating inside her ears. She had heard the sound of leaves rustling in the tree outside her window. She had heard a kettle whistle, and a baby cry somewhere in the building. And then a single word had strolled through her mind.

*Solitude.*

Perplexed, she had opened her eyes, and had thought about what her heart was trying to tell her. She had realised that, in her entire life, she had never been on her own for as much as two whole days. She had lived with Norah up until the day she had been married, and ever since that day, she had only been apart from Jimmy on the few occasions when she stayed at her grandmother's or he visited his parents.

Solitude. Angie understood.

While she waits for her plane at the domestic terminal, drinking black coffee from a disposable cup, Angie notices that her hands are shaking, but more with excitement than with nerves. Taking a deep breath, smelling the aroma of the coffee, she is surprised that she's not nearly as sad, or guilty, as she had expected to be.

Angie's heart has spoken, and she feels reassured by what it has told her. Knowing that she is doing the right thing, she has decided to stay with her grandmother only for two weeks, and then spend the rest of her time off – a whole month – on her own.

&

On Saturday, Angie and Pearl visit the country markets, where they buy home-made blueberry jam to have with the scones that they have baked, and seeds for Pearl's herb garden. They walk the few blocks back to Pearl's house along wattle tree lined streets, and sit on the front porch of Pearl's timber cottage, which overlooks the emerald green hills, partially curtained by mist.

Over Devonshire tea, Angie tells Pearl what she's planning to do. As she speaks, she notices that her grandmother is sipping her tea with a look of deep concentration in her eyes, staring at a point beyond the misty hills. She has lost a lot of weight since the last time Angie saw her and the pronounced wrinkles in her forehead make it look as if she were frowning.

'I'll probably need to use some of the money you gave me to set myself up, so it's important for me that you approve, Grandma.' Angie says.

'You're old enough to make these decisions without anybody else's approval, pet,' Pearl says.

'I know, Grandma. And I felt so sure yesterday! But last night, as I lay in bed, I started to have serious doubts. I started thinking about Jimmy reading my letter and imagining his reaction. Did he cry? Was he angry? Was he indifferent? That letter was one of the hardest things I've written in my life. No matter what I said, I knew no words could adequately express what I felt. I found myself wishing he had called me here, even though I asked him not to.'

'Jimmy didn't call, but Norah did – she rang first thing Friday, as soon as she found your letter. She accused me of plotting with you, of being a bad influence, all sorts of things. She threatened to drive here immediately; to take you back home to your husband.'

'See? That's why I couldn't tell her anything,' Angie says, putting her mug of tea down on the table. 'I know this will sound crazy, but sometimes it seems to me that mum loves Jimmy more than she loves me. When I was ... you know, a bit 'high', I felt that she took Jimmy's side against me. Suddenly, the two of them were like an old married couple and I was their teenage daughter. Ugh! I know my perceptions were distorted, but I'm still having trouble overcoming that weird thought.' Angie clears her throat, trying to rid her voice of the bitterness. 'And what did you say to mum when she rang?'

'I told her that a mother must try to be supportive of her daughter, even when she believes that she might be making a mistake.' Pearl turns around and combs Angie's hair with her fingers. 'But you also need to understand, pet, that if you want her to be supportive and understanding, you need to try and reciprocate.'

'So you think I'm making a mistake?' Angie asks, grabbing her grandmother's hand.

'Quite the contrary, Angie. I know you're doing the right thing,' Pearl says. 'Do us a favour, will you? Can you go inside and fetch the photo album that's sitting on the coffee table? The black leather one. I want to show you something.'

Angie brings the album and Pearl leafs through it until she finds the photos taken last Boxing Day, when Angie, Jimmy and Norah came to visit.

'Here!' she says, pointing at a photograph. 'They say a picture speaks a thousand words.'

In the photo, Angie and Jimmy are sitting on the same wooden bench they are sitting on now, on the veranda. Jimmy looks rather serious, leaning on the armrest, wearing a black T-shirt. Angie is leaning away, towards the opposite side, and looks terribly unwell. Her face is a sickly green, her hair is lifeless, the bags under her eyes are dark and heavy, her smile is artificial, and there is no spark in her eyes.

The picture makes Angie's stomach churn.

'Oh my God! Grandma, why on earth did you keep this photo? I would've torn it to bits the moment I saw it! I look like a corpse. Look at my eyes; they're hollow.' She tries to remove the photo, but it has been glued to the page. She shuts the album with a bang. 'I guess I was still recovering from my last depression, and it shows.'

Pearl takes the album from Angie's lap, and finds the same page again.

'Look at the other pictures, taken the same day.'

There's one of Angie busy with the barbeque, one of the three women opening presents in the lounge, one of Pearl and Angie arm in arm, smiling under the shade of a lemon tree.

'See? You look fine in all of them,' Pearl goes on. 'But when you are next to Jimmy, it's as if there were a black cloud hanging over your head, or rather, over his head. He's carried that weight all his life, and he's used to it, but it was crushing you to death.

'I kept that picture because I wanted to show it to your mother, when the time came. And I gave you that money back in July because I already knew that you'd need it, sooner rather than later.'

Angie covers her mouth with her hand. She looks at the

other pictures with cloudy eyes, and can only nod in agreement.

'So,' Angie finally says, swallowing her tears, 'You think there is no hope for Jimmy and me?'

'There is always hope, pet. But I'm afraid you've done everything you can. It's up to Jimmy now. This is the way I see it, Angie: three years ago, you fell into a rabbit hole, and had to find your own way out, but the hole that brought you out wasn't the same one you fell into. You've come out at a totally different place and Jimmy needs to make his own journey to meet you there.'

Angie has lost her voice again; all she can do is nod. She wishes she had thought of that metaphor when trying to reason with Jimmy. Perhaps it would have helped him understand. She takes a sip of her tea but it has gone cold.

'I have no doubt that Jimmy loves you, pet,' Pearl says, ruffling Angie's hair.

'Neither do I,' Angie manages to say, unable to hold the tears any longer.

'And, as the Good Book says,' Pearl goes on, 'Love can endure all things.'

Pearl pulls Angie's face towards her shoulder, as she did with her own daughter not long ago. 'I really hope that somewhere along the way, Jimmy is able to chuck away some of his baggage. But there's something else you could do in the meantime, Angie.'

'What is that?' Angie says, in between sobs.

'You can make peace with your mother. She's coming next weekend.'

Angie spends the following week by her grandmother's side. The guilt that had attacked her belatedly begins to subside.

They go for a walk every day as soon as they get up, then they work in the garden, feed Pearl's hens, collect their eggs, take turns to do the cooking, and watch TV after dinner. Some mornings Angie drives to the nearest beach in Pearl's old Gemini, and on the Friday they even venture all the way to Merimbula. In between, they have long talks.

Pearl teaches Angie her foolproof scone recipe: all you need is one cup of flour, one cup of cream and one cup of fizzy lemonade. Mix it, bake it, and voila. She shows Angie how to make yoghurt using freeze-dried culture, and how to cook porridge the way they do it in Scotland. She makes everything look so easy.

At night, working on her stories with pen and paper, Angie hears her grandmother coughing hour after hour, even though she insists that she's sleeping well. She still won't hear of going to the doctor, and continues to self-medicate by taking lemon lozenges, a measure of whisky in her tea, and inhaling the steam of boiling water with eucalyptus leaves.

Going through the family albums, Angie learns all about her grandfather, Alexander Moore, who died before Angie was born. He had been a dairy farmer with a heart condition and a passion for the music of his forefathers. There are several photos of him wearing traditional Scottish clothing and playing the bagpipes. After his death, Pearl had sold their farm, ten kilometres west of Cobargo, and had bought the cottage in the village.

There are dozens of photos of the twins, as children and teenagers. Even though Norah and Jo were identical, more so as children - with the same haircuts and clothes - Angie can always tell one from the other. Jo used to smile with only half her mouth, which gave her a mischievous look. Norah smiled with her whole face back then, radiating light. Angie can almost imagine her mother's face lighting up like that. In fact, she can remember seeing that smile as a child.

'Dr Suenho said I could've been mildly depressed ever since I was seven. Could it be that mum has never recovered properly from the breakdown she had that same year?' Angie asks her grandmother, looking up from the album.

'I hope not,' Pearl says, shaking her head. 'Your mother is no spring chicken, and I would hate to think that she has spent the best decades of her life suffering from depression without even knowing it. At least you have plenty of time to make up for the years lost; you're in the prime of your life.'


On Saturday, Norah has hardly had time to put her bags down and sit on the lounge when Angie comes running from the kitchen and lands on her knees in front of her. She smears her mother's lap with tears, unable to speak. Slowly, the words come.

They spend the night talking and crying. Pearl supplies tea and tissues. In the early hours of the morning, when Pearl has to bring toilet paper because they have gone through all her tissue boxes, they finally call it a night.

Over breakfast the next day, Norah tells Angie she had left Jimmy a message telling him she was driving to the Sapphire Coast first thing on Saturday. As she was loading her bags into the car on Saturday morning, Jimmy had turned up at her doorstep, his T-shirt on inside out. Feeling awfully sorry for him, Norah had asked if he wanted to come, and he had said that he intended to respect his wife's request to be left alone.

When Norah was about to drive away, he had tapped on the window and had asked her if she would be back next Saturday, for their usual weekly dinner.

'He didn't even ask you about me?'

'That's his way of coping, I guess.' Norah says.

'I see.'

'Come home with me, Angie,' Norah pleads. 'You don't have to go back to living with Jimmy straightaway. You can stay with me.'

'No, Mum.' Angie says. 'I have to do this. I need to learn to live on my own.'

'I've been living on my own for twenty-five years, and it isn't exactly paradise, Angie.'

'Mum, I only plan to be on my own for a few weeks, not a lifetime. And you can visit me.'

'And where do you plan to stay?'

'Don't know yet. Maybe I could housesit for someone who's going on holidays. I've seen a few ads.'

Norah looks across the table at her mother, who has remained silent throughout this conversation, but Pearl is away in a world of her own. She often is these days: she stares into the void, completely disengaged from her surroundings. It's so unlike her.

The feeling that Pearl won't be around for much longer comes to Norah again. A shiver runs up her spine. She makes up her mind to visit her mother more often. Perhaps come and stay with her for a while – give Angie some space.

'What if I wasn't at home? Would you stay at my place then?' Norah tries one last time.

'Muu-uum!' Angie exclaims, rolling her eyes.

'Fair enough,' Norah says, and smiles her faint smile. 'Fair enough.'

# ~ Solitude ~

**Angie's Diary, Thursday, January 4th 2001**

I'm writing this sitting on the deck of a rented cottage, overlooking a national park. It's that time of the day, between afternoon and night, when the world sits still – as if it were holding its breath. The day was mine, the night is mine, these precious hours are mine. There is no rush, no doctor's appointments to keep, no uni assignments to write, no having to get up early to go to work tomorrow.

I've been staying here for over two weeks now. I had to sign a three-month lease, and was reluctant at first, but one look at the place was enough to make up my mind. It's small, but it's clean and bright, with polished floorboards, high ceilings and a deck with an awesome view. It has one bedroom and a sunroom, where I've set up my study (bought a second hand-computer and everything), and it's only a ten-minute walk from the train station.

Mum insisted on buying me a mobile phone for emergencies. She had dinner with Jimmy two weeks ago, before she went to stay with Grandma Pearl, and she says that he seems to be doing okay. I suppose I'll have to call him soon, to tell him that I have to stay here for at least another two months, but I'm dreading his reaction, or worse, his non-reaction. Don't they say that the opposite of love is not hate, but indifference?

In between catching up with my friends, I've kept busy settling into my new place, devouring books and writing furiously. Something resembling a novel is starting to come together. Its working title is Avoiding Elena. I've chucked away a lot of the Mills and Boon stuff and I'm exploring the relationships between the three characters in depth.

Dave, who has never stopped caring about Mario, can only deal with the situation by resorting to denial. Elena, who threw herself into Dave's arms because she was feeling neglected, is beginning to feel the weight of remorse.

Mario has finally sensed this, and suspects that there is something terribly wrong with Elena, although he cannot yet ascertain what it is, and cannot bring himself to ask. After all, he has never been very good at expressing his feelings.

## Tuesday, January 9th, 2001

Yesterday I called Tiger after nearly eighteen months. I had been writing all day, and the more I wrote about Dave, the more embarrassed I felt about the way I behaved with Tiger the year before last. I felt I needed to apologise.

He was sorry to hear that I've decided to have a trial separation from Jimmy, but he sympathised when I said we were no longer communicating – he had felt the same all those years ago, when he decided not to pursue their friendship.

I asked him how his love life was going. He said that he has recently started dating his secretary, and things between them are going well.

Now that he has my mobile number, Tiger promised to call me regularly, and he called today. I told him our talks have been enormously helpful, and that he's a very good listener.

'A couple of my mates have said the same, you know?' he said. 'I've been thinking of going back to uni, to study psychology. Be the one who listens, and nods, instead of the one who lies down on the couch and rambles on.'

'Dr Suenho never made me lie down,' I told him.

'I guess she's a psychiatrist, not a psychoanalyst,' he explained. 'Are you still seeing her, by the way?'

'I've sort of graduated now – she only wants to see me once a year. My GP can write my prescriptions.'

'You must be proud,' Tiger said. 'I'm still seeing my shrink once a month.'

'I'd be prouder if I didn't need to take medication,' I said.

'C'mon Angie! There's nothing wrong with having to take a few pills to compensate for a chemical imbalance in your brain. It's the same as diabetics having to take insulin because their pancreas has stopped making it. The important thing is that it's working for you – it doesn't work for everyone.'

After hearing Tiger say that, there is no doubt in my mind that he would make a great therapist, although Dr Suenho would probably think his comparison was a little simplistic.

**Wednesday, January 10th 2001**

I'm writing this on the plane, heading for the Sapphire Coast. Last night I opened my eyes, just after midnight, and there was an old man sitting at the end of my bed. I wasn't afraid because I knew who he was – I had seen him in photos, although he was much younger in them. He was wearing a tartan kilt and a white shirt, with several medals pinned to it.

'Grandpa Alex!' I exclaimed, sitting up. 'What are you doing here?'

He didn't answer but just looked at me serenely, his head tilted to the side, a sad smile on his lips.

'Is Grandma okay?' I asked, realising the reason for his visit.

'Don't you worry about a thing, child,' he said. His voice was deep and gentle. 'Everything has been arranged already.' With this, he got up and gave me a kiss on the forehead, waking me up.

I grabbed my mobile and called Grandma's number. Mum answered – she had been about to call me. Grandma had passed away in her sleep, sometime between 10.00 pm and midnight.

'I was reading a book,' Mum told me, 'and at about midnight realised I hadn't heard your grandma cough once since she went to bed. So I went to check on her and...' She couldn't finish the sentence.

I asked her to remain calm and since I still have one week off, I jumped on the first available plane.

**Saturday, January 13th 2001**

Grandma died of pneumonia – just like Aunt Jo supposedly did. The funeral was almost surreal to me, as if we were burying a distant relative. I couldn't shed a single tear during the preparations or the ceremony. Mum had held herself up very well during the week, but broke down at the service.

Only a few weeks ago, Grandma told me that I should try to be Mum's pillar. I was glad that I was able to remain strong, if somewhat impassive, offering her my shoulder to cry on.

Jimmy was there too. He had asked Pete, his brother, to

drive him, and they stayed overnight at the pub in the village. When Jimmy hugged me to give me his condolences, it was like hugging an old, dear friend. He smelled faintly of mothballs – his suit has been stored away for years.

It dawned on me that the six weeks were up, and I still hadn't had the courage to speak with him. I figured that it was then or never, so when we went back to the cottage for supper, I told him about the three-month lease.

Without showing any emotion, he said that I know where to find him when the lease is over. After he left, I found myself wishing that he wouldn't make it so easy for me to stay away.

It was nearly midnight when I said goodnight to Mum, after we had finished washing up. When I came to my bedroom, I found an envelope sitting on my pillow. It had my name on it, written in Jimmy's neat, square handwriting. The note inside read:

> Dear Ange,
> You know that I've never been good at expressing my feelings, and now, more than ever, I'm a bit paranoid about saying something insensitive, like comparing our marriage to a disease. So I'll tread carefully. Anyway, at this stage, there's only one thing I wish to say.
> It's a quote that I'm afraid has been used to death. But its original author was a very wise man – the author of The Prophet, a book you and I have read together, remember?
> Khalil Gibran said: 'If you love somebody, let them go, for if they return, they were always yours. And if they don't, they never were.'
> Over the past few weeks, while waiting for you to return (or not), I've truly come to understand the meaning of his words.
> With love, always,
> Jimmy.

**Sunday, January 14th, 2001**

Sinéad and Georgie offered to pick me up from the airport this afternoon, when I got back to Sydney. Mum stayed back to clean up Grandma's house. I would have liked to help, but I have to go back to work tomorrow – after a six-week break, I couldn't ask for more time off.

When I arrived at the airport, Georgie was waiting for me by herself. She said Sinéad had come down with a migraine and had gone to bed. Georgie drove me home and I asked her to come in for a cuppa.

We sat on the deck and I started to tell her about Grandma – not about the funeral, or her death, but about how dear and resilient and wise she was, and how much I will miss her. The things I couldn't say last week because I was afraid of upsetting Mum. All of a sudden I was sobbing and hic-cupping, drowning in belated grief. Georgie moved closer, held me in her arms and told me that she knew how I felt. Her mother passed away a year ago, and she still wakes up at night pining for her.

Next thing I knew, she was kissing me. And I didn't stop her.

Myriad thoughts went through my mind: I thought of the six-second kiss that started Elena and Dave's affair. I thought of my best friend, lying sick in bed. I thought about the times I had been so close to kissing Tiger when I was euphoric, and yet it had never happened. I thought of my husband, who hadn't kissed me like this in a long time. I thought about the fact that never, in my wildest dreams, would I have imagined being kissed in this way by a woman.

I wasn't counting the seconds, so I don't know how long it was before I shakily pushed Georgie away from me and told her that it would best if she went home. She nodded and left without saying another word, and I sat on the deck for a long time, holding my head in my hands to stop it from pounding, trying to make sense of what just happened. I was still out there when Sinéad called me on the mobile. She was in tears – our conversation went along these lines:

Georgie and I have just broken up.

What?

Don't play the angel, Angie. She told me what happened. She told me she's attracted to you.

But I'm not attracted to her!

She said you kissed her!

*She kissed me!*

How can I ever trust you again?

Sinéad, I've just come back from burying my grandmother, and I was emotional and upset. Sometimes crazy things can happen during a crisis.

Oh yeah. And how many of your crises have I seen you through? How many crazy things have I seen you do? I could have overstepped the line too, but I never did, because you were my friend, my sister! And now … everything has changed!

Listen, why don't we both sleep on this, and calm down? Believe me, I am as bewildered as you are by what just happened. I'm back to work tomorrow – could you meet me at the bookshop after five, to talk? Sinéad? Sinéad, are you there?

But she had hung up.

When Angie locks up the bookshop at five-fifteen the next day, she finds Sinéad waiting outside, leaning against a post. To Angie's surprise, she's smoking a cigarette.

'I thought you quit months ago!' Angie says, approaching her friend.

Sinéad exhales smoke, shrugging her shoulders. She's wearing dark glasses and black clothes, looking as if she were the one who had just returned from a funeral.

'I'm sorry about last night,' Sinéad says, keeping her distance. 'I was wrong to blame you for what happened. I was very upset, and had a bitch of a migraine.'

'I know. As long as you know that I'd never do anything to hurt you, Shine.'

'I need a drink,' Sinéad says, and starts walking. 'Where can we get a beer?'

They walk to the local bar. On the way, Sinéad tells Angie that Lillian, her long-time girlfriend in Northern Ireland, had left her for a guy.

In the pub, Sinéad slides her glasses to the top of her head. Her eyelids are pink and puffy. Two middle-aged men sit at a table next to them, giving them sleazy looks. In the next room, several slot machines dingle and bleep. Angie wishes they would have gone somewhere else. She drains her glass of wine in one gulp.

'I came to Australia to mend a broken heart, and I'm leaving with a broken heart.' Sinéad says, taking a sip of her beer.

'What do you mean you're leaving?' Angie says, feeling her cheeks on fire. 'I thought you wanted to stay.'

'I had a long talk with my mum last night – she was always against the idea of my moving here permanently. It didn't take her long to convince me to go back straightaway. I'm leaving in a few days, just before my visa expires.'

'That soon! And it's all my fault! '

'Remember how we once talked about people coming into your life for a reason, a season or a lifetime? I reckon *she* came into my life for a season, and I came into your life for a reason.' Sinéad says, before downing the rest of her drink.

'A reason!' Angie repeats, shifting in her chair. 'What do you mean?'

'I was meant to be there for you when you were unwell and felt that nobody else understood you. Now you've got your health back and you've made heaps of friends, like Kim, Sim and Mandy. You have your mum, and Jimmy, who's patiently waiting for you. You've even got Tiger, by the sounds of it, not to mention *her*, if you felt that way inclined.'

Sinéad pauses, looking at Angie with a blank expression. It's a long, uncomfortable pause. She then bursts into laughter, pointing her finger at Angie.

'Cheer up, sister. It's not the end of the world. I'll survive, and so will you,' she says.

'That wasn't funny!' Angie says, frowning.

'You don't need me anymore,' Sinéad says. 'And that's a good thing.'

'That's all rubbish. I'll always need you!'

'Listen, Angie: it was always on the cards that I'd be going back when I finished my degree, wasn't it? It's time for me to go home and think about what I'm going to do next. It's just something I have to do. I know you will understand, because you are doing the same thing right now. Well, sort of in reverse. Instead of going home, you left home, so you could sort things in your head.'

Angie nods, unconvinced, and gets up to order more drinks. On her way to the counter, she remembers the last words Sinéad said to her the previous night. Everything has changed.

∾

It is only the day after Sinéad has left that Angie feels lonely for the first time since she's been living alone. That night, lying in bed, her senses amplify every sound and movement around her, and she can't sleep. She can hear the floors creaking, the pipes humming, the tree branches scratching the roof, the possums running on the deck.

Even though it's summer, Angie finds herself shivering in the dark. She turns on the lights. Her thoughts go to Jimmy, who's also lying in bed on his own, like her. Then she looks at the time, and realises that Jimmy hasn't even finished his shift. It's only 10.45 pm.

Angie's mobile is right next to her, sitting on her bedside table, next to the pile of books she has borrowed from the library. She's tempted to call Jimmy, but she punches Tiger's number instead.

Tiger is about to open a bottle of pink champagne when the phone rings. Holding the receiver between his ear and his shoulder, he struggles with the cork.

'Tiger, it's Angie. I hope I didn't wake you up.'

'Hey Angie! No, you didn't. I just got home. Are you okay?'

'Not really,' Angie says. 'My best friend has gone back to Ireland, and right now I feel lost without her. She said that I'll get over it, because I have other friends now. But this has made me think about Jimmy and you. For years, you went through thick and thin together and then – Poof! You fell out, just like that.'

'Listen Angie, it wasn't "just like that" --'

'No, you listen,' Angie interrupts. 'The thing is, you made other friends, but he didn't. At least he had me, but now that I'm not there, I'm worried that he's becoming too isolated. I wish you could give him a call, ask him how he's doing.'

'Angie, you know I can't do that. We've spoken about this already,' Tiger says.

He covers the receiver with his hand and whispers 'Won't be long,' to his secretary, who's sitting on the sofa holding an empty flute. His secretary nods, and putting the flute down, walks over to Tiger, takes the bottle, and opens it with one single, confident twist.

'I know we spoke about it,' Angie says. 'But I still can't understand --'

'Listen, Angie,' Tiger gently cuts in. 'I have company. Can I call you tomorrow?'

'Shit, Tiger! You should've told me straight away! I thought I heard something pop. Champagne, uh?'

'Never mind,' Tiger says, blushing. 'Actually, why don't we meet tomorrow, for dinner? There's something important that I left out the last time we spoke about Jimmy and I. It may help you understand. How about seven at the Spanish restaurant in Liverpool Street, where we met the other day?'

'The other day? You have some warped sense of time, Tiger. That was nearly three years ago, before this roller-coaster even started!' Angie says, laughing. 'Never mind. I'll be there at seven. Thanks and ... have fun!'

Still sleepless, Angie turns her computer on - the hours usually fly when she writes - but she finds that she can't put a word down. To pass the time, she starts reading what she's written so far, starting from the beginning. Her heart beats faster when she reads one particular scene from the first chapter, and she wonders about the 'something' that Tiger had left out of their previous conversation. Could it be what she has always suspected?

All of a sudden, Dave touches her cheek, as if to make sure that she's real.

'I wish some of the girls I dated were more like you ...'

Elena blushes and looks away. He knows he should stop, but doesn't. 'Elena, there's something I have to tell you – '

'No,' she interrupts. 'You do not have to. I know.'

'What do you mean?'

'I know you are attracted to me. I always knew.'

# ~ The book of revelations ~

The next day, Angie finds herself at the Spanish Restaurant feeling as nervous as she had felt that night almost three years ago. To keep her mind occupied while she waits – as usual, Tiger is late – she gets up and walks around the place looking at the photos that hang from the walls, each one depicting an aspect of Spanish life.

There's a black and white photo of a matador striking a bull, labelled 'Juan Belmonte (1892–1962)'. There is a photo of a group of members of the guardia civil – the Spanish paramilitary force – wearing their traditional three-pointed hats.

Another picture shows a group performing a flamenco dance. In it there is a beautiful woman in her late thirties, singing and clapping her hands. She's wearing a bright orange dress, a black knitted shawl, and a red carnation in her hair. Two teenage girls in equally dazzling costumes are dancing on high-heeled black shoes, holding one hand up in the air and lifting their frilled skirts with the other. The fourth member of the troupe, a middle-aged man, accompanies them on the guitar.

Angie realises that she has seen this photograph before, years ago, right here. She came to this restaurant to celebrate Pete's birthday, only days before she chose the place for her first meeting with Tiger.

The legend underneath the picture reads 'María Elena Rodriguez, the renowned Andalusian Flamenco Singer, performing with her family at the Seville Expo in 1992.'

Angie had seen this picture only a few days before Elena materialised in one of her dreams, apparently out of nowhere. Her unconscious had recorded not only the Spanish beauty's features, but also her name.

While pondering all this, Angie sees a bald man enter the restaurant out of the corner of her eye, but she doesn't look away from the picture. For a moment, she has forgotten why she's here. Just then, the bald man taps her on the shoulder. Angie turns around, and gasps.

'Tiger! Why on earth did you shave your head?'

'It's trendy, and easier to keep,' he explains, pulling out a chair for Angie to sit down. 'It's been like this for ages.'

'Well, I last saw you when I wrote off Mum's car, and that was nearly eighteen months ago. You had hair then.'

Tiger doesn't kiss her on the cheek, as he has always done in the past. He seems as nervous as she is. They order several tapas and a jug of sangria.

As soon as their meal arrives, Tiger dives into the heart of the matter.

'Remember, Angie, when Liz died?'

'Yes, you told me about it. You rang Jimmy, and he wasn't very attentive, so you decided that that was enough to piss you off for life.'

'Well, it wasn't quite like that. It's true that he wasn't very attentive over the phone and that ticked me off, but we arranged to meet in person the next day. I'd been drinking all afternoon, so by the time he arrived at my place, after work, I was well and truly smashed.'

੨

Jimmy knocks on the door and it falls open, so he lets himself in. Tiger is sitting on the floor in the middle of the living room, an empty bottle of scotch at his feet, another one clutched in his hands. The stereo is playing Tchaikovsky at full blast. There are two tumblers on the coffee table, but he's drinking straight from the bottle.

'There you are,' Tiger slurs. 'Drink?'

'Look at the state you're in!' Jimmy says, walking over to the turntable and lifting the needle off the record. It screeches.

'Ouch!' Tiger screams. 'Careful!'

'C'mon, I'll put you to bed.'

'Nah, no bed for me. Not until we make a toast,' he shakily pours a glass for Jimmy.

'Tiger, you know I don't drink alcohol. You saw what it did to my mother.'

Tiger holds his chin and scrunches his eyes while he thinks of a toast.

'To the dead! No. No. Hold on. To women. Yes, to all bloody women!' he says, holding the bottle up. 'Your mother included!'

'C'mon Tiger, pull yourself together. Liz was lost long before you met. You couldn't have done anything to save her,' Jimmy says. Leaning over his friend, he peels Tiger's fingers off the bottle, one by one.

'Maybe she was,' Tiger says, reluctantly letting go of his treasure. 'And I didn't love her anyway. In fact, I've never loved her or any of the dozens of women I've slept with.'

'What nonsense! Your problem is the exact opposite: you fall in love too easily. Didn't your shrink tell you that?'

'Funny you should mention my shrink. I rang him today. Since you wouldn't listen to me yesterday, I had to make an emergency appointment. He charged me a bloody fortune, but at least he was there for me. We talked about Liz, and Ruth, and Tanya, and Laura, and all my other lousy attempts at having something that would resemble a relationship. He said I should stop trying to go against my nature; that I should accept who I am.'

'What on earth are you talking about?' Jimmy says, kneeling on the floor, close enough to Tiger to smell his alcohol breath.

'I'm no good with women, Jimmy – because I'm gay. There.'

'Fuck off, Tiger. If this is your idea of a drunken joke, it's not funny.'

'I am gaaaay, I'm gay,' Tiger sings at top of his lungs, mimicking an operatic voice. 'And the only man I love I can't possibly have.'

Tiger latches onto Jimmy but Jimmy pushes him away and jumps to his feet as if propelled by a spring.

'I love you, Jimmy – I've always loved you,' Tiger mumbles, hugging his knees and rocking back and forth.

'Tiger!' Jimmy exclaims. 'Get under the fucking shower and sober up NOW!'

'No!' Tiger says, leaning on the couch to help himself up. With considerable effort, he manages to stand tall. 'This is my place,' he says, sounding sober all of a sudden. 'I can do whatever I want here. I can be whoever I want to be. If you don't like it, then piss off.'

Still shocked, Jimmy turns around and walks out, just like that. Out of Tiger's place and out of his life.

∾

Angie's vision blurs, and she rubs her eyes furiously – thankfully she's not wearing any makeup today. After a few seconds, she comes to, and realises that the photograph of the flamenco dancing family, hanging on the wall behind Tiger, has changed. The four members of the troupe are no longer dancing. They are all bending over with laughter – they are laughing at her.

'Earth to Angie,' Tiger calls. He's looking more relaxed now that he has uttered his confession.

Angie adjusts her eyes. The phantoms behind Tiger dissolve and he comes into focus. He doesn't look as handsome without hair – his head has the shape of an egg.

She nods to let him know that she's still with him.

'I had never really intended to tell Jimmy how I felt about him,' Tiger goes on. 'In time, I'm sure he would've come to accept my nature, but he just couldn't hack the fact that he was the object of my affection.'

Angie suddenly bursts into laughter.

'So you think it's funny, uh?' Tiger says, raising his eyebrows.

'No, not at all … it's just that I thought … I had always thought …' She stops until the laughter recedes. She touches her cheeks – they're sizzling. 'I had this crazy idea that you were secretly attracted to me. And to think, that it wasn't me at all, it was… oh, my God, how embarrassing!'

Tiger also laughs, shaking his head. 'Yes, I remember the story you sent me, years ago. Believe me, I've always liked you, but not in that way. I'm sorry to disappoint you, Angie.'

'I'm not disappointed. I'm relieved, I think…' Angie says, and stirs the fruit in her sangria in order to avoid Tiger's gaze.

'Jimmy is a good man, Angie,' Tiger says, in a serious tone. 'And you're a good woman. You're a good couple. I'd never come between you, no matter which one of you I was attracted to, if you get my drift.'

'I guess I do. But there's one thing I don't understand. How come you're still trying to get on with women? You said you were dating your secretary.' Angie says, taking a mouthful of sangria.

'Ha!' Tiger exclaims, smiling mischievously. 'I like how people always assume that all secretaries are female.'

Angie chokes on her drink, spitting half of it on the table. They both laugh for a long time.

'It's so good to hear you laughing the way you used to,' Tiger says, when their laughter recedes. 'Last year you freaked me out, you know, the way you laughed. It sounded so much like Jimmy's mother, when she used to roam around the house in a drunken stupor, either laughing out loud or sobbing like a baby. In fact, your whole demeanour reminded me so much of her it wasn't funny.'

'Gwyneth?' Angie says, with a furrowed brow. 'You've had too much sangria, Tiger. You've lost the plot. You must be thinking about someone else's mother. Gwyneth Fletcher doesn't even drink, and she instilled that in Jimmy.'

'Of course she doesn't. I'm talking about a time long before she joined AA, silly.'

Angie slumps in her chair, looking like she's about to faint. She's hardly had the chance to assimilate Tiger's first revelation when he drops another bombshell on her.

'What on earth are you talking about?'

'Far out,' Tiger says under his breath, seeing Angie's reaction. 'I... I always assumed you knew. I assumed...' His voice trails off.

Angie remains silent for a long time, as several pieces of a puzzle audibly click into place inside her head.

'Angie, are you okay? Do you want a glass of water?' She hears Tiger say.

'Well, now you need to tell me the rest of it.' Angie manages to say in a whisper.

'I'm sorry, but if Jimmy didn't tell you then I have no right to. This is his life, not mine,' Tiger says, resolutely.

'But --'

'Listen, Angie: all of this happened years before he met you. After Jimmy's mum joined AA and both her and her husband became Christians, they turned into living proof that people can really be born again. Trust me; I've seen it with my own eyes. I should've known that Jimmy would want to protect his parents' reputation.'

'His parents' reputation? Were they both alcoholics?'

'Oh Angie...'

'Tiger?' Angie pleads. 'If he hasn't told me by now, then he never will, and I need to know - it's my life too. It's my marriage we are talking about. If my laughter freaked you out last year, imagine what it did to Jimmy. Imagine what it was like for him to live with a woman who was behaving the way I was.'

'C'mon Angie,' Tiger says, signaling to the waiter. He sounds weary. 'Let's go back to your place and we'll talk there. It's too damn noisy here.'

Angie nods. She feels like a yoyo again, her reactions having jumped from shock to laughter, then to disbelief and now to distress throughout the course of one meal. The voice of inevitability starts to hiss in her ear. 'Here we go, going over the edge again,' but with so many other issues at hand, Angie has no time for it right now. She flicks it away, like a fly, and follows Tiger into the night.

❧

After Tiger leaves her place, Angie stays up until dawn, trying to make sense of the vague details about Jimmy's past that Tiger has reluctantly told her.

She finds it impossible to reconcile the image of the drunken mother and the violent father with the church-going, squeaky-clean middle-aged couple she has known for twelve years. But she can now understand why Jimmy always kept his distance from his folks, whereas his brother Peter never made an effort to hide his hostility towards them, spoiling every family function. Each one had found their own way to cope with the traumas of their childhood.

What Pearl had said about Jimmy carrying a crushing weight on his shoulders makes perfect sense now. At first, Angie feels her bewilderment giving way to anger and frustration. Not only has Jimmy chosen to bear the burden of his turbulent childhood on his own, knowing that it is still weighing on him and affecting his relationships, but he has also kept to himself the real reason behind his falling out with Tiger. She never questioned him about his parents, for she knew nothing about their past, but she had asked Jimmy countless times about Tiger.

As Angie weaves these astonishing new revelations into the book she is writing, she sympathises with the character of Mario more and more, and begins to understand why he is the way he is and behaves the way he does. And as Mario finds some kind of redemption in the pages of her manuscript, Angie finally begins to cry, her anger turning to sorrow for the real-life Jimmy. She wonders what it would take for him to be able to exorcise the demons of his past.

In the story, Elena cuts off her affair with Dave, and wanting to make a clean break from both Dave and Mario, she goes back home, to Seville, for three months. She tells Mario that she needs to spend some time with her ageing parents, who she hasn't seen in ten years. Mario tells her that he will be there, waiting for her, when she returns.

On the eve of Elena's departure they make love, with a passion they haven't demonstrated to each other in a long, long time.

# ~ Fate's Call ~

Not long after Tiger has left Angie's place, Jimmy finishes his shift at work. Bending under the weight of his backpack he makes his way to the train station. His teeth are chattering as he walks down George Street. There has been a southerly change and he has been caught unawares, wearing a short sleeved shirt. He stops at the pedestrian crossing and presses the button, thinking that he can't wait to get to the station, where at least there is some shelter.

'Do you have the time, mate?' a young man, standing next to him asks.

'Ten past eleven,' Jimmy says.

'Shit!' the man says, and slams the button again.

The lights change. Jimmy is about to step onto the road, ahead of the young man, when his mobile rings. He climbs back onto the curb and reaches into his shirt pocket, thinking that the only two people who could be calling at this time would be Norah, or Angie. It could be an emergency.

'Jimmy!' It's a very familiar voice, one he hasn't heard for about seven years.

'Tiger?' is all Jimmy can say.

'Sorry to call you like this, out of the blue, but it's important --'

There is a shriek of brakes.

'FU-U-UCK!!!' Jimmy screams. He has just seen a car, speeding through the red light on the opposite side of the six lane road, hit the young man who had asked him for the time.

'I see that you're still pissed off with me!' Tiger exclaims.

Jimmy can't take his eyes off the road. A man has gotten out of the car, and is running towards the pedestrian, who is lying motionless on the pavement. Other cars have stopped, and several people are quickly making their way towards the scene.

'Listen mate, I've just seen someone get hit by a car,' Jimmy says, his voice trembling. 'This guy might be fuckin' dead! I've got to go. I'll call you when I get home – I still have your number.'

'You go, man!' Tiger says. 'Please call me, no matter what time it is – I'll be up.'

After making sure the traffic has stopped, Jimmy runs across the road.

'Someone call an ambulance!' the driver howls, kneeling on the floor next to his unintended victim.

'I'm onto it!' Jimmy screams, dialling the emergency number.

On the train home, after giving his witness statement to the police, Jimmy thinks about the premonition he has had all his life that he would die in a car accident. It had never occurred to him that it wouldn't be as a driver, but as a pedestrian. This was the accident he was meant to have died in, he thinks, and due to a fluke, to a phone call from Tiger of all people, he hasn't.

The last time that he phoned the hospital to ask about the casualty, he was told that he was in a 'critical condition.' He wishes he had Angie's number, to phone her and tell her what has happened. As his next of kin, she could have been the one receiving a call to inform her that her husband is in critical condition, instead of the young man's next of kin.

It is after midnight when Tiger's phone rings. Jimmy is obviously still affected by the night's events, rambling unintelligible things about having lived a life half-lived all this time, for nothing. He keeps mentioning the young guy who had asked him the time and then ran to his possible death. He keeps repeating that Tiger has saved his life. He keeps saying that he was a fool to have let Angie leave the way she did, for not disobeying her wishes and actively pursuing her. He could have died tonight, without letting her know how important she was to him, even if she is no longer the same person she was when they first met.

He has forgotten to ask Tiger the reason for his earlier call. Tiger had wanted to warn Jimmy that he had been forced to tell Angie about his parents' history, but after what has happened, Tiger gathers he doesn't need to go into any of it. In fact, it's Jimmy who brings it up.

'My mother once said that the Alcoholics Anonymous believe that the day they take the first step to become sober is the first day of their new lives,' Jimmy says when he has calmed down a little. 'This is exactly how I feel now. I've been given another chance, to set things right. I could've died tonight; with so much unfinished business it's not funny. Tomorrow is the first day of my new life.'

'So what are you going to do with it? This new life?'

'After mother joined AA, she gave us all a flyer with the twelve steps. I memorised them at the time and would you believe, I still remember them! Step four is "make a fearless inventory of ourselves", and step eight is "make a list of all persons we have harmed, and be willing to make amends" – I guess that's a good place to start.'

'That's a bloody good place to start,' Tiger says. 'But you can't make an objective inventory of yourself on your own. You'll need professional help – would you like my shrink's details?'

'Shit, Tiger. Some people never change. Are you on commission or something?' Jimmy says, but Tiger can hear a faint smile in his voice.

Tiger sighs, thinking that it was worth a try. He then finds the courage to say: 'Hey, Jimmy – please put my name down on that list. You know, when you're ready. I too would like to make amends.'

Angie, exhausted and with cloudy eyes, types the very last sentence of *Avoiding Elena*, giving it a fairy tale ending that could only happen in a work of fiction. It's 5.00 am on the Saturday, and she's been up all night writing. She's feeling physically and emotionally worn out, as if she had just given birth to a child. It's a rather light first draft, weighing only thirty thousand words, but Angie has no doubt that it will develop into a healthier, longer volume in the coming months.

Alas, by fixing Elena and Mario's marriage she still hasn't discovered the magic formula that will save her real life relationship. But if Dr Suenho has been able to help her manage something as life-changing as mental illness, Angie reasons, there must be a professional out there who can help her and Jimmy deal with its aftermath together. She still has the note with the phone number for the relationship counselling service that Dr Suenho gave her almost a year ago.

Most importantly, she thinks, there must be someone out there who can help Jimmy deal with his own issues, just as she has been dealing with hers – otherwise they, as a couple, don't stand a chance.

Before turning off her computer, there is one last thing she wants to write.

> Dear Shine,
> Trust you got home safely. The reason I'm writing is that last night I had dinner with Tiger, and learnt the truth behind his falling out with Jimmy. It's too complicated to explain here, but it was something similar to what happened with you, Georgie and me. I am still saddened by the way Jimmy and Tiger's friendship slipped between their fingers, and I don't want the same to happen with us.
> I didn't have the chance to tell you that I've received an inheritance from my grandma. She gave me some of it earlier this year, but there was more. She wanted me to have a third of the proceeds from the sale of her cottage.
> I'm in a position to either put a deposit on a property or start a small business, and have decided that I'd really like to own a little bookshop. I know that you love books as much as I do, and thought we could be partners. Perhaps you could come back to Australia on a business visa? What do you say?
>
> Love, Angie

She pushes the "send" button and switches off the computer.

The four-word reply will take one excruciating week to arrive.

> Thinking about it. Hugs, S.

❧

It's Easter Saturday, 2001. Jimmy and his brother Peter are driving along the old Pacific Highway, heading to their parent's place on the Central Coast, where they are staying for the rest of the long weekend. Peter is listening to the rugby, cheering and cursing all the way. Jimmy has a knot in his stomach, but is encouraged by the cloudless sky that lies ahead.

His parents are next on the list of people Jimmy wants to make amends with. The first was Angie. She is still living alone, but has agreed to undergo marriage counselling on the condition that Jimmy also finds a therapist to help him deal with his own issues. Jimmy finally gave in, and Dr Hamilton, their family doctor, recommended a local counsellor.

After a couple of very tense sessions full of uncomfortable silences, Jimmy mentioned that he was attempting to follow some of the twelve steps. The counsellor had immediately referred him to AL-Anon. He explained that this organisation is for relatives and friends of alcoholics who want to recover from the effects of living with a loved one's drinking problem. Jimmy thought it couldn't be that effective seventeen years after the fact, but decided to give it a go. At the first meeting Jimmy felt, perhaps for the first time in his life, that he had found his tribe. And well, the rest is--

'Tsk, tsk, tsk. You're sliding to the right again!' Peter says, interrupting Jimmy's thoughts.

'Well if you turned that bloody radio off, maybe I could concentrate better,' Jimmy snaps, clasping the steering wheel. It's only been a few weeks since he obtained his L-plates. Even though the old, winding highway is almost deserted now that everyone else uses the freeway, he's still shaking.

'Mate, if you don't like my footy, you can get yourself a paid driving instructor,' Peter says, elbowing his brother in the ribs.

Jimmy smiles. Despite the apprehension caused by driving, and the impending visit to his parents, he feels peace at the centre. Today, at least.

As his mother used to say when she was recovering: one day at a time.

# EPILOGUE:
# VICTORY SONG

*No hay mayor crimen que matar un sueño,
ni mayor virtud que realizarlo.*

*(There's no greater crime than to kill a dream,
nor greater virtue than to make it happen.)*

- Old Spanish proverb

# ~ Victory Song ~

Closing chapter of *Avoiding Elena*,
by Angelica Fletcher

My mother named me Victoria because she says that even though I had a very difficult birth, and she almost lost me, I was born smiling - as if celebrating my victory over death.

I am now seventeen years old and live in Seville, Spain, with my mother Elena, my father Mario, and my sister Maria. My sister and I never get tired of hearing the story of how we came to live here, when we could have lived our lives on the other side of the world.

See, my mother and my father met in Australia and lived there for many years. In fact, my father was born there, and had never thought about leaving the country. Ever since he was a child, he suffered a terrible fear of flying and would not even think about getting on a plane.

One day, my mother tells me, she decided to come home, to Seville, the place in which she had grown up, to reflect upon her life and her marriage, because things were not going very well between her and my father. Originally she wanted to stay here for only three months, but three months turned into six.

Soon after she arrived, having a lot of time on her hands, she had joined the local choir. After their first performance, in which she had a small solo part, a man approached her and asked if she was interested in a singing career – he was a tutor and had been very impressed with her voice; she would make an outstanding flamenco singer.

Mother was delighted, and started training. It soon became evident that at the age of thirty-four, she had finally found what she most wanted to do in life. When the time came to return to Australia and to her husband, she found herself at a crossroads.

There was yet another complication. On the last night my parents had spent together, they had conceived me. Six months had gone by, and mother still had not found the courage to tell my father that she was pregnant.

One day, as she was crying, torn between two lives and two countries, someone had knocked at her door. It was my father, who had defied his phobia of flying to come after her. When he saw that she was heavily pregnant, he fell to his knees, and said that he was willing to move to Spain, if that was what would make her happy. Mother jokingly says that the real reason he stayed was that he couldn't face another plane trip.

My mother once told me that her name means 'shining light'. I can see how true this is whenever she sings: she can light up an entire hall with her voice. Her exuberance is contagious, and her audience loves it. As I write this, I can hear her starting to warm up her vocal chords in the lounge room – and my father accompanying her on the guitar, which he learnt to play after he moved here. Maria and I do the dancing, and we perform, as a family, several times a week.

They are calling me now. I better find my shoes and join them.

# Acknowledgements

My heartfelt thanks go to the people and organisations who contributed in one way or another towards the making of *Exuberance*. Elizabeth, friend and editor, who meticulously and patiently copy-edited the manuscript. Varuna, the Writers' House in the Blue Mountains, where I spent an unforgettable week as one of the recipients of the Varuna Awards Residential Masterclass in 2005, and where I completed the first draft of this novel under the guidance and mentorship of Peter Bishop, who was then the Creative Director of Varuna.

Debbie Golvan, of Golvan Arts Management, who believed in this book, read it thoroughly and made many valuable suggestions to the content and structure. The Hon. Jeff Kennett AC, founding chairman of Beyondblue, who took the time to read an early draft and endorsed it as 'offering a well-constructed account of bipolar'. Michelle, who gave me so many pages of excellent feedback. Viv, who revised all the tenses when I restructured the timeline. Katie, who checked the 10th anniversary edition. My mum, who has been my biggest fan since I won my first national writing competition in Bolivia, at age fifteen. Peter, for all his patience and support. And my best friend Mark, who was my sounding board, who read endless incarnations of this novel; and whose relentless belief in *Exuberance* and its message of hope and new possibilities motivated me to finally having it published.

For research and inspiration, I have mainly relied on my own experience with bipolar II and on two works by Dr. Kay Redfield Jamison: *Touched by Fire* and *An Unquiet Mind: a memoir of moods and madness.*